MISSING ON 30A

By

Deborah Rine

MISSING ON 30A is a work of fiction. The characters, incidents and dialogue are drawn from the author's imagination and are not to be construed as real.

MISSING ON 30A: Copyright © May 2020 by Deborah Rine. All rights reserved. No part of this book may be used or reproduced in any manner whatsoever without written permission except in the case of brief quotations embodied in critical articles and reviews.

ISBN: 9798645883324

MISSING ON 30A is dedicated to my wonderful, devoted readers. Thank you!

Books by Deborah Rine

Banner Bluff Mystery Series:
THE LAKE
FACE BLIND
DIVERGENT DEATHS

Contemporary Novel:
RAW GUILT

Emerald Coast Mystery Series:
THE GIRL ON 30A
ENVY ON 30A
(MISSING ON 30A)

Memoir and Fantasy
VERONA WITH LOVE

Deborah Rine can be contacted at:
www.deborah-rine-author.com
http://dcrine.blogspot.com/
Facebook and Twitter

"The secret of health for both mind and body is not to mourn for the past, worry about the future or anticipate troubles, but to live in the present moment wisely and earnestly." Buddha

MISSING ON 30A

Part I

Chapter 1

Claire sat there and smiled, as Anne Bergner explained they no longer needed her services.

"We just love having you visit, Claire. You're such a breath of sunshine, but it's easy for me to order the purses and sandals online from the Letízia website."

Claire continued to smile a plastic smile. She nodded, then picked up the glass of sweet tea, Anne had poured for her and took a small sip. Anne and Tom Bergner had been some of her first customers. They ran their store, The Sweet Sands Shop, in perfect sync. They both wore sky blue shirts and khaki shorts, and they often finished each other's sentences.

"You understand, don't you? I don't want to hurt your feelings." Anne looked down at her neat little pudgy hands and then looked up. "But it's also a little cheaper that way." She gave Claire a sheepish grin.

"I understand. No problem. I'm glad you'll continue to order our products." Claire gathered up the catalogues she'd brought and stuffed them into her briefcase. All she wanted to do was get the hell out of there. She had the same childish feeling she'd had in middle school when Sheila Bennet had said she didn't want to be friends anymore.

She stood and slung the bag over her shoulder. "Well, I better get going." Out in the store, Tom was helping a client pick out one of the very same purses Claire had convinced them to carry last month. Well, too bad. They were on their own now. She waved to Tom. He smiled awkwardly and then she was out the door.

The Sweet Sands Shop was located in Destin. Claire took Highway 98 back east towards Lemon Cove. She banged the steering wheel in frustration as she drove. Sweet Sands was the second store that week that claimed they didn't need her. For the last three years, she had worked hard to build up an extensive clientele of gift shops that carried the Letízia brand of leather products. Her region had been northern Florida. Southern Florida was covered by Gabriella Santos. Claire had always felt she and Gabriella were in competition. But

Gabriella was Lucca Silva's fiancée and Lucca was Claire's boss. So, there was no way she could ever win.

She yawned. It was nearing five o'clock and the traffic on 98 was extra heavy. As she drove along, she thought about Anne's words: that it was cheaper to buy from the Letízia website. That hadn't always been the case. She sighed again in frustration. So be it. The Sweet Sands Shop was gone. At least she wouldn't have to drive there anymore and drink that sweet, sweet tea. It probably would have made all her teeth fall out.

As she approached Highway 331, her phone dinged. She slowed down and stopped behind the long line of traffic at the stoplight. Then she picked up her phone, and read the text. It was from Lucca. We will be terminating your contract as of next Monday. Sorry. There is no good way to tell you. Thought a text was better than a call. Talk soon.

Claire stared at the message, frozen. Was this for real? Was it a joke? Had Arnold Schwarzenegger swooped in and terminated her? She read the message again and again. It still didn't make sense. Behind her, a barrage of honking horns sounded. How long had she been sitting there? She didn't know. The road ahead was clear, the stoplight green. She pushed down on the accelerator and took off like a rocket. She barreled along, barely aware of the traffic around her. Terminated. Fired. This couldn't be happening. After all the hours of planning, marketing and cold calling, it was over.

At Highway 283 she turned south towards Grayton Beach. From there it was a short drive to Lemon Cove and home. She held it together until she pulled into the carport, then she burst into tears and cried like a baby. She knew she was acting irrationally, but this text was a shock. All along she'd thought she had a good working relationship with Lucca. What had happened? It disturbed her that she hadn't had an inkling this was coming. Her numbers had been good last month, maybe not quite as good as the month before…but still. With tears running down her cheeks, she picked up her phone and punched in Lucca's number. The phone rang and rang. She hung up and tried again…and again. No answer. Then she sent a text: You owe me an explanation. She stared at her phone and willed it to ding a response, but there was nothing.

Claire pulled herself out of the car and retrieved her bag and her purse. She and her husband, Dax, lived in a house right on the beach. It was built on stilts that were actually heavy pilons constructed to make the house hurricane safe. There were three parking spaces under the house, an outdoor shower and an enclosed stairway that led up to the dwelling above. She tapped in the code and pushed open the door into a well-lit entryway decorated in tones of grey and turquoise. Normally she found the colors soothing, but not today.

Claire trudged up the interior staircase to the first floor. At the top of the stairs, a small foyer opened out to an enormous great room. She gazed at it as if she'd never seen it before. The area felt spacious and cozy at the same time. Comfortable sofas and armchairs in tones of turquoise and yellow on white formed attractive groupings. A round teak dining table was surrounded by captain's chairs with green and turquoise plaid cushions. Green plants and a couple of ficus trees added to the charm. The white kitchen cabinets and marble counters were a backdrop to colorful Italian pottery and sleek kitchen appliances. One wall was all windows that opened onto a wide deck with a view of the beach and the Gulf of Mexico.

The room felt stuffy. She went over to the windows, pulled back the curtains, and opened the sliding glass door to let in a light breeze. In the kitchen, she opened the fridge and pulled out a bottle of pinot grigio. She poured herself a generous glass and took a long sip. She needed to calm down. There must have been a mistake. Tomorrow she would talk to Lucca and all would be solved.

She sighed and gave herself a shake. It was time to think about dinner. Dax should be home in a few minutes. She pulled the makings of a salad out of the fridge, along with a plastic bag of chicken breasts that had been marinating all day in her special vinaigrette. Dax would grill the chicken as well as a couple slices of Texas toast. Working quickly, she made the salad and put the bowl in the fridge. She slathered butter on thick slices of bread and sprinkled them with grated parm, garlic salt and herbs. Claire glanced at her phone. Still no calls. It was six o'clock. Dax should already be home. Maybe she'd have time for a quick shower.

Claire went upstairs to the second floor. The master suite was done in warm beige and peach colors. As in the great room below, a deck ran the length of the house. Sliding glass doors opened onto a fabulous view of the beach. Next to the bedroom was a cozy sitting room where she and Dax liked to hang out on cool evenings. Dax called it Claire's boudoir. There was a deep sofa and a matching armchair as well as a turquoise and beige chaise lounge that was Claire's favorite place to curl up and read.

She pulled off her clothes, dropped them in the hamper, and turned on the shower. In the full-length mirror, she studied her body. From jogging and yoga, she had maintained her figure: slim but curvy. She undid her ponytail and let her sun-streaked blond hair fall around her shoulders. Then she approached the mirror and studied her face. Her eyes, blue-grey-green like the ocean, were smudged from crying and her small, straight nose was red. Her lips trembled slightly, a sign that she was still feeling emotional. Dax thought she was beautiful, but she knew better. She was attractive, maybe pretty, but certainly not beautiful.

Claire showered quickly, then dried off and put on an old grey tee-shirt and a pair of pink-plaid sleeping shorts, her go-to outfit for relaxing. Downstairs, she checked her phone again. No texts, no calls. Not even from Dax. That was odd. She was sure he'd said he would be home by five. She called his cell, but got voicemail. No response when she texted him, either. Could something have come up that prevented him from calling her? Back when Victoria Palmer had been killed at the Magnolia resort, Claire hadn't heard from him for nearly twenty-four hours.

Dax was Chief Deputy Sheriff for the Emerald Coast. An ace detective, he'd worked for the FBI for several years before joining the Sheriff's Department and eventually becoming the major operating officer. Normally, things were relatively calm up and down 30A. He spent most of his time managing the department, doing paperwork and attending meetings.

Claire put a call into the station. It rang once before someone picked up. "Sheriff's Department, Officer Nilsson speaking."

"Hello, Roger. It's Claire Simmons. I wondered if Dax was there?"

"Oh, hi Claire. I don't think so, but I'll check."

Claire liked Roger Nilsson. He was a nice young officer who'd only joined the force a year ago. A minute later he was back on the line. "No, Claire. He's not here. I'm told he left early today; said he had a meeting."

"Did something come up this afternoon? Some incident that needed his expertise? I don't know, an assault...a major crime?"

"Not that I know of. Things seem pretty calm this evening. Thank goodness," he added.

"Right. Okay, I'll just wait until he shows up. Thanks, Roger."

Claire put the chicken back in the fridge and wrapped the toast in plastic wrap. To kill time, she watered the geraniums on the deck and the plants in the great room. Then she went into the den at the back of the house. Supposedly, she and Dax shared this office space, but the truth was he didn't work at home. He kept some guns and legal papers in a wall safe behind a picture of Rosemary Beach, and he had two locked drawers in the desk. She had no clue what he kept hidden away in there. The rest of the room was Claire's domain. She had file cabinets, a printer and a scanner. On the wall was a map of the area covered with bright-colored push pins indicating the location of her clients.

She sat down at the desk, opened her laptop and looked at her schedule for the next day. Yoga at eight, then she would visit three shops. At eleven she had a meeting with Alexia Cosmos in Seaside. They planned on lunch afterwards at the Great Southern Café, which was just a hop, skip and a jump from Beach Mania, Alexia's store. In the afternoon, she'd drop by two shops in Panama City Beach she hadn't visited in a while. She planned on showing them the latest leather purses. She had several models in her inventory.

Then it hit her. Why go there? Why show them anything? Why spend the gas or the time? She'd been fired. Why drive up and down the Emerald Coast when there was no future in it...or any money. She sat back and wrapped her arms around her chest, feeling pinpricks of tears behind her eyes. Come on, Claire. Toughen up. You'll talk to Lucca tomorrow. You'll tell him he's making a big mistake.

Claire went back into the kitchen and refilled her glass of wine. It was eight o'clock and still no word from Dax. She should probably eat something, but she wasn't about to cook chicken for herself. In the pantry, she found some Ritz crackers and peanut butter. She made a couple of cracker sandwiches and put them on a plate with some cherries, then carried the wine and her plate outside to a chair on the deck. The sun was setting, and the sky was a panoply of radiant colors: pink, red and orange. As darkness approached, she munched on her crackers and thought about her options. If Lucca was for real, she would need to find a new job. What could that be? Never would she go back to the corporate world she'd fled three years ago. Never. If Lucca had really fired her, she had to find something else to do. But what?

Chapter 2

Claire made sure the outside lights were on at the back of the house for Dax. Then she went upstairs. Curled up on the chaise, she tried reading Where the Crawdads Sing. The night before, she'd had to force herself to put it down. Tonight, she couldn't concentrate on the novel. She turned on the TV and clicked on Netflix. Maybe there was a movie that would grab her, but after ten minutes, she turned it off. She kept yawning. She might as well go to bed and try to sleep. Tomorrow would be another day.

Before plugging in her phone, she tried Dax one last time. The phone went immediately to voicemail. She tried texting. Nothing. With a sigh, she plugged in her phone and burrowed under the covers. There must have been a homicide or something major that was keeping him busy. In spite of everything, she fell asleep. Lately, she was always tired.

A while later, something woke Claire. A buzzing noise. Was it her phone? Slowly, she came to and reached over to nudge Dax. But he wasn't there. Buzz, buzz. It wasn't her phone. It was the doorbell. As she got out of bed, she glanced at the clock. Four AM. Who could be at the door at this hour? Buzz, buzz. Worry cut through the lingering sleep daze. She pulled on a robe, then hurried into the study and looked outside. A police car was down there, its lights flashing.

Claire ran downstairs, almost tripping on the bottom step, and pulled the door open. Bob Rogers was there, his face a pale oval in the flashing lights. He held his hat in his hands. With hunched shoulders, his stocky frame seemed diminished. He looked as though he had aged ten years since the last time she'd seen him.

"Hi Claire," he said in a subdued tone.

Fear bloomed in the pit of her stomach. "Bob. Why are you here?"

"I don't know what to say. I feel so terrible." His eyes were pools of pain and sympathy. "Dax...Dax is dead."

She couldn't make sense of the last three words. "Dax is dead?"

"Yes. He drowned."

"Drowned?" This couldn't be. This was nuts. Dax was a strong swimmer.

"Some kids found his body on the beach in Seaside."

Claire shook her head. "Dax is a great swimmer. You must be mistaken."

Bob had tears in his eyes. He and Dax were close friends. "I saw the body, Claire. It's him."

"I don't believe you. It must be somebody else." Her voice was raw and hard, and rose by an octave as she went on. "Dax can't be dead. He had a meeting tonight. He wasn't swimming. It makes no sense." She felt like hitting him.

He stepped back and raised his hands. "Please, Claire. Calm down."

"Calm down? Calm down? When you tell me my husband is dead?"

"I'm so, so sorry, Claire. I didn't want to come here and tell you this."

She was shaking with anger and fear. "I want to see. I want to see Dax's body. You have to prove it to me."

His tone was patient. "I can take you to the morgue tomorrow."

"No! I want to see him now. Where is he?"

"Still down there where he was found. They're waiting for the Medical Examiner from Fort Walton Beach.

"Let's go." She moved toward the patrol car. Bob held up his hands again, but she pushed past him. "Take me there. I want to see him. I'll prove you're wrong." She yanked at the handle of the front passenger door. The thing wouldn't budge.

He went around the car, opened the driver's door and clicked the passenger door lock. She pulled the door open, sat down heavily and banged the door shut. Bob slid in, started the engine, and turned off the flashing lights. He backed down the driveway and they took off. She could feel him glancing over at her periodically. He sighed several times. Then he said, "This might be really hard, Claire."

She said nothing. Ten minutes later, he pulled into a spot near the Van Ness beach access on the edge of Seaside. "You don't have to do this," he said, his voice breaking.

She turned and looked at him. "You don't get it. I have to know. Now please open the door, so I can get out."

The second she heard the lock click, she pushed open the door and slid out of the patrol car. Only when her bare feet hit the pavement did she realize she was still wearing her old tee-shirt, her sleeping shorts and no shoes. But it didn't matter what she looked like or if her feet got scratched. She strode down the cement sidewalk and began to run when she came to the wooden walkway over the dunes. Ahead, the sky was clear and sprinkled with stars. The Gulf looked like a sheet of glass. To the left, she could see bright lights as she reached the top of the stairs leading down to the beach. There were several vehicles pulled up in the sand, lights flashing. She could see a small crowd of people.

Bob was huffing and puffing behind her. She didn't wait for him, but took off down the stairs and ran toward the lights and cars. As she approached the scene, she saw yellow caution tape flicking in the breeze. Inside the taped off area, a man was bent over a figure in the sand. They were only a few feet from the water. It must be low tide, she thought. She raced along the hard sand toward a couple of officers with their backs to her, unaware of her approach. She leaped over the tape, took two more running steps and fell on her knees near the body.

"Hey, lady. Get out of there."

"Jim, grab her. She'll destroy evidence."

Someone grabbed her arm, but she shook it off.

Then she looked at the face of the man lying supine on the sand. It was Dax. But it wasn't, not really. This face was expressionless, like a Greek marble statue of a god. His mouth was thin and lifeless; his eyes were closed; his forehead smooth. Gone was the Dax whose mouth smiled at her with love. Gone were the eyes that crinkled in laughter. Gone was the spark of joy he radiated. Dax was gone. This was just his body. This was the shell of his soul. He was gone.

She kept staring, hoping for a reaction, a movement, anything. A strange, frozen calm took hold of her. She reached out a hand and smoothed his chest. Then she bent and kissed the lips that were no longer Dax. They felt cold and hard. She pulled back and looked up. The man inspecting the body—the medical examiner, she thought dully—looked down at her with pity.

Behind her, she heard voices. "It's his wife."

"Yeah, but she shouldn't be in there."

She felt gentle hands lifting her up. It was Bob. "Claire, come away. Let me help you."

She let herself be led away. Bob lifted up the yellow tape and she bent under it. Everyone stared at her, their faces lit by the red and blue flashing lights. They looked like carnival clowns at a three-ring circus. But this time she was the main act.

Chapter 3

At home, Bob said he would stay with her until a friend or relative came. Did she want him to call someone?

She wiped her eyes with the bottom of her tee-shirt. "I'll be all right. I'll call my parents and some friends. Don't worry." She could feel more tears running down her cheeks, like an uncontrollable soft drizzle.

Bob looked anxious and uncertain, but he clicked the car door open and she got out. Without looking back, she said, "Thank you." And fled to her own front door.

With shaking fingers, she taped in the code and pushed the door open, letting it slam behind her. Inside, she pounded up the stairs. The house was dark and too quiet. She turned on the light switch at the entrance to the great room. All the canister lights came on. Then she went around the room, turning on all the lamps and the kitchen lights. She shouted, "Alexa, play Dax's mix." Van Halen filled the room.

Claire made a pot of coffee, grinding the beans and filling the basket. As the coffeepot dripped, she emptied the dishwasher, placing each glass, each plate in the cupboard with careful precision. At the back of the top shelf in the dishwasher was Dax's favorite mug. It was dark blue and had his name on it. Someone at the FBI had given it to him. She clasped it in her hands, studying the white printing. Then, with terrific force, she threw it across the room. It smashed into a thousand pieces in the corner next to a ficus tree.

Her body sagged against the counter as she covered her face with her hands and sobbed. What would she do without Dax? He had been her best friend and her passion. How could she cope with being totally alone again? The tears didn't stop for a long time.

Eventually, the storm of grief slackened. Claire sighed, still shaky and groped for the paper towel rack. She pulled off a square and wiped her face with it. The scent of the coffee nudged at her, so she poured herself a cup and added a splash of milk. She sat on a stool at the kitchen island and took a cautious sip of the hot brew. The coffee didn't taste quite right. Lately, it had made her borderline nauseated. The beans must be out-of-date. She took another sip. Her world had been turned upside down. She'd lost her job and the love of her life. They said bad luck came in threes. What would happen next? Maybe a hurricane would blow the house away.

She sipped more coffee, holding the cup in both hands. Without wanting to, her mind went back to the body on the beach. Dax had been so cold. She would have liked to cover him with a warm blanket. She thought back to the kiss she'd given him, and involuntarily touched her lips. That kiss would be the last time she touched him forever.

Something nagged at her through the fresh surge of grief. What was it? She thought back to the bright lights beaming down on Dax. She remembered the kind eyes of the ME. She remembered the cold, lifeless body…and then it hit her. The bathing trunks. They were bright fluorescent orange, something Dax would never wear. Something a teenager might choose, or a surfer dude, but not Dax. He was way too conservative. He usually wore trunks that were dark blue or black.

Claire set down her coffee and raced upstairs to the bedroom, where she walked into the closet and opened the bottom drawer of Dax's dresser. There they were, three pairs of bathing trunks: dark blue with a red stripe, plain blue, and black with a white stripe. With a shaking hand, she grabbed her phone and tapped in the number to the sheriff's office. A female voice came on the line. "Sheriff's Department."

"I need to talk to Bob Rogers," Claire shouted. "It's an emergency."

"Bob's gone home. Who is this?"

"It's Claire Simmons. I have to talk to Bob now."

The woman's voice softened. "Oh, Mrs. Simmons. I'm so sorry for your loss."

"Thank you, but I need to talk to Bob. Could I have his cell phone number?"

"Just a minute, Mrs. Simmons."

Claire heard some mumbling in the background. Then a man's voice came on the line. "Hello, Mrs. Simmons. This is Detective Drakos. I'm so sorry for your loss. The entire department is in shock. We all loved and respected Dax." He coughed and cleared his throat.

It struck Claire that she would be hearing those words again and again: I'm sorry for your loss. She knew Drakos. He was a stern, gruff guy with piercing dark eyes and a deceptively laid-back manner. Dax had told her that when he was on a case, he was relentless, like a dog with a bone. Maybe she should tell him what she was thinking.

"Thank you, Detective. I called to talk to Bob Rogers. He took me over to the beach in Seaside. He dropped me off back home a little while ago." She took a breath. For a moment she saw Dax on the sand again and felt a little light-headed. She sat down on the edge of the bed. Drakos said nothing. He was giving her time. "I have an idea about Dax. I…" She trailed off, suddenly unsure of herself.

"Maybe I can help you." His tone was patient and kind.

She tried again. "It's about the swim trunks. The ones Dax was wearing on the beach."

"Yes…go on."

"Those weren't his trunks. They were fluorescent orange. Dax would never wear something like that. He was supposed to be home at five. He wasn't planning on swimming. He had a meeting. Why would he turn up dead on a beach wearing someone else's bathing trunks? Something is terribly wrong." She was breathless when she'd finished her incoherent recitation. Did Detective Drakos think she was nuts?

"So, he wasn't wearing swim trunks you recognized, is that right?"

"Yes, and I'm wondering where he went yesterday. When I called the station yesterday evening, they told me he left for an appointment in the early afternoon. Where did he go?"

There was a long pause and a hacking cough. "It's five in the morning. When the day shift comes on in a couple of hours, I'll ask around and find out what Chief Simmons was working on yesterday. Then we can figure out where he went." He spoke clearly and patiently, as if dealing with a child.

Claire's brain was hopping around. "And where's his phone? Maybe if we found his phone, we could figure out who he talked to and where he went."

"I'll look into that. We can access his phone records. But—"

He sounded like he was placating her. She cut him off. "Yes, please do that and get back to me. Thank you, Detective."

She hung up before he could say anything else. She was shivering and tears were streaming down her face again. Oh, God this can't be happening. Frantically, she looked around the bedroom. Dax's side of the king-sized bed was smooth and neat. He would never sleep there again. She threw herself down and clutched his pillow to her chest, sobbing. "Dax, I need you. Don't leave me."

Chapter 4

After she'd cried herself out, Claire went into the bathroom and splashed cold water on her face. She needed to call someone. But she wasn't up to talking to her parents yet, or Dax's family. That would require a strength she didn't have.

She dialed Olivia's number. The phone rang and rang and then she got voicemail: "Olivia, here. Leave your number." She couldn't tell Olivia Dax was dead on a voicemail recording. She hung up, then dialed Morgan. It would be three in the morning in California, but she needed to talk to someone who knew her well.

The phone rang two times and then she heard Morgan's voice. "Hello, Claire. Wow! Why are you calling me at three in the morning?" She sounded energetic, not groggy at all.

For a moment Claire couldn't respond. Then she took a breath. "I'm sorry if I woke you..."

Morgan laughed. "Don't be sorry. I'm wide awake. I can't get comfortable in any position. Right now, I'm lying on the sofa like a beached whale."

Claire remembered that Morgan was seven months pregnant. How could she have forgotten? Her voice caught on the next words. "I needed to talk."

"What's up? You don't sound good. Tell me."

At first, Claire couldn't speak. Maybe if she didn't tell anyone Dax was dead, then he wouldn't be. Like that riddle...if no one hears a tree falling in the forest, does it actually fall?

"Morgan..." She swallowed. "Morgan...Dax is dead."

Morgan's shock came clearly over the phone line. "What? Dax? What happened? A car accident?"

"No...they say he drowned while swimming. But, see, that's impossible." She told Morgan everything and then she began to cry again.

"Oh, my God. You poor thing. I'm coming, Claire. I'll get the earliest flight out."

"You're pregnant. You probably shouldn't fly."

"Give me a break. It's not like this baby is going to pop out anytime soon. I want to be there for you."

"Really? That... that would be...wonderful," Claire said between sobs.

"Okay. I'm going to check on flights. I'll text you as soon as I know when I'll arrive. Be strong, I'll be there soon."

"Thank you, thank you." Claire hung up.

A short while later, she got dressed in jean shorts and a blue 30A tee-shirt. In the bathroom, she brushed her teeth, splashed water on her face and pulled her hair into a tight ponytail. Downstairs, she told Alexa to turn off the pounding music. She hadn't even realized she'd left it on since Bob brought her home, and now it was giving her a headache. Then she put on the kettle. If she couldn't handle coffee, maybe tea would settle her stomach.

The clock told her it was five-thirty. In New York it would be six-thirty. She should call Dax's sister, Jenny, and break the news. Jenny lived in Bronxville, a suburb of New York City. Claire placed the call. After four rings, Jenny picked up.

"Hi, Claire. What's up?" Typical Jenny, very direct and no time for niceties.

For a few seconds, Claire was speechless. Then she took a breath. "I've got bad news."

"Bad news?"

Claire could imagine Jenny, suddenly alert. Dax's sister was pretty, thin, and driven. Dax used to say she was like a pointer intent on its prey.

"Yes, very bad news. Dax is dead." Her voice caught. She hated making this call. Jenny had been Dax's closest sibling.

Silence. Then Jenny said, "You're joking, right?"

Was this something Claire would joke about? "No, I'm not."

Suddenly Jenny's voice was raw with emotion. "Oh, my God. What happened?"

"They say he drowned while swimming in the Gulf."

"That's bullshit. Dax was an ace swimmer. In high school he broke all the records."

Hearing Jenny's anger, so like her own, felt good. Claire felt empowered. "You're right. It is bullshit. I've spoken to a detective and he's looking into what happened." She told Jenny about the orange swim trunks and the unanswered questions about where Dax had been earlier in the day.

Jenny agreed it all sounded suspicious. "You know, Dax has been in a lot of precarious situations, but he's always pulled through. He must have been onto something. Listen, what can I do for you? Do you want me to fly down?"

Jenny had three kids and a big job in finance. Not easy for her to get away or unload her responsibilities. "No, I've got a friend coming to stay with me. But would you please tell the rest of the family?" Dax had another sister and three brothers, plus a bunch of nieces and nephews. Calling each sibling and telling them their brother was dead, was more than Claire could handle right now.

"Sure. They'll all be devastated. Dax was everyone's favorite brother and uncle." Jenny began to sob. "God, I really loved Dax."

"Me, too. I'll be lost without him," Claire whispered.

They were quiet for a minute.

"What about a funeral? You need to make plans," Jenny said.

Claire felt a flash of resentment at Jenny's need to take over and manage things. "I'll get back to you, Jenny. Thanks." Then she hung up, like she had on Detective Drakos. A funeral? She had only learned Dax was dead three hours ago. Was she supposed to have the funeral arranged by seven AM?

The tea kettle was whistling, an ear-splitting scream. Claire screamed back at it. Then with fumbling hands, she turned off the gas. For a moment she held on to the counter and closed her eyes. Then she found a mug and an Earl Grey teabag. She poured in the boiling water. While the tea steeped, she went into the broom closet and got out a broom and a dustpan. She swept up the mug she'd smashed earlier and dumped the shards into the garbage can. The tears began again. Why had she broken Dax's favorite cup? She should treasure it. She should treasure everything Dax had ever touched.

Chapter 5

An hour later, Claire heard the doorbell. At first, she thought, Maybe it's Dax. Then she caught herself. Dax was never coming home again. Maybe it was Detective Drakos with information. She hurried down the stairs and opened the door. Lights flashed in her eyes, and a couple of blurry faces pushed microphones at her.

"Can you tell us what happened, Mrs. Simmons?"

"Why was the Sheriff swimming in the Gulf?"

"What would you like to share with the public?"

Claire slammed the door shut and stood trembling in the entryway. The press had already been clued in to Dax's death. She ran back upstairs. When she entered the great room, she saw someone peering through the window. They'd used the outside staircase to get up on the deck. Moaning, she ran over to the windows and closed all the curtains. Who were these people? Did they have no morals, no sensitivity? All that mattered to them was the story for their newspaper or the five o'clock broadcast.

Claire called 911 and told the dispatcher what was happening outside her door. Of course, the woman began by saying, "I'm sorry for your loss." Then she told Claire they would send officers over to block off the area around her house. Claire would be protected.

She hung up, then went into the office and looked down at the scene below. Several TV vans clogged the street. She went upstairs and out on the deck in front of the bedroom. Peeping over the edge, she could see a small crowd of people talking and laughing. A couple of guys seemed to be filming the house. They were all there to get the big scoop. She felt like screaming at all of them to get the hell away from her house. She'd just lost her husband and now she would be a prisoner in her own home.

Claire paced up and down, so angry she felt nauseated. This tension was making her sick. She needed to calm down.

Fifteen minutes later, the police arrived. They forced the newshounds and gawkers away from the house and blocked the driveway with two patrol cars and stationed more officers on the beachfront. Daxton Simmons had been their boss and they were there in force to protect his widow. Widow. Claire felt the full weight of the word. A widow was an old, wrinkled woman dressed in black. But she was thirty-two, too young to be a widow.

The officer in charge came to the house briefly and told her they would be there day and night. He said she should contact them if she had any problems. He also said he was sorry for her loss. It took an effort not to slam the door behind him when he left.

Moments later, her phone rang. She looked at the screen. It was Lucca. For a split second, she debated whether to take the call. She didn't have the energy to talk to him now. He would have to wait. But there was another call she had to make.

She tapped in her parents' number. Her dad answered the phone, "Hey, sugar plum. Glad you called. We're on our way out the door. We're meeting the Jensens for lunch."

"Dad." Her voice broke. She couldn't continue.

"Claire. What's the matter?"

"Daddy. Dax is dead." She began crying in earnest—deep, painful sobs.

He let her cry for a moment, then he said, "Oh, honey. Tell me about it."

Claire could almost see her dad's kind eyes and his sorrowful expression. It made her cry even harder.

"Claire, I'm here. Take your time. Take a deep breath." Her father's voice was warm and soothing. He had always been her go-to parent when she'd had a problem as a kid. Mom was great, but she usually got too upset herself and wasn't helpful.

Claire took a deep breath, composing herself enough to speak. "Dax drowned. They say he drowned in the Gulf. Some kids found him on the beach this morning. I went down there and identified the body." She swallowed another sob.

"Oh, honey, I wish I'd been there for you. That must have been hard."

They talked for a while, and she told him everything. Then her mother came on the line and she repeated what she could manage.

"Claire, we'll come down there." Her mother's voice trembled. "We'll be there tonight."

She felt grateful at the idea, and also overwhelmed. "No, Mom. Not now. I've got Morgan coming. When I know more about what's happening, I'll get back to you.

"Are you sure?"

"Yes, I'm sure." Dad would understand, she thought. He'd talk Mom around. They spoke a little longer and then Claire hung up.

The rest of the morning was spent fielding calls from Dax's brothers, sisters and cousins. She'd hoped to avoid these conversations when she'd asked Jenny to pass the word. But they all wanted to tell her how sorry they felt and wanted to know when the funeral would be. It exhausted her to talk to them, but it kept her from thinking about the enormity of what had happened.

***

Morgan texted she would arrive at four o'clock at Panama City International. Claire was determined to pick her up at the airport. But how could she get out of the house without being mobbed? She rang the police officer in charge, and together they organized a plan. Some ten minutes later, she left the house. The police kept people back while she got into her car, and they blocked the road to prevent the media from chasing her down.

When Morgan came out of the airport terminal, Claire was waiting in her car at the curb. Morgan looked as elegant as ever in a grey knit maternity dress that clung to her curves and her protruding belly. Her thick blond hair was swept up in a smooth French chignon. As usual, she wore her pearls and strappy sandals. Claire got out and came around the car, and they had a long hug. Both of them were crying. When they pulled apart, they each managed a shaky smile. Then Claire put Morgan's bags into the trunk of the BMW, and they took off.

In the passenger seat, Morgan patted Claire's arm. "It's so wonderful to see you."

"It's wonderful to see you. You're my life-saver." Claire felt the tears beginning to spill.

"Go ahead and cry. It's good to cry," Morgan said.

"I'm sick of it." Claire gripped the steering wheel and took several deep breaths. "Are you hungry? Do you want to go somewhere for a late lunch or an early dinner?"

"Am I hungry? I'm always hungry. I could eat an entire pizza by myself." Morgan giggled.

Just her presence made Claire feel calmer. "Is there some place you've missed since you moved to California?"

"Hmm, let's see. I've missed a lot of places: Pescado, Stinky's, Amici's, the Cowgirl Kitchen, the Great Southern Café…just to name a few."

"How about we go to Amici's. You can have your pizza and I'll have that chicken piccata. Dax and I used to split it…" Claire didn't finish her sentence. What was the point? What Dax and she had done together was over.

Morgan patted her hand. "Yes, let's go there."

Claire gave her a tremulous smile, then pulled out a tissue from the box on the console and dabbed at her eyes.

When they entered the restaurant a little while later, Clarissa welcomed them. A fresh-faced college girl who went to school in Panama City, she'd often been Claire and Dax's server. She beamed at Claire and then looked past her. "Hey, ya'll. Where's the Sheriff? He's my man." Her eyes were wide and bright.

Claire didn't know what to say. Would she need to tell everyone she met that her husband was dead…over and over and over?

Morgan stepped in. "The Sheriff can't be with us this afternoon." She smiled and held out her hand. "Hi, I'm Morgan."

Claire smiled gratefully at Morgan. That had been the perfect answer.

Clarissa and Morgan shook hands. "Where would you guys like to sit?"

They picked a table in the back and ordered drinks, San Pellegrino with lime for Morgan and a glass of pinot grigio for Claire. "I'm so glad you're here," Claire told her friend. "But I'm surprised you were able to leave. What about the California Magnolia? And what about Carter?"

Morgan worked as wedding planner at the California Magnolia Spa and Resort, a hotel chain owned by her father and uncle. Previously she had worked at the Magnolia on the Emerald Coast. A couple of years ago, she had met Carter Perry when he was a groomsman at Victoria Palmer's celebrity wedding. Carter was a professor at UCLA, and Morgan moved out to California when they got engaged.

"Carter insisted I come. He felt you needed a friend. As for the resort, they're renovating the restaurants and redesigning the gardens, so there are no weddings for me to organize for four months during construction. It works perfectly, because I'll be off until the baby is a couple of months old. And right now, I don't feel much like working. I feel literally like the elephant in the room." She laughed, and Claire tried to join in.

"So, any idea if it's a boy or a girl?"

"There have been many prognostications. It's a boy because I'm carrying it high. It's a girl because I have 'the mask.' But I don't believe any of it. We'll just wait and see."

"What's the mask?" Claire asked.

"Apparently, your face takes on a tint and is fuller."

Claire studied her. "I don't see a mask. You look as beautiful as ever."

Morgan blushed. "I sure don't feel that way."

When the food arrived, Morgan devoured several slices of pizza, but after a couple of bites of the chicken piccata, Claire put down her fork. She just wasn't hungry, and she had cramps.

Morgan leaned toward her. "Are you all right? Maybe going out for dinner was a bad idea."

"I'm just not hungry. I'm too upset." She picked up the glass of wine and took a long sip.

"Do you want to talk about Dax?" Morgan said gently.

"No. Not here. Not now. Let's wait until we get home." Another sip of wine. "Hey, tell me about the latest weddings."

Morgan picked up another pizza slice. "The latest was between two gay guys. They wore matching pink tuxedos and had over-the-top mountains of flowers, Wagyu filets and cases of Dom Perignon. It was really elegant, and they were a lot of fun to deal with."

Morgan continued to talk, and Claire listened with part of her brain so she could nod at the right moments, but her mind's eye kept returning to the image of Dax on the beach. The ME would have transported the body somewhere by now. Where had Bob Rogers said the ME came from? She thought it was Fort Walton Beach. Would they do an autopsy? That thought gave her the shivers.

"What do you think?" Morgan was looking at her, eyebrows raised.

"What?" Claire said. "Sorry, my mind wandered." She felt terrible, being so rude to Morgan.

Morgan looked sympathetic. "Don't apologize. I know you're going through hell and it must be almost impossible to concentrate. Let's get out of here."

Clarissa boxed up the leftover pizza and chicken and soon they were back in the car driving down 30A.

Chapter 6

At home, Claire drove up to the blockade. Media people were still there hanging out. Several photographers snapped her picture while reporters swarmed as she drove in.

"Mrs. Simmons, do you have any comment about the death of your husband?"

"Is there anything you'd like to say?"

The police let her drive through and then closed ranks. She pulled into her parking space under the garage, then looked over at the empty spot where Dax usually parked. That gave her pause. Where was Dax's car? Were the police looking for it? Maybe its whereabouts would point to where he'd gone and who he'd met. Once inside, she would text Detective Drakos and ask him to look into it.

She and Morgan got out. Morgan still looked shaken by the media scrum. They went inside the house and up the stairs to the first floor.

Morgan looked around the great room. "I've always loved this room. The colors are so cheerful, and with those twelve-foot ceilings, you can really breathe in here." She walked over to the windows and pulled back the curtains. "What a fabulous view."

She reached for the sliding glass door, but Claire hurried over and pulled the curtains shut. "They're out there watching me. I don't want anyone taking my picture for their early morning TV show."

Morgan turned, frowning. "I didn't see anybody."

"Well, maybe they're gone now, but this morning some guy came right up on the deck and peered in."

Morgan's eyes widened with concern. "Wow, that's terrible. I'm so sorry."

"Let's go upstairs We can relax in my little sitting room. We can open the blinds up there and you'll get your view of the beach."

"Sounds great. But first, I want to get out of these clothes."

While Morgan was freshening up, Claire went in to use the bathroom. All afternoon, she'd had cramps, something she didn't usually have with her period. She looked into the toilet and felt a shock. There was bloody discharge in the bowl. Then she noticed her panties and shorts were stained. It looked different from her usual flow. She cleaned up and changed her underwear, battling a jolt of anxiety. When had she had her last period? She'd been keeping track on her phone these last few months. She found the app and realized she'd missed her period last month. Now nearly two months had passed. Usually, she was as regular as rain. But with all the stress at work, she hadn't paid close attention. Could she have been pregnant?

No. Oh, no. She ran out into the hall and banged on Morgan's door. Immediately, Morgan opened up. She'd changed into shorts and a voluminous pale-yellow shirt. "What's the matter? What happened?"

"I think…I think I was pregnant. But I…I miscarried, just now."

"What?"

"I've been cramping this afternoon…and I saw clotting. On my underwear. I don't…that's not normal, it's not…"

"When did you last have your period?"

"Almost two months ago. But I've been feeling lousy and tired these last couple of weeks. Somehow I never put two and two together." The reality of it hit her then, and Claire burst into tears. Bad things did come in threes: losing Dax, losing her job, and losing her unborn child.

Morgan took her into her arms and smoothed her hair as she cried.

Chapter 7

Claire and Morgan were curled up at each end of the sofa in her boudoir, drinking warm milk with cinnamon. Morgan said it would calm Claire down so she would be able to sleep. Morgan didn't believe in taking sleep medications.

"Tomorrow, you'll need to go see your gynecologist and make sure you're all right." Morgan said.

Claire had googled miscarriage and read about it. Now she felt even more fragile than before. "I don't know how I didn't realize I was pregnant. I hadn't been feeling so hot lately...nauseated off and on. I should have guessed." She took another sip of the milk. "My boss Lucca was here a month ago and I was so busy planning his visit, I just forgot about my period. Oh gosh, Dax would have been so happy...and so sad." Her eyes filled with tears.

Morgan leaned over and patted her leg. "Somehow you'll get through all of this."

The doorbell buzzed downstairs. "I'll go. You stay put." Morgan pulled herself up, rolled into a sitting position and then stood.

A few minutes later, Morgan ushered Detective Drakos into the room. He was of medium height with a full head of black hair. His face bore the ravages of teenage acne. His avocado green dress shirt was open at the neck, and under his sizeable paunch, a tired brown belt valiantly held up wrinkled grey pants. On his feet were scuffed cowboy boots. His dark, deep-set eyes roved around the room before settling on Claire. She made an effort to stand up, but he gestured for her to stay where she was.

Claire gestured to a flowered slipper chair. "Please sit down. Would you like something to drink?"

"No, nothing, thank you." He sat on the edge of the chair.

Claire leaned forward. "Did you find out where Dax went? Do you know who he met with? What about his car? Did you find it?"

Drakos held up his hands. "Hold on. I have something important to tell you." He set his hands on his knees, and his eyes zeroed in on hers. "Mrs. Simmons, we believe your husband was murdered."

Claire's eyes widened and more tears welled up. "How?"

"He didn't drown in the Gulf. The autopsy revealed no saltwater in his lungs. That means he was already dead when he went into the water." Drakos pulled out a small notebook and flipped the pages. Morgan sat down close to Claire and held her hand.

"The coroner believes he was injected with something," Drakos went on. "There was a puncture wound in his arm. It's still too soon for a complete blood test to nail down the drug that killed him."

A fresh wave of cramps hit, making Claire feel woozy. She bent over and hugged her knees.

"Are you all right?" Drakos asked, his bushy eyebrows knitting in concern.

Claire lifted her head and sank back against the sofa pillows. "Yes, please continue. I need to know everything."

Drakos looked at Morgan, who nodded. The detective glanced back at his notebook. "Chief Simmons's wrists and ankles had been bound by some kind of soft ligature...not a rope. Maybe a piece of cloth."

"So, he was tied up, injected with some drug, died, and got dumped in the Gulf." Even to herself, Claire sounded robotic.

Drakos looked down at his notebook. "Yes."

"What else?"

"Not much. As yet, no one in the department knows where Chief Simmons went yesterday afternoon. The department is working several cases right now, but the Chief was in a supervisory role. He wouldn't have been out talking to suspects or following up on complaints. That wasn't in his job description."

"What about his car?"

"We haven't found it yet. When we do, that should narrow our investigation." Drakos tapped his notebook with a stubby finger. "Maybe you can help. Is there anything you remember from the last couple of weeks? Anything your husband said, or did, out of the ordinary? Any strange phone calls?"

Claire closed her eyes and thought back over the last few weeks. It was all a blur. Nothing stuck out. She searched her mind, feeling desperate. Then something came to her. It wasn't much, but..."I can only think of one night, a few days ago." She took a breath. She could see Dax in her mind's eye, out on the deck, dressed in his boxers. "I woke up and Dax wasn't there beside me. I got up and found him outside on the deck. He was leaning his elbows on the railing, looking out at the water. I asked him what he was doing out there. He told me he couldn't sleep. Then he said something like, 'You know how when you pull on a loose thread and before you know it you've pulled out the hem of your shirt?' I was half asleep and not quite sure what he was getting at. I probably nodded. Then we went back to bed. In the morning we never discussed what he meant."

"When you pull on a loose thread..." Drakos scribbled in his notebook.

Claire felt her spirits sink lower. Was that the only lead they had?

Chapter 8

Claire lay on a chaise out on the deck. Stars twinkled overhead. She didn't know what time it was. Probably very late or very early depending on how you looked at it. She held a full glass of chardonnay, and an open bottle sat within arm's reach. A couple of empty bottles lay on the wooden floor. On the side table was an elegant gold and burgundy urn. Claire clicked her glass against the urn. "To our love and true friendship, my darling."

She took a sip of wine and sloshed some on her tee-shirt. The wetness felt pleasantly cool. They were all finally gone. The last week had passed in a blur. Wednesday, she and Morgan had gone to the gynecologist and learned that she had in fact miscarried. The doctor pressed some antidepressants on her after she told him of Dax's death. They turned out to be a godsend at certain times during the week. She'd taken one this morning, which probably meant she shouldn't be drinking…but right now she couldn't bring herself to care.

Wednesday afternoon, Drakos had talked to the media. He had displayed Dax's picture, asked if anyone had seen Chief Simmons on Monday afternoon, and if so, would they please contact the Sheriff's Department. She'd learned that Dax had pentobarbital in his blood, a drug often used to euthanize dogs. Drakos said Dax was injected with a large amount and had died quickly. When the kids at the beach discovered his body, he hadn't been in the water long. The two teenage girls and the guy had told Drakos they hadn't seen anyone in the vicinity, but they'd been pretty high and wouldn't have been aware of much.

The police hadn't found Dax's car or his phone, and so far, no one had come forward with a sighting of Dax or his vehicle. He'd apparently disappeared into a spinning vortex.

Now, a week after his death, the media presence outside Claire's house had faded away. The fickle press had moved on to cover Senator Juniper's massive luau. The esteemed Senator had recently acquired a mansion in Lemon Cove that was built on the site of Citrus Haven, the house where Claire had lived when she first arrived on the Emerald Coast. Guests at the luau included Hollywood stars and Washington movers and shakers. The front page of the Northwest

Florida Daily News couldn't get enough of all the big names and beautiful people. They no longer cared about a local sheriff who had died like a dog.

Last Thursday Dax's siblings and extended family had arrived. They stayed in hotels, motels and AirBnBs. Claire's parents, her brother Tim and his family stayed at the house. Tim and Beth Ann had three rambunctious children. Dax's family included a lot of babies, children and teens. The house became beach central. All day babies cried; children ran in and out; mothers scolded; dads drank beer. There were lots of tears but also lots of laughter. When Claire walked into the great room at a moment of hilarity, they all looked sheepishly at her. But she was glad they were laughing. Better to laugh, than to cry.

Her father entertained the kids with his repertoire of magic tricks. As a girl he'd taught her how to hide a coin and how to pull one from behind an ear. At other times her brother Tim played his guitar and got everyone singing.

Local friends and staff from the Sheriff's Department brought food and drink: mountains of pasta salads, pans of lasagna, barbequed wings, chocolate cake and peach pies. Dax's brother grilled hot dogs and burgers, and his sisters and cousins washed the dishes and swept up the sand, while Claire wandered around in a haze.

Morgan had taken over much of the funeral planning. Her frequent consultations with Claire had mainly consisted of proposals to which Claire nodded assent. The service took place in The Chapel at Seaside. Hundreds of people attended, and many had to stand around outside the small church. They held the reception afterwards at the Magnolia Resort and Spa, where Morgan had been the wedding planner before moving to California. Claire remembered the food was beautifully displayed, but she didn't remember eating any of it. Mostly, she remembered shaking hands with hundreds of people and trying to smile over the hollow, dead feeling inside.

Monday, Dax's family cleared out. Claire's parents left Tuesday morning.

"Are you sure you don't want us to stay? I could take care of you," her mother had said. But Claire could see how exhausted she was. Her pale blue eyes were bloodshot and her back seemed to be bothering her.

"I'll be fine, Mom. I have to learn to be alone again." She turned to her dad. He looked tired, too. He had just finished a bout of chemo before they came, and the past week had exhausted him.

"You'll keep in touch, baby girl?" He had tears in his grey eyes.

"Yes, Dad, I will…regularly."

Claire hugged them both and watched as they got into the car. "Drive carefully," she'd called out as they pulled away.

Tuesday afternoon, Claire and Morgan went to see Dax's lawyer. When Dax and she got married, they had kept their finances separate, but he'd insisted on putting her name on the deed for the house they owned jointly along with the cars. At the lawyer's office, Claire learned that Dax had a healthy stock portfolio as well as several investment properties she hadn't known about. There was also a two-million-dollar life insurance policy. Claire would be fine financially...more than fine. She wouldn't really need to work if she handled her finances properly.

Late Tuesday, Claire drove Morgan to the airport.

"I don't know how to thank you for everything you've done for me," Claire told her as they stood outside the terminal, Morgan with her luggage in hand. "Without you I would never have gotten through the past week."

"I think you're stronger than you realize," Morgan said. "I also think you should stay busy. What about Lucca and the job with Letízia? Did you ever talk to him?"

"No, I let his messages go to voicemail. I suppose I should call him, but I don't have anything to say." She sighed. "Letízia is over for me. I've got to start a new life."

They hugged for a long time. Claire promised to keep in touch and Morgan left.

When Claire got home, she started to drink. She'd been drinking ever since. She was going through all the bottles of wine people had contributed this past week. With shaking hands, she set her glass of chardonnay down, picked up the urn, and hugged it to her chest while tears trickled down her cheeks.

Chapter 9

Claire drifted awake. She felt warm, curled up under a blanket. Where was she? With effort, she opened her eyes. Bright light seared into her brain. She quickly closed her eyes and rolled over. When she opened them again, she was staring at a yellow-and-white geometric pattern. After a moment she recognized a sofa pillow in the great room.

Her head felt like it had been squeezed in a lemon press. She turned back over and tried to sit up. Nausea and dizziness washed through her. With an effort she pushed the blanket off, sat up, and shoved her hair out of her face. When she looked up, shock jolted her. She wasn't alone. A man sat in an armchair across from her. He wore a high-necked dark green vest over a long-sleeved black shirt, black pants, and leather sandals. He was reading a book, his lips pursed in concentration.

She cleared her throat and managed to say his name. "Seijun."

He looked up. "Hello, Claire. How do you feel?" His voice was rich and melodious. Biracial, with a Japanese father and a Caucasian mother, Seijun was a Buddhist who'd instructed Claire in Zen meditation. He exuded spiritual serenity and emotional calm.

"I feel horrible." Her voice was scratchy and her mouth felt dry. "How did I get in here?"

"My dear, your friend Morgan phoned me. She was worried about you. She had been calling you, and you didn't respond. So I came over. I found you on the deck and carried you inside." He crossed his legs at the ankle. "May I say, you were drunk as a skunk."

"How about shit-faced," Claire said.

"I wouldn't use that term."

She made an effort to stand, but dizziness made her fall back against the sofa pillows. Then her face scrunched with worry. "Where's Dax? He was with me."

"He's there beside you on the table." Seijun spoke softly, and his eyes reflected concern.

Claire turned her head and saw the urn beside a bowl of seashells. It looked gaudy in the sunlight. Tears pricked in her eyes. How could there be more tears left in her? She reached out and pressed her palm to the urn's hard metal curve, then pulled her hand back as if she'd been burned. That wasn't Dax. Nor were the ashes inside. He was gone. She wrapped her arms around her chest and drew in some deep breaths.

Seijun studied her. "Why don't you take a shower, change your clothes and come back down for some coffee and maybe a couple of Tylenol. We'll talk."

Slowly, she got up off the sofa and headed for the stairs. She took a long, hot shower and brushed her teeth, then dressed in jeans shorts and a turquoise halter-top. In the closet, she found her favorite flip-flops, and slipped them on. Just dressing in clean clothes made her feel tons better.

Downstairs, Seijun was standing by the center island where he had set a place for her. She smelled breakfast, and for the first time in a while it didn't make her feel sick. He handed her two pills and a glass of water. After she dutifully swallowed them down, he poured her a cup of coffee and gave her a plate of scrambled eggs and whole wheat toast.

"I don't know if I can eat anything."

"I bet you can. You probably haven't eaten much for two days. You'll feel better when you get something in your stomach."

"What day is it?"

"Friday."

"So, I drank all day Wednesday and Thursday."

He poured himself some coffee. "I came over at nine last night. After I brought you in, you slept for twelve hours."

Claire blushed. "I've never done that before…gone on a binge. I normally don't drink all that much." She looked down at her hands.

"Well, there were mitigating circumstances. Dear Claire, it's all right to suffer."

"Yes." She glanced over at the gold and burgundy urn that looked so out of place amidst the Florida décor. "Dax wouldn't have approved of my drinking like that. He was the epitome of self-control."

"I'm sure the man I knew would understand," Seijun said.

Claire picked up her fork and took a bite of the eggs. They were creamy, just the way she liked them. The toast was buttered and still crisp, incredibly delicious. She ended up gobbling down everything. While she ate, Seijun sipped his coffee and gazed out at the rolling surf.

Finally, she set down her fork. "Thank you, Seijun. You saved me from myself. I've been an idiot."

"Not an idiot, just a grieving widow. Centuries ago, you would have been literally pulling out your hair."

Claire leaned back in her chair and crossed her arms, closed her eyes, and sighed. "Now I need to think about what to do next. It seems like a monumental task." She turned to face Seijun. "Along with losing Dax, I also lost my job." She paused, because the rest was harder to say. "And I lost a baby. I miscarried last week."

Sadness crossed his features. "You have much to grieve. You need to mourn before you can move on. Don't bury your pain or try to suppress it with alcohol."

"You're right, I shouldn't do that. When Morgan left and I came home to this empty house, all I wanted to do was lose myself." She smiled tremulously at Seijun. "I think I learned my lesson."

He set his coffee mug down and spread his hands on the white marble counter. "You could return to meditation. It would give you some release, help you handle your deep sorrow."

"I haven't meditated for a long time." She remembered the positive feelings meditation always gave her. But she'd lost so much, so fast. Then again, what else was she going to do? She had to pick up the pieces sometime, somehow.

Seijun seemed to sense what she was thinking. "Join us on Monday night. It will help you."

"Okay, I'll do that."

Seijun bowed slightly and took his leave. Claire accompanied him down the stairs and out the door. They did not shake hands or hug. Claire said, "Thank you," and he nodded and got into his car. Once he'd left, she emptied the mailbox, which was full of sympathy cards. She took them upstairs and dumped them on her desk in the office. She would get to them later.

Claire spent the next hour cleaning up. She threw away the empty wine bottles from the deck and cleaned out the previous week's leftovers from the refrigerator. She carried several plastic bags down to the trash bins, something she hadn't done for a long time. Dax had always taken out the trash. As she closed the lid, she glanced up and saw a car at the end of the driveway. As she narrowed her eyes for a better look, the car sped away. Probably some wayward journalist who thought there was still a story here. Whatever.

Upstairs, Claire emptied the dishwasher and wiped down the counters. Then she watered the plants she'd neglected for days. The geraniums on the deck looked really sad. She removed several dried-up blooms. Down on the beach she saw a couple walking along the shore. They waved and she waved back. The water today was a deep shade of blue. Little whitecaps caressed the shore. Claire sighed. She wanted to share all this natural beauty with Dax…but now she was so very alone.

She headed back inside, where she sat down and attacked the email and text messages on her phone. She sent several messages of thanks to people who were sorry for her loss. Lucca had texted many times. It looked like he didn't know about Dax. One message said Letízia would be sending a direct deposit of five thousand dollars in severance pay to her bank. She sent a quick thank-you response and left it at that. For her, their relationship was over.

Next she called Morgan, who had left several messages, and assured her she was feeling better. "I spent two days drinking and crying, but that's done now. Though I'm not sure what comes next."

"You've got to make a plan for each day. You need a purpose," Morgan said. "I know you. You'll be miserable if you have too much time on your hands."

"You're right. Tomorrow, I'll go to yoga and meditation. That'll kill some hours."

The one person she did want to respond to in person was Alexia Cosmos, a gift shop owner and client who'd become a friend. Alexia had written a lovely note with a touching poem included. Claire vaguely remembered seeing her at the funeral. She texted her and they made a date for two-thirty that afternoon.

Chapter 10

At two-fifteen, Claire left the house. She noticed a car parked down the road, and idly wondered if it was the same one, she'd seen earlier. She knew the house two doors down was for sale. Maybe people were checking it out.

Claire got into her car and drove down Lemon Cove Drive. To her right were a series of houses that backed on the beach, to her left a thick wooded stretch that was part of the Point Washington National Forest. A quarter mile down, the road veered to the left and continued another quarter mile towards Highway 30A. Along this stretch, large houses were set back among the trees on both sides. At 30A, Claire turned east towards Seaside.

Seaside was a picturesque little town right on the Gulf, full of quaint restaurants and kitschy shops. Highway 30A ran right through it. On the other side of the road, opposite the beach, a horseshoe-shaped street curved around a wide, grassy bowl that served as an amphitheater. Along the semicircular road were elegant little boutiques, restaurants and a bookstore. Alexia Cosmos owned the Beach Mania gift shop in Seaside, as well as stores in Destin and Panama City Beach. In addition, she owned three Baby Beach Bunny shops that specialized in adorable clothes and toys for children.

Claire parked the car in the horseshoe curve across from Beach Mania. Before getting out, she checked herself in the mirror. With no make-up and her hair pulled back in a ponytail, she looked strung out. There were dark circles under her eyes and her lips were peeling. She shrugged. How she looked didn't seem to matter anymore.

Tina, the shop clerk, looked up as Claire entered the store. "I'm so sorry for your loss," she said, her eyes filling with tears over a shaky smile. "Everybody is. We all liked the Chief."

Claire made an effort to smile back. "Thank you."

"Are you here to see Alexia? She's in the back. I'll go get her."

While she waited, Claire perused the shop. In one corner she saw a collection of Letízia purses and beach bags. They sold well in this Seaside location. Oh well, Letízia was a thing of the past. She wouldn't have to tote those boxes of samples around anymore. She fingered a bright red sundress. It was soft and would probably cling just right. But she didn't see cheerful red dresses in her immediate future.

"You're too thin, Claire," Alexia's deep voice carried through the room. She was a formidable woman, classically beautiful, with thick dark hair swept back from a strong face. Today she wore a sleek black sheath, chunky jewelry and heels. She swept up to Claire and pulled her into a warm hug, then held her at arm's length. "I bet you haven't been eating. Let's go and get you some ice cream."

Claire nodded. Alexia's brisk warmth made her feel weepy again.

Alexia hugged her close and then patted her back. "Tina, we're going out for some gelato. Hold down the fort."

Claire followed Alexia outside. They went down to the corner and turned left toward Heavenly's Shortcakes and Ice Cream. Claire still felt a little off, probably from all the wine she'd consumed over Wednesday and Thursday. She ordered limoncello gelato, and Alexia got two scoops of salted caramel. They sat down outside in the shade. Claire ate a spoonful of limoncello. The cool citrus flavor was deliciously sweet and fresh.

"Claire, how are you doing? Tell me the truth." Alexia never minced words.

"I don't know. I'm still a little numb." She glanced at Alexia and smiled ruefully. "I've cried a lot and I drank myself silly for a couple of days."

"That all sounds normal. I'm all for crying…and I've had too much to drink on more than one occasion." Alexia ate a spoonful of ice cream. "Are you going back to work soon, or are you taking some weeks off?"

Claire stirred the gelato, making a thick yellow soup. "I'm not going back to work for Letízia. I was fired. I figured you probably knew."

Alexia frowned. "No, I didn't. I did see an email from the company recently, but I didn't bother to open it."

Claire continued to stir the gelato. "I got fired a few hours before Dax was killed. They're expecting you'll order directly from the website. Anyway, they don't want a middleman…or woman." She looked up; her eyes clouded over.

"I'm sure it's all about the bottom line.

Claire nodded and kept stirring.

Alexia tapped her spoon on the ice cream dish. "Do you want to work?"

Tears brimmed and spilled over. "I don't know what I want. I'm just floating right now. It's only been nine days."

Alexia patted her hand. "If you want a job, I've got one for you."

Claire patted her face with the mini paper napkin. "A job? Where?"

"Here in Seaside. Tina is running the shop, but she's a single mom with two kids. She just can't be here as much as she needs to. And I could use help as a second in command in running the Beach Mania and Baby Beach stores."

"You mean a role like the one Amy had before she died."

"Yes. I know you're over-qualified; what with an MBA from Duke and those years when you ran the marketing department with that British firm. What was it called?"

Claire's gelato had turned into lemonade. "Safetynaps."

"Right. Safetynaps. What did they make again?"

"Adult diapers."

Alexa smiled at that. "I'd say you've had a varied career." She tilted her head. "Would that be something you would consider? Working for me?"

Claire sighed, balling up the napkin in her hands. "I don't know, Alexia. Right now, I can't think what I want to do."

"Take your time. You need to grieve. But when you're feeling stronger, give me a call."

Claire felt more tears coming. Alexia's kindness, practical help and no sorry for your loss, had done her in.

***

Before heading home, Claire walked over to Amavida and bought some Eclipse Blend dark roast coffee beans. Dax hadn't liked that blend. She drank it back when she was single, before she met Dax. Well, she was single again.

What else did she need? She couldn't think. As she walked back to the car, she passed happy families coming up from the beach carrying buckets, folding chairs and beach balls. The parents were laughing, the children giggling. Clearly, they'd had a great day. In comparison, Claire felt empty. She just needed to get through this day and then sleep would bring her relief.

She drove homeward down 30A in the late afternoon light. The world had taken on a golden glow. With all the traffic, she had to go slowly. Her gaze scanned the sidewalk and settled on a big sign posted on the front of a brand-new town home. She'd seen several like it up and down 30A. The sign depicted a stylized bouquet of white lilies and red roses tied with red and white ribbons. Underneath was written, Lilly Rose Hamlin, Emerald Coast's #1 Realtor. Claire was somewhat ignorant of the real estate market, but she knew it was what made the area tick.

The traffic began to move. Minutes later, Claire turned onto Lemon Cove Drive. As she drove down the road, she spotted a red car up ahead. A young woman jumped out and waved her down. Claire slowed to a stop. The young woman stood in front of Claire's car and talked into her phone for a few seconds, then came around to Claire's window. Claire rolled it down.

"Hi, I'm looking for Cottage Street. Is it right down there?" The girl pointed down Lemon Cove Drive. She wore heavy pancake make-up and her eyelashes were thick with black mascara. A tight purple shirt stretched across her full bosom, above equally tight black leggings. Two inches of dark roots showed in her blond hair.

"Cottage Street is in Grayton Beach," Claire said. "You have to go back east on 30A, then turn right on DeFuniak. That's Route 283. I know there's a Cottage Street off of Hotz. You'll find it."

The woman stood there, scratching her head. "Where do you live?"

"Down this road." Claire tried not to sound annoyed. Where she lived wasn't any of this stranger's business. Why didn't she use the GPS on her phone to get where she was going?

The woman's hand rested on Claire's open window. She wore silver rings on every finger, including her thumb. The thumb ring resembled a twisted snake with little green eyes. "This looks like a pretty glitzy neighborhood," she said.

"Yes, it's nice."

The woman didn't move. Claire felt impatient. "Listen, I've got to get going. Nice to meet you."

"Yeah, okay. Thanks." The woman turned away and walked slowly back toward her vehicle, stopping briefly in front of Claire's car and bending as if to pick something up. Once she was out of the way, Claire gunned the engine and zoomed down Lemon Cove Drive. What a nutcase, she thought. As she made the turn along the beach, a dark car flew past her. Idiot. They'll cause an accident, speeding like that.

At home, Claire parked and then grabbed her bag and the coffee. As she reached the door, she saw it was open a crack. Her first wild thought was, Dax is home. Then apprehension gripped her. Who'd entered her house while she was gone?

She stepped inside and called out, "Hello. Anyone here?"

No answer, just silence. She slowly climbed the stairs, listening hard for any sound, ready to bolt if necessary. Nothing.

As she entered the great room, she screamed. The sliding glass door to the deck was open, the curtains whipping in the breeze. The furniture was turned upside down, cushions tossed left and right, lamps smashed on the carpet. In the kitchen area, the cupboards were open and the drawers upended. Cutlery and pots and pans littered the floor. The urn lay among them turned upside down over a mound of chunky grey dust.

Chapter 11

After Claire called 911, she hurried back outside and locked herself in the car. She'd been too afraid to go upstairs and check out the second floor. She leaned her forehead against the steering wheel, trembling.

Before long, Detective Drakos arrived with the first responders. After they looked inside the house, he came back outside and knocked on her window. Claire lowered it.

Drakos had his notebook and pencil in hand. "Can you tell me how long you were gone this afternoon?"

Claire leaned back and closed her eyes. "I left about two-fifteen for Seaside. I had ice cream at Heavenly's with a friend. I must have been gone about two hours."

"Have you seen anyone lurking around these last few days?"

Claire's eyes shot open. "Yes. There was a dark sedan parked in the street when I left. I might have seen it earlier when I took out the garbage and got the mail. I'm not sure." She sat up straight and met Drakos's gaze. "As a matter of fact, it might have passed me when I drove home. I remember a dark car, speeding." That made her think about the quirky girl who had stopped her to ask for directions. She told the detective about the woman. "Maybe she was a lookout? Stalling me so whoever did this could get away." Claire banged the steering wheel with her palm. "Damn, I could have caught the guy."

Drakos wiped sweat from his forehead with the back of his hand. "That might not have been a good idea. Who knows who these people were? You're better off not running into them."

"I should have written down the license plate or noted the kind of car."

"What about the woman? What kind of car was she driving?"

"Something red. I really didn't notice the model. But I can tell you what she looked like and what she was wearing."

She gave Drakos every detail she could remember. After the detective wrote everything down, he tapped the notebook on the roof of her car. "Ms. Simmons, you're going to have to get out of here so we can work. Can you think of somewhere you could go?"

"Can you just call me Claire?"

"Okay, Claire," Drakos said patiently. "Can you spend the night somewhere with friends?"

"What about Dax?" She clenched her hands in her lap. "Did you see what they did?"

"Yes. We'll do our best to—"

"Put him back in the jar?" she snapped, her tension boiling over.

"Yes." His dark eyes assessed hers. "I understand you're upset. This is the last thing you needed. But your house is a crime scene and we need to go through it, room by room."

"Did they tear apart the bedroom too?"

He nodded.

She realized her nails were digging into her thighs. "Okay. I'll leave. Can I get my pjs?"

"No. We'd prefer you didn't enter the house." He tucked his notebook into his shirt pocket and turned away.

Claire banged the steering wheel again. "Fuck, fuck, fuck." She rolled up the window, started the car and backed out around the police vehicles, then drove off down Lemon Cove Drive at breakneck speed. Let them give her a ticket.

When she reached 30A, she jerked the car to a stop. Still fulminating with anger, she looked at the spot where the woman in the red car had blocked her way. Claire should have just driven around her instead of stopping to help. That way she would at least have seen the guys who broke into her house. She closed her eyes and tried to remember what kind of car the woman was driving, but to no avail. With everything awful that had happened lately, she'd been too self-involved to notice much that went on around her.

Claire turned right on 30A. Where could she go? The Watercolor Inn, maybe. She could probably get a room for the night. As she approached Grayton Beach in the gathering dusk, she remembered the scummy woman in the red car had mentioned Cottage Street. Right, like she really wanted to go there. Just the same, Claire turned on DeFuniak and made her way to Cottage. She drove slowly down the short street, looking for a red car. Of course, there wasn't one. She'd been played.

She turned around and retraced her route, trying to think where to go. And then it came to her. Maybe she could stay with Aunt Irma. Her house was only a few blocks away on Hotz Street.

Minutes later, Claire pulled up in front of a yellow clapboard house with a wide porch, surrounded by a white picket fence. The porch lights illuminated a swing and some deep cushioned chairs, as well as the white painted steps dotted with pots of herbs and bright red geraniums. The inside of the house was dark, except for a warm glow from the kitchen. Hopefully, Aunt Irma was still awake. She got out of the car and locked it, opened the fence gate, and walked up the garden path. The sweet perfume of the rose bushes enveloped her as she ascended the steps.

Claire knocked timidly. No response. She gently pushed the door open and called out, "You-hoo. Aunt Irma?"

A familiar voice answered. "Is that you, Françoise?"

"No, it's Claire. Claire Simmons." Françoise was a neighbor of Irma's.

"Claire. Wonderful. Come on back." Aunt Irma's voice was warm and inviting.

Claire went through the dining room to the kitchen. Aunt Irma was seated at the small round kitchen table. A copy of People Magazine lay open in front of her on the flowered oilskin tablecloth. Aunt Irma smiled up at Claire, her bright blue eyes full of welcome. She wore a light blue nightgown covered by a tattered grey sweater, and a long white braid trailed over one shoulder.

"Land sakes, I'm so glad you've come for a visit," she said. "I've been worried about you."

Claire felt her eyes brimming. Aunt Irma stood and waved her to an empty chair. "Sit down, sit down. What can I get you? A glass of wine?"

Claire shuddered. "No thanks. I've had way too much wine lately."

Aunt Irma came around the table and gave her a hug. "Would you like some tea? I've got sweet tea. Or maybe hot?"

"Hot tea would be good. Thank you." Claire sat, grateful for Irma's quiet calm.

"Are you hungry?"

It hit Claire that she was. "Yes, I am." She spotted the cookie jar on the counter. "Maybe I'll have a cookie."

"Did you have dinner?"

"No. I can't get in my house. I've been kicked out."

Aunt Irma frowned. "You need to tell me all about it. Meanwhile, I'm going to make you a sandwich. Do you like chicken salad?"

Claire actually smiled for the first time in a week. "I love chicken salad."

As Aunt Irma brewed a pot of tea, sliced a loaf of homemade bread and made the sandwich, Claire told her what had happened that afternoon. Aunt Irma nodded and hmmmed several times. While Claire ate the sandwich and sipped her tea, Aunt Irma sat down and folded her hands on her magazine. "So, these guys were looking for something in your house?"

"Seems that way. I think it had to do with Dax." Her throat tightened, and the next bite of sandwich went down hard. "I think he was killed because he discovered something or knew something. Maybe they thought he'd hidden an incriminating piece of evidence, or written down a name…I don't know."

"It could be a drug deal, or some real estate scam. There's lots of money changing hands around here with all the housing developments being built." Irma sipped her cup of milky tea. "Barb went to the last county board meeting. She thinks some shysters are running the county. Lots of fishy deals."

Claire picked up a barbeque potato chip from the bowl Aunt Irma had set out and took a bite. "The Sheriff's Department said Dax wasn't working on anything that would have caused his death. I mean, his cases were all normal, everyday stuff. He spent most of his time shuffling papers." In her mind's eye she could see Dax pacing the great room, frustrated because he didn't see the action he had as a FBI agent or as a detective. I'm bored, Claire. I don't know if I'm cut out for this job, he'd complained.

"I'll ask Detective Drakos if he knows anything about Dax and the county board." Claire stretched her arms over her head. She felt relaxed, better than she'd felt in a long time.

"You need a place to stay tonight, right?" Aunt Irma said.

"Yes, I was hoping I could sleep on the sofa."

"You can have Amy's old room. I had another girl here for a while, named Ruby. It was the strangest thing, one day she just up and left."

Amy had been Claire's good friend when she first moved down to the Emerald Coast. She'd been killed by a drug lord. Claire and Irma had both mourned her death.

"What do you mean, she up and left?"

"She moved out and left all her stuff. I got a text from her a couple of days later. She always texted me. Never called. She said she was going to Texas and to dump her clothes and things. I finally sent her stuff up to the post office in DeFuniak Springs. She came from there; I had her address." Irma picked up a potato chip crumb and rubbed it between her thumb and middle finger. "It was the oddest thing. I never heard from her again."

Chapter 12

Claire awoke to the delicious aroma of cinnamon and brown sugar. Eyes still closed, she stretched her arms over her head and yawned. Dax is downstairs making breakfast. She smiled, thinking of the satisfied grin he'd give her when she appeared in the kitchen: Look what a great husband I am. Then the painful truth came crashing over her like a mammoth wave. She wasn't at home and Dax wasn't downstairs. This trick of the imagination kept happening…as if Dax was there, but just out of reach. She had to pull herself up short and face reality.

Nonetheless she'd had the best sleep she could recall since Dax died. She glanced at the clock beside the bed and saw it was eight already.

Claire got out of bed and padded over to the small wooden desk chair where she'd laid her clothes the previous evening. Irma had given her an old flannel nightgown to sleep in, so soft it had probably been washed a million times. She pulled on her halter top and jeans shorts. In the bathroom, she splashed water on her face. After drying her face and hands, she pulled open the mirror above the vanity, looking for mouthwash. Instead she found, a bottle of Tylenol and several small bottles of prescription drugs, each labeled Ruby Branson. Irma must have forgotten to empty the cabinet. Claire picked up one bottle and looked at the label: Xanax. Another bottle contained Valium pills. Apparently, Ruby Branson had suffered from major anxiety. A couple of inches from the Valium bottle, Claire noticed a pink packet of birth control pills, about half full. Amazing, how much you could learn about someone by looking into their medicine cabinet. Why would Ruby leave all this stuff behind…particularly the birth control pills?

Downstairs, Aunt Irma was bustling around the kitchen. Claire saw a pan of cinnamon rolls on the stove. "Yum. Those look delicious."

Aunt Irma turned around and gave her a big smile. In her house dress, with her silvery hair in a neat bun and her sparkling blue eyes, she looked like everyone's idea of a fairytale godmother. "How did you sleep?"

Claire smiled back. "I slept well, and I feel great."

"Good. Last night you looked really strung out. Sit down and have some coffee and one of these rolls. You'll have to tell me what you think. It's a new recipe."

Aunt Irma poured coffee into a yellow mug with a sprightly daisy on the side. She handed Claire a plate with a giant cinnamon roll and a small bowl of sliced peaches. "Would you like some bacon and eggs?"

"No, this looks perfect. What a treat." Claire cut into the roll with her fork and took a bite. The creamy frosting and gooey cinnamon interior were out of this world. "Mmm, these are wonderful. I give this recipe an A-plus."

"I've got my book club coming over for coffee this morning. I'm glad the rolls pass muster."

Claire continued to eat as Irma told her about the book club and an annoying member who talked all the time. "I love Judith, but she thinks she knows everything."

"I know people like that. They need to be the center of attention."

"What are you going to do today?" Irma asked.

"Go home and start cleaning. I have a big job ahead of me."

"I wish I could help. Why don't you call a friend?"

"That's a good idea. I'll try Olivia. You know her. She's the one with the dark curly hair. She works for McDonald's."

"Really? Doing what?"

"She's an inspector. She goes around and does surprise visits, making sure the restaurants are clean and up to code and the food is being prepared properly. I guess McDonald's is pretty strict."

"Interesting. I never heard of a job like that. What about your job? When are you going back?"

Her good mood deflated somewhat. "I'm not. I was fired. It happened just a few hours before I learned Dax was dead." She couldn't bring herself to talk about the miscarriage as well. No one else needed to know about that.

"You poor thing. Two blows in one night." Aunt Irma's eyes were full of sympathy and she squeezed Claire's hand across the table.

"Right now, I can't think about finding a job. I need to find out what happened to Dax. That will be my job."

Irma looked worried. "Shouldn't you leave it to the police? Whatever business Dax was investigating must be serious, very serious...and dangerous. They killed Dax and they tore up your house. Don't get involved, Claire."

"I've got to know what happened. Dax was everything to me."

Irma raised her eyes heavenward. "Dear God, keep her safe," she murmured.

***

Before leaving Aunt Irma's house, Claire stepped out on the porch and called Detective Drakos.

"Hello, Mrs. Simmons...Claire." His scratchy voice sounded as though he'd just finished smoking a pack of cigarettes.

"Can I go home?" She sat down on the porch swing.

"Yes, we finished a few hours ago. There's an officer on duty outside the house and a cleaning crew inside."

"Cleaning crew? I didn't think the Sheriff's Department supplied cleaners."

"It's courtesy of a local business. They've been there for about an hour."

"Did you find useful fingerprints?"

"Not really. There were just too many big hands and little hands to count."

All the funeral guests. For a moment, she'd forgotten. "Right, I had fifty or sixty people in and out of that house last week." She pushed the swing back and forth with her toe. "Anything else?"

"You'll have to go through your stuff and figure out if something is missing, and make a report."

Claire sighed. Just now, the job sounded overwhelming. "What about Dax's car or his phone? Any news?"

Drakos coughed and cleared his throat. He was stalling, she could tell. "Listen, Mrs. Simmons..."

"Claire."

"Claire. This is police business. We are actively investigating Chief Simmons's death, but I can't divulge each step of the process."

Red hot anger flashed through her. "That's bullshit. My husband was murdered, and I have a right to know what is being done to catch his killer or killers. I'm not just any random wife. I was married to a cop. I know how these things go."

"I know that, Claire. But you've got to be patient and let us do our job."

She stood and paced up and down the porch. "I don't need to know all your precious investigative secrets. I just want to know if you found his car or his phone."

He sighed heavily. "We didn't."

"What about his land line at the department? Did you check his phone log?"

"Yes."

"And?"

He cleared his throat again. "There were two calls to an unidentified number that afternoon. One around two and one at three-thirty. We tried to track that phone through triangulation, but it's gone silent. Which means it was probably a burner."

Claire thought about Dax's car. It was a classic white BMW, fairly distinctive hereabouts. It must be parked somewhere along the coast. "Maybe you should have the TV and radio stations put out a plea to look for the car. I'll bet someone's seen it."

Much too eagerly, he said, "Good idea. I'll see to it. I've got to go. You could help us by making that list of stolen articles, if there are any."

"Right, Detective..." But before she could ask another question, he'd hung up.

Claire went inside to thank Aunt Irma for taking her in on such short notice. Irma hugged her. "Land sakes, child. You're welcome anytime. If you're lonely at home, come back and stay a day or two."

Before taking off in her car, Claire tapped in Olivia's number on her cell phone.

Olivia picked right up. "Hey there, I'm so glad you called. I've got the day off. Just got back from a three-day jaunt. I saw the worst facility ever. They're giving McDonald's a majorly bad name. My report tore the place apart from top to bottom. But forget all that. How are you?"

"So-so. Trying to figure out my new reality. Listen, I'm wondering if you could help me out. I've got a clean-up job at the house." Claire explained what happened the previous afternoon.

"Oh my God, that's the last thing you needed. Poor you! Sure, I'd love to help. I feel guilty because I haven't been there for you this past week."

"Please don't. I had Morgan, my family and all of Dax's family...too many people, honestly."

"Where are you now? At a motel?"

"No, I'm at Aunt Irma's. Remember Amy's landlady?"

"Yes, she's such a dear. So, what's the plan?"

"Can you meet me at my house in a half hour?"

"I'll be there. See you then." Olivia sounded strong and sure. Although she hated to admit it, Claire needed someone by her side when she entered her home again. Olivia would give her strength.

Chapter 13

Claire turned onto Lemon Cove Drive and slowed down at the spot where she had run into the quirky woman in the red car. She stopped, got out, and looked around at the pavement, remembering that the woman had picked something up off the ground, but she didn't see anything. It had probably been another ploy to keep Claire from driving home.

When she arrived at the house, Olivia was there talking to the officer on guard. As Claire approached, she realized it was Officer Nilsson, the young rookie she'd spoken to the evening Dax died. She waved hello. Olivia had parked her Jeep next to one of two white vans in the driveway. Claire pulled into her parking spot, got out, and joined Olivia. They hugged.

"Officer Nilsson tells me there's already a cleaning crew in there," Olivia said. A few inches shorter than Claire, she looked ready for action in ripped jeans, a red plaid cotton blouse with the shirttails tied in front, and brown booties on her feet. Her dark curly hair was tied up in a red scarf.

"Right, I'm sure the police dusted for fingerprints. So that's a big cleaning job. Whoever broke in dumped everything we own all over the floor, so in addition to cleaning the floors and the furniture, we need to put things back in drawers and cupboards."

"What were they looking for? Do you have any idea?" Olivia asked as they walked toward the entrance.

"No clue. But I think it had to do with Dax's death. He must have had something they wanted."

Olivia patted Claire's back. "I just hope they found what they were looking for, or they gave up…for your sake. That means they won't be back."

Claire nodded and glanced at the two parked vans. A logo painted on the driver's door of the nearest one said Lilly Rose Hamlin, Inc. underneath a stylized bouquet of lilies and roses.

"Look at that. How come we've got Lilly Rose cleaners? Weird," she said.

Olivia squinted at the logo. "Maybe they work for the county part time."

They went inside. From upstairs they could hear voices, vacuum cleaners and loud music playing. It sounded like there was a mariachi band in the great room. On the landing, they found a Hispanic lady dressed in a pink maid's uniform, pushing a vacuum cleaner. On the shirt pocket was the Lilly Rose logo and the name Lucinda. She turned off the vacuum and smiled broadly.

"Hello, we're cleaning up. Big mess." She raised her eyebrows.

"Yes, I know. Thank you." Claire smiled back and gestured to Olivia. "We're going to put things away."

"Good. We not know where things go," Lucinda said.

"Did the Sheriff's Department send you here?" Claire asked.

"No. Is Miss Lilly Rose."

Claire looked at Olivia, whose puzzlement reflected her own. She drew her brows together. "Lilly Rose Hamlin? Why?"

"Miss Lilly Rose wanted to help, so we come."

This was getting odder by the minute. "Well, I'll have to pay you something."

"No, no. This is gift for you." Lucinda beamed at Claire again.

"Okay. I'll call Ms. Hamlin and thank her."

Lucinda shrugged and turned the vacuum on again.

Four more Hispanic women were working elsewhere in the house. The one out on the deck, where the intruder had turned the planters upside down, was sweeping up the dirt and replanting the pots. Another woman was working in the kitchen. The great room was back to normal already.

Claire nodded toward the kitchen area. "Olivia, could you help her put the pots and utensils away? I don't care if the fry pans are where the mixing bowls used to be. Just put them away someplace."

"Sure." Olivia moved off, and Claire went upstairs where she found two ladies in green uniforms working, one in the bathroom and one in the boudoir. They had stripped the bed and Claire could hear the washing machine running. She said hello and got busy putting her underwear back in drawers and folding up her tee-shirts. After she'd hung up her dresses and pants, she turned to attack Dax's stuff, starting with the pile of pants just inside the closet. But she couldn't. She sat down on the bed and looked down at her clenched hands. Her gaze settled on her wedding ring and her beautiful diamond engagement ring. Remembering when Dax had surprised her with it, she felt tears coming on. What was the point of those rings now? But she didn't want to take them off. Although Dax was no longer with her in body, he was still here in spirit.

Olivia came pounding up the stairs. "What can I do up here?" Her eyes swept the room. Through the open closet door, she saw the pile of Dax's pants. She walked over and picked up a pair, frowned at it, and then eyed the rest. "Look at this, Claire. Whatever these folks were after, it must've been pretty small. Right? Otherwise they wouldn't have turned all the pockets inside out. What could they be looking for?"

"I don't know. I guess you're right, something small." Claire felt weighted down, as though a ton of bricks lay on her shoulders.

Olivia draped the pair of pants on the end of the bed and sat down beside her. Very gently, she said, "What do you want to do about Dax's clothes?"

The tears were coming now. Olivia slipped her arm around Claire's shoulders. "We can either hang everything back up or we can pack it up and give it away. You tell me. I'll do the work."

Claire closed her eyes and sobbed, leaning into Olivia, who pulled her into a hug. "You'll get through this. I'm here for you," she crooned in Claire's ear.

Finally, the sobs subsided. Claire took a deep breath and straightened. "Let's give it to these cleaning ladies. I bet they know someone who might need good clothes. And the uniforms, I can give them to the department. Maybe someone would appreciate that."

"Excellent idea. Do you want to do the packing? Or shall I?"

Claire rubbed her eyes with her palms. "You do it. It's too hard for me."

"Why don't you check out the office downstairs? They've pretty much cleaned the desk, but everything from the drawers and files is piled in boxes."

"Okay." She went to the doorway, then looked back. "Olivia, thank you."

"No problem. I'm glad I can help."

Downstairs, Claire glanced into the great room. Someone had placed Dax's urn in the center of the dining table, as though it were a vase of flowers. She wondered what she should do with the ashes. She and Dax had never talked about death. Should she sprinkle them somewhere meaningful or keep them in a closet until she was old and grey?

She turned and went back through the foyer to the office. Lucinda had vacuumed and wiped everything down. She'd placed everything from the file cabinets and desk drawers in four boxes that were lined up on the desk. Before attacking the boxes, Claire took the picture of Rosemary Beach off the wall. There were scratches on the frame. The intruders had probably thrown it on the floor. Claire set the picture aside, tapped in the code for the safe, and opened the door. It looked as though no one had tampered with the contents. She pulled out the two guns and laid them on the desk along with a box of ammo.

Underneath the guns, she found the file folder with their birth certificates, wedding certificate, their passports and a bundle of fifty-dollar bills. Dax liked to have cash on hand. In the very back, she spied a plastic sandwich bag. Claire reached in and pulled it out. Holding the edges gingerly, she looked at what lay inside. It seemed to be a pair of lacy pink underpants. Not anything she'd ever owned. Whose? As she looked at them more closely, she realized the front was stained with a dark reddish substance, like dried blood. She dropped the bag with a little scream.

Chapter 14

Claire must have screamed louder than she thought. A few seconds later, Lucinda appeared at the door to the office, looking worried. Claire turned her back to Lucinda, quickly picked up the baggie, and pushed it back in the safe. Then she turned around and forced a smile. "I just had a little shock. It's nothing. Sorry to frighten you."

Lucinda glanced over at the two handguns on the desk. Her eyes widened and she backed out of the room. She was obviously not a fan of firearms. Claire put the guns back in the safe along with the bullets. In another life, she had been a pretty good shot. She'd spent childhood summers with her grandparents, and her grandfather had taught her to shoot a rifle. At this stage of life, she had no desire to shoot, although Dax had offered to take her out to the range multiple times.

Claire spent the next hour sorting files and filling up the desk drawers. It kept her mind busy and off the pink lace panties. She threw away dried-up markers and pens that didn't work. There were several brochures about houses for sale and real estate developments along the Emerald Coast. Claire didn't remember seeing them before. Maybe Dax had been looking into buying real estate.

Aggressively, she threw away the files from Letízia. Now the file cabinet was almost empty. She glanced up at the wall map of the Emerald Coast, with all the pushpins that indicated the location of her Letízia clients. What had seemed so clever when she first came up with it seemed silly now. Looking closer, she noticed some black markings...a little x here and there. She couldn't remember what they signified.

The robbers had pried open Dax's two desk drawers. Claire didn't know what had been in them, or if the intruders had found what they were searching for. As Claire worked, her thoughts returned to the safe where the bloodstained panties were hidden. Were they a clue to Dax's death? Why had he put the panties in his and Claire's personal safe rather than taking them to the lab to have them analyzed? Was that what her intruders were after? Should she give them to Drakos? So many unanswered questions.

By late afternoon, the cleaners had left. Claire tried to give them a generous tip, but they refused the cash. Miss Lilly Rose would not approve, they said. However, they happily accepted the bags of clothes Olivia had sorted. Claire looked away as they loaded the garments into their cars. She knew it was the right thing to do but it pulled at her heart strings.

Olivia gave two more big garbage bags of clothes to the officer on duty guarding the house. Nilsson had left, and his replacement was a new officer Claire didn't know. Afterwards, she and Olivia inspected the house, going from room to room.

"I don't think this house has ever been this clean and neat," Claire said.

"They did a great job. So why do you think Miss Lilly Rose sent the cleaners over? Was she a friend of yours?"

"No, I've never met the woman. I've heard she's pretty formidable...a tough-as-nails businesswoman. I'll write her a thank you note, maybe take her out for lunch."

"For sure you'll have to acknowledge her gift."

Back in the great room, they looked around at the shiny floors and spotless kitchen. Olivia's eyes rested on the urn on the dining room table and then on Claire. Softly she said, "Do you have plans for Dax's ashes?"

Claire sighed. "No. For now, he's staying with me. But I don't think that urn should be on the dining room table. I'll take it upstairs later."

Olivia suggested they drive over to Watercolor and have a drink at the Wine Bar. Claire figured she could allow herself one glass.

***

The next few months were strange. Claire felt as though she was floating through life. She couldn't seem to drum up a sense of purpose. Every day she called Detective Drakos and asked him if there was anything new with the investigation. Every day he told her the investigation was still active, but he had nothing to report.

"What about the car?"

"It hasn't been found."

"What about his phone? What about phone calls?"

"Claire, I have nothing to tell you."

"I feel so frustrated. Will we ever know what happened?" Claire pleaded.

"Sometimes these things take a long time to solve. I won't give up, though, not ever," he assured her.

She knew he was being kind, but she hung up without saying goodbye.

A month after the break-in, the Sheriff's Department pulled the security guard and Claire was on her own. In the meantime, she'd installed burglar-proof sliding glass doors on both floors upstairs. The entryway door was reinforced steel and she'd installed a security system and cameras, so once the friendly sentinel was gone, she felt relatively safe. And of course, there were the revolvers. Claire had taken the Glock 22 upstairs and placed it in the top drawer of the bedside table.

***

Claire went to yoga three days a week. Some days she walked over and some days she took the car. Rhea Bell, the statuesque blond owner of Sunshine Yoga, had been friends with Claire for a long time. Rhea welcomed her with a hug at each session, something she'd never done in the past. Claire went through her paces, but she failed to get that wonderful high at the end of class. The same thing happened when she went running on the beach. She just felt blah. She and Dax used to run together, and when they arrived home, she would feel the adrenalin pulsing through her veins. Sometimes, after a run they took a shower together. She remembered the feel of his hands on her body under the warm spray…

She went up to Atlanta and spent a week with her parents. She'd intended to spend two weeks, but her mother's constant questions and her dad's concerned gaze drove her back home.

A little while after that, Claire went out to California and visited Morgan. The baby, a girl, was adorable and practically never cried. They'd named her Harper and Morgan asked Claire to be Harper's godmother. At a service at the Episcopal Church, Claire had sworn to keep the baby safe in God's name, but she felt uncomfortable because she wasn't a regular churchgoer. And right then, she was angry at God for taking away the greatest joy of her life.

Claire and Morgan took long walks on the beach and talked and talked, but neither of them ever mentioned the miscarriage. Claire could sense that Morgan felt sorry for her and was trying to bolster her up, just as her parents had done. It made her want to escape. She felt a sense of relief when she was back on the plane, on her way back to the Emerald Coast.

At home, she wandered the house. Every room vibrated with Dax's spirit. He inhabited their bedroom, laughed in the great room, pounded up the stairs calling her name.

Nothing held her interest: not TV, nor books nor magazines. Rarely did she sit down in front of her laptop or scroll through her phone. Facebook and Instagram detailed everyone's happy lives. What did she have in common with any of those people?

Once in a while, she cooked a simple dish, but most days, it was a frozen Lean Cuisine or some crackers and cheese with a couple of carrot sticks. She drank one or two glasses of wine most nights…but she never got drunk.

Off and on during those long days, she went over and over the last couple of weeks before Dax was killed. She tried to remember what he'd said, where he went, who he called…anything that would give her a clue to his murder, but she came up with nothing.

A couple of times a week, she attended the Zen meditation sessions at Kōfuku, a shop that carried Letízia purses and was one of her previous clients. Seijun held the sessions behind the shop, in a Japanese sand garden bounded by a wall. A narrow path led to a koi pond complete with a small, elegant bridge over the water. The Zen group gathered in a little gazebo at the back of the garden. Claire tried to empty her mind of random thoughts, but she seemed to have no control over her brain. Dax always infiltrated her mind and she found herself reliving precious moments when they were together.

At the end of one session, after the others had left, Seijun beckoned to her to follow him. That day he wore a long forest green kimono and matching full pants. He made his way through the sand garden to the koi bridge, a container of fish food in his hands. At the top of the bridge he sprinkled the nuggets of food in the pond. Together he and Claire watched the orange, black and yellow fish dance in the water. Seijun radiated a sense of deep calm. He looked down into her eyes, and she smiled a tremulous smile.

"Claire, let me tell you a story."

She nodded; her mouth dry.

"A senior monk and a junior monk were traveling together. At one point, they came to a river with a strong current. As the monks were preparing to cross the river, they saw a young and beautiful woman also attempting to cross. The young woman asked if they could help her reach the other side.

"The two monks glanced at one another, because they had taken vows not to touch a woman. Then, without a word, the older monk picked up the woman, carried her across the river, placed her gently on the other side, and continued on his journey.

"The younger monk couldn't believe what had just happened. After rejoining his companion, he was speechless, and an hour passed without a word between them.

"Two more hours passed, then three, until finally the younger monk could contain himself no longer. He blurted out, 'We are not permitted to touch a woman. How could you have carried that woman on your shoulders?'

"The older monk looked at him and replied, 'I set her down on the other side of the river. Why are you still carrying her?'

"This simple Zen story has a beautiful message about living in the present. We can choose to think about past actions or events, but they will ultimately weigh us down and sap our energy. Or, instead, we can choose to let go of what doesn't serve us anymore and concentrate on the present moment. Until we can find a level of peace and happiness in the current circumstances of our lives, we will never be content, because now is all we will ever have."

Claire nodded. "It's hard, though. Really hard."

"Dax loved you," Seijun said. "He would want you to unburden yourself and choose to live in the present. If you can't yet do that for yourself, perhaps you can do it for him."

Chapter 15

Alexia had called several times, but Claire always refused her invitations to get together. That day, after her talk with Seijun, Alexia called again. "Hello, Claire. I'm going to be in Rosemary Beach this afternoon. How about an early dinner at La Crema?"

Claire thought about what Seijun had said about living in the present. If she didn't go out for supper with Alexia, she would huddle in her boudoir all evening, trying to bring Dax up in her mind. Lately, she'd had trouble remembering exactly what he looked like. The previous evening, she'd sat on the floor with his picture in her hands and pretended a conversation with him. How pathetic was that?

Claire took the plunge. "Sure, I'd love to. What time?"

Silence at the other end. Obviously, Alexia hadn't thought she would accept the invitation.

"Wonderful," Alexia said, finally. "How about five-thirty? We'll have a glass of wine, share a couple of tapas and maybe some gooey chocolate concoction."

"Okay, and...thanks, Alexia."

After she hung up, Claire studied herself in the mirror. She looked terrible. Her hair was long and stringy, and the dark circles under her eyes appeared to be permanent. Her clothes hung on her and her nails were ragged. She checked the time on her phone. Eleven o'clock. She called the Magnolia Spa. When Natasha answered, she identified herself and said, "Is there any way I could get my hair cut and a mani-pedi this afternoon?"

"Sure, Claire. Come right now and we'll get you taken care of." Natasha spoke with a distinctive Russian accent. A tall, muscular redhead, she gave a killer massage. *Maybe I should get one of those, too,* Claire thought.

Claire took a quick shower and put on some clean shorts. They hung on her hips, so she threaded a scarf through the beltloops and stuffed her tee-shirt in the waist to hold them up.

When she arrived at the Magnolia, she said hello to the parking attendants and briefly hugged Hans at the front desk. They all knew her because of her friendship with Morgan. She headed to the spa, where Natasha gave her the onceover. The Russian girl frowned and lifted a section of Claire's lank hair. "You haven't been taking care of yourself."

Claire nodded. She knew she looked a mess.

"We'll take care of you. You'll walk out of here today a new woman." Natasha clapped her hands. Seconds later, a petite Asian woman arrived and led Claire away.

First, she had a facial. Afterwards, in the mirror, her face appeared smooth and glowing. A handsome Italian hairdresser cut her hair in layers, so it framed her face in soft waves. Her nails were trimmed and painted a perfect blue. Lastly, Natasha insisted they do her make-up. When she left the salon, she did feel like a new woman. And she hadn't paid a cent. Apparently, Morgan had told them that when or if Claire came in, she should get a complete makeover and Morgan would pay for it all.

At home, Claire went through her wardrobe. Nothing seemed right, but she finally settled on a turquoise, white and pink flowered sundress that had always been a little tight. Now, it was a little loose. She left the house at five, making sure everything was buttoned-up tight and all the outdoor floodlights were on for her return.

Alexia was already seated at a table outside when Claire arrived at La Crema. She looked up and did a double take. "Wow. You look fabulous."

Claire smiled. "Thanks. You wouldn't have thought so if you'd seen me this morning." Then she told her friend about the afternoon at the Magnolia Spa.

"You did the right thing. You look really great. I love the haircut. It's cute and chic."

Claire couldn't help but giggle. When was the last time she'd laughed, really laughed? It threw her for a loop. Was it too soon? Should she be happy? Claire dropped into a chair, feeling guilty. Alexia was smiling at her. Claire shook herself. Live in the present. Don't be weighed down by the past. You're having a fun time with Alexia. It's okay.

They ordered and shared several tapas dishes: delicious crab cakes, crispy Brussels sprouts, goat cheese-stuffed piquillo peppers, and lobster-stuffed mushrooms. Claire ate with pleasure for the first time in months. They shared a bottle of crisp Sancerre.

As they ate, Claire told Alexis what her life had been like since Dax's passing. Then she related the story Seijun had told her that morning. "I'm going to try and get out of the house and learn something new."

After a pause, Alexia said, "Do you want to come and work for me? The job is still open."

Claire nibbled on her bottom lip, then looked up. "I'm very grateful, but I don't think I want to go back into retail. I want to shut the door on that stage of my life. Please don't take it the wrong way."

Alexia's eyes twinkled. "Don't be upset. I had a feeling you wouldn't want to run a store. But I wanted to offer you the possibility. It's no big deal. I admire you and I know you'll do well, whatever you decide."

Relief washed through her. "Thank you, for understanding."

They decided to go all out and share the hot chocolate molten cake. As Claire scooped up a bite on her fork, she looked over at an adjoining table. An amazingly beautiful woman was just sitting down. An emerald green dress with a low décolleté set off her creamy white skin and matched her bright green eyes. Her full lips were painted a luscious pink, and thick auburn hair was piled on top of her head. She glanced at their table and then gave a little cry of recognition. "Alexia, how are you?" she said, in a marked Southern drawl. "I haven't seen you in ages."

"I'm so glad to see you," Alexia drawled back. Then she turned to Claire. "Let me introduce Lilly Rose Hamlin. I'm sure you've heard of her?"

Before Alexia could say anything more, Claire blurted out, "Oh, I'm so glad to meet you. I'm Claire Simmons. I wanted to thank you in person for sending your staff to clean my house. I've been remiss, taking so long." Claire got up and went to Lilly Rose's table, one hand outstretched to shake.

Lilly Rose took it and beamed up at her. "My pleasure. I was glad to help out."

Claire smiled down at her. "One thing I've wondered…how you knew it had been trashed."

Lilly Rose shrugged. "I can't remember. Someone must have told me." She gestured toward the chocolate cake. "Y'all better lap up that pool of chocolate before it cools down."

***

Lilly Rose was waiting for someone. She ordered a glass of wine and the three of them chatted for a while. "I'm sorry for your loss," she told Claire. "Losing your husband at such a young age must be terrible. Do you have children?" She seemed truly interested, her manner warm and sympathetic.

For once, I'm sorry for your loss didn't bother Claire. Tears glistened in her eyes as she answered. "Thank you. No, no children."

"What do you do? Do you have a job?"

Before Claire could respond, Alexia said, "She used to represent Letízia. You know, those adorable purses?"

Lilly Rose nodded and took a sip of her wine. "What happened?"

"They're going totally internet sales. I was told they no longer needed my services," Claire said.

Alexia ate a bite of cake. "What's crazy is, she was a fabulous sales rep. She built a network all over northern Florida. Right, Claire?"

Claire blushed. This was high praise from Alexia.

"I wanted her to work for me, but she turned me down," Alexia continued.

Lilly Rose scrutinized Claire. Claire was glad she'd done some personal maintenance that day.

"Have you ever considered real estate? I bet you could apply your merchandising talents to selling houses."

"She's really smart. She's got an MBA from Duke," Alexia said.

Claire laughed. "Oh my gosh, Alexia, enough already."

Lilly Rose peppered her with questions, and she ended up telling the woman about her job at Safetynaps and then her move down to Florida. In the midst of their conversation, Lilly Rose's guest arrived—a tall, well dressed gentleman, lean and nice looking. She paused in her questioning and gestured toward him. "Harrison Reed, let me introduce Alexia Cosmos and Claire Simmons."

Harrison Reed's neatly combed hair was a burnished copper, and his brown eyes sparkled with flecks of gold. He had a friendly, amused expression. Claire guessed people liked him immediately.

"Ladies, I'm delighted to meet both of you. But I feel like I've interrupted something."

"Sit down, Harrison. I'm getting to know Claire. I think she should join our team."

Harrison raised his eyebrows. "You must have made quite an impression on Miss Lilly Rose, Claire. She doesn't usually make such quick decisions."

Claire didn't know what to say. She'd never considered a job in real estate. A five-star realtor friend back in Atlanta had told her being a realtor was a twenty-four-hour, seven-day-a-week job. You had to be ready to jump when a client needed you. Claire had thought it sounded exhausting, with little time for a private life. Harrison, Lilly Rose and Alexia were all staring at her, apparently waiting for a response. Was this a job offer?

"My goodness, thank you, Ms. Hamlin. I don't know what to say."

"Ms. Hamlin? Oh, no. Please call me Lilly Rose. Think about it, will you? No pressure. But our agency would love to have you."

They chatted for a few more minutes. When Alexia and Claire got up to leave, Harrison got to his feet as they said their goodbyes.

What nice people, Claire thought as she drove home.

Chapter 16

The next morning Claire had an email from Lilly Rose Hamlin. It contained the names and contact information of several real estate licensing programs and information about licensing in the State of Florida. Claire saved the email, but she felt iffy about the prospect of working in real estate. Was this something she really wanted to do? She needed to think it over.

Wearing a cotton bathrobe over her night gown, a mug of coffee and her iPad nearby, Claire sat outside at the glass table on the deck. It was the first time in weeks she'd enjoyed the weather, instead of being oblivious to the beauty of the Gulf and the beach. She spent a little while watching the smooth, rolling waves and little lacy wavelets caress the shore. The sky was a brilliant blue, the water several shades of turquoise. She sighed. She should be grateful for the day. She closed her eyes and tried to feel at peace.

Then she heard a voice shouting, "Hello. Is this your beachball?"

Claire looked up. Some distance away, a guy down by the shore was facing her, beachball in hand. She'd seen him before, running along the beach. Claire got up and approached the railing. "No, it's not mine," she called out. "Maybe it belongs two houses down. Some kids live there."

"What?" he shouted back. Then he gestured towards her. "Permission to approach."

Claire smiled and waved for him to come closer.

The guy looked like a surfer dude, fit and well-muscled. He had longish sun-bleached blond hair and wore ragged jeans shorts. He jogged towards her, carrying the ball. "What did you say?"

"I said it might belong two doors down where some kids live." Claire gestured to the east, where the kids' house was.

"Okay, I'll toss it over there. I don't want to get too close, in case someone shoots at me."

Claire laughed. This must be a joke. "What do you mean?"

He gestured westward, towards Lemon Cove. "Down there, this guy's got sentinels out on his deck. They shout at you to get away from the house. They've got AK-47's."

"Wow! I never run that way. Are you talking about Senator Juniper's house?"

"I don't know whose house it is, but it's gigantic."

When Claire first moved down to the Panhandle, she lived in a carriage house attached to a mammoth mansion that had burned down. Senator Juniper had bought the property and built a new castle. She had no desire to run down that way. Too many bad memories.

"He must be enforcing the customary use law. You know, you have to stay down by the high tide mark," Claire said.

He squinted up at her. He had brilliant blue eyes. "I thought that was overturned in Walton County."

"I'm not sure where things stand right now." Claire pulled at the folds of her bathrobe and tightened the belt.

"My name is Hobbs. Hobbs Scranton."

"Nice to meet you. I'm Claire." She avoided using her last name. She didn't want to hear I'm sorry for your loss. "I promise, I won't shoot at you. As far as I know, my neighbors aren't worried about beachgoers. People are generally pretty laid-back around here."

"Good to know. Well, I better get going. It's getting late." Hobbs waved and jogged down to the water's edge, then headed east. She watched as he ran, his gait smooth and rhythmic.

Over the next several days, she saw him now and then when she was on the deck in the morning. Since she wasn't pressured by a job or social activities, she usually went running later in the day. But one morning, she was jogging back early from Grayton Beach and Hobbs overtook her.

"Hey, good to see you out here." He was sweating profusely. A red-checked bandana around his forehead kept the sweat from running into his eyes.

"I'm not as lazy as you might think. I usually run later in the day, but today I felt compelled to rise and shine."

"Do you mind if I keep you company?"

"Sure, fine," Claire said.

They jogged along for a few minutes without talking.

"What do you do besides drink coffee?" he asked, grinning at her.

"Is that a criticism?"

"No, just a question."

"I actually do nothing…except drink coffee." It felt good to be bantering.

"Meaning?" He was breathing heavily, just like she was.

"I had a big job in corporate America…then I came down here…worked in retail. Now, I'm unemployed."

"Are you looking for a job?"

"Not really. I've had some…some difficulties in my life…I guess you could say I'm in the process of healing."

Hobbs didn't respond. Their labored breathing was synchronized: in-out, in-out.

As they neared her house, she veered off up the beach. "I'm going to head home."

He stopped and she could feel his eyes on her back. "Take care," he yelled. Then he took off.

As she walked up the beach toward her house, she berated herself for getting personal. Her business was her business. Why had she blurted out that she was healing to this beach bum? He probably worked as a dishwasher in some restaurant along 30A, or on a fishing boat.

The next day when she got home from yoga, she found an exquisite arrangement of flowers in a cut-glass vase placed in the shade by the door. A card was attached. It read: Sorry, Claire, if I was insensitive yesterday. Have a beautiful day. Hobbs

Chapter 17

For the next few days, Claire avoided running on the beach. She didn't want to run into Hobbs. Instead, she ran up Lemon Cove Drive and along the bike path on 30A. She drank her coffee inside at the kitchen island instead of out on the deck. A week later, she got a call as she was buttering a piece of toast. It was Drakos. "I've got some news."

Claire's heart sped up. "What is it?"

He cleared his throat. "We found the car."

"Where?" Claire was breathless.

"In an old garage behind an empty house in Fort Walton Beach. Some kids were walking along, when their dog got off its leash. It ran across the yard and into this garage through an opening in the wall. The kids slid through the crack after it and found the car. Being kids, they fooled around for a while. Their mom heard them whispering about it at home later. She questioned them and called us."

"Did you learn anything? Fingerprints? Fibers? Strands of hair?" She was thinking about forensic shows on TV.

"The car's been towed to the lab. At this point, I don't have any additional information for you. But I'll keep you in the loop."

She sighed. "Okay, thanks. I appreciate that."

His tone softened from strictly professional to friendly concern. "How are you doing?"

"Fine, I guess. Listen, did they find Dax's phone in the car?"

"No, no phone. I imagine whoever took it removed the SIM card and smashed it up. We have no way of tracking it now."

Claire sighed again.

"Are you keeping the doors locked and the security system on?" Drakos asked.

"Yes, sir, I am. I feel safe."

"Good. I'll keep in touch." Drakos hung up.

Claire laid down her phone and took a bite of toast. It was dry and tasteless. She pressed her hands to her face and started to cry. Finding Dax's car probably wouldn't lead to his killer. It had only brought fresh pain, like opening a deep wound.

She was bent over sobbing when she heard a gentle knock on the glass door to the deck. Startled, she looked toward it. Through the sheer curtain, she could see Hobbs. He had the nerve to come up from the beach. Anxiety struck as she realized the door was partly open and the security system wasn't on. She'd turned it off when she went out to water the geraniums. She could ignore the knock. But what if he came in? Maybe she should run to the safe and get a gun. But no, Hobbs had given her those nice flowers. She should thank him for the bouquet, at least.

Claire straightened up and wiped her eyes with her palms. Then she went to the door and pulled back the curtain.

Hobbs looked like he was dressed for work, in dark green cargo shorts and a matching polo shirt with a logo on the breast pocket. The tentative smile on his face gave way to concern as he noticed her red nose and watery eyes. "Are you all right? I just wondered how you were doing. Did something happen?"

Claire opened the door wide. "What the fuck. Come on in. I don't care if you're a robber or a murderer." Then she broke down. "I think, I'm just lonely," she said between sobs.

Hobbs stepped through door. "What can I do to help?"

"Can you give me a hug?" she whimpered.

"Sure." He held out his arms.

Claire stepped into his embrace and cried her heart out. When she'd calmed down, she pulled away, embarrassed. Heck, she barely knew the guy. She glanced over at the vase of flowers he'd given her that she'd placed in the center of the dining table. They had long since withered and died. Claire felt guilty. She hadn't even thought to replenish the water in the vase.

"I'm sorry, I didn't thank you for the flowers. They were beautiful. Really special." She must look a mess. She had on her chill outfit: the old grey tee-shirt and flannel sleeping shorts. Her hair hung limp like the flowers. She hadn't taken a shower and probably smelled like last night's pepperoni pizza.

She took another step back from him. "Oh, look, I got your clean shirt all wet with tears."

Hobbs glanced down. "No problem. It will dry out, and get a lot dirtier today." He gestured at the flowers, "I figured out who you were. I felt like an idiot interrogating you the other day. I can imagine you didn't want to talk about your husband's death to a complete stranger. You must be suffering."

"My husband's death," Claire repeated. "I like that. Okay, not like. But I prefer the word death to all the euphemisms: my loss, or his passing, or his demise. Say it like it is. Dax is dead and gone." She walked around the kitchen island, tore off a piece of paper towel, wiped her face and blew her nose. "Do you want some coffee?"

"Sure, that would be great."

"By the way, I've been avoiding you. Let's put all our cards on the table."

"I figured. That's why I decided to knock on the door." Hobbs smiled, and his eyes lit up.

While the coffee dripped, Hobbs walked around the great room, checking out the paintings, the furnishings and the view. "This is a fabulous room."

"Thanks. We took our time decorating. Many of the pieces are special finds Dax and I picked out together."

They took their coffee outside to the deck. Claire's eyes twinkled. To her surprise, she was enjoying herself. "I guess I don't have to hide inside anymore."

"No, you don't. If you find me in your space, just wave me off."

"Deal, but like I said, I've been avoiding people and the truth is I'm probably lonely."

Once they were settled in deck chairs, Hobbs said, "So, what was this about me being a robber or a murderer?"

Claire explained about the break-in. "I got a new security system and I've been careful about keeping the doors locked…except not today."

"Do you think the burglars might be back? Have you figured out what they were looking for?"

"No. I'm hoping they found whatever it was and will leave me alone."

"What was your husband working on?"

"No one knows. The detective on the case hasn't come up with anything much, until today. They found Dax's car in Fort Walton Beach. It's being analyzed in a lab." She didn't want to talk about Dax anymore. She was tired of going over and over that last week in her mind, trying to remember what he'd said or done that could give her a clue to his death. "What does EGL mean? I see the logo on your shirt." She leaned in for a closer look at the design.

"It's a stylized Sabal palm tree, the state tree of Florida."

"Right." Claire could see that now. "And EGL?"

"The initials of my company, Emerald Green Landscaping." The corners of his eyes crinkled. "You're speaking to the owner and chief landscape architect."

"Gosh, I don't know anything about plants or landscaping. How did you learn to be a landscape architect?"

"I went to the University of Florida in Gainesville. It's about the best program in the country. Then I did various internships."

Claire frowned. "Oh, I think I've seen your trucks around."

"You probably have. We've got clients up and down 30A. Right now, we've got a big job north of Highway 98. Have you heard of the Bramble Bay Estates?"

"No, I don't think so. Tell me about it." Claire took a sip of coffee.

"It's a big development of condos and single-family homes. There's a nine-hole golf course, hiking and biking paths, lakes and a lazy river canal they've built for canoes and kayaks. We're doing the landscaping. It's massive." Hobbs was leaning forward, his excitement palpable.

"Wow, that does sound impressive."

"Sales are being handled by Lilly Rose Hamlin. She's a tough cookie. Do you know her?"

Claire felt swept up by his enthusiasm. "Yes, I do. She actually offered me a job."

"Well, you should take it. You could be part of this new venture."

They talked a while longer, until a pause in the conversation came and he glanced at his smart watch. "I better go. I should be on location at Bramble Bay, but I had an early meeting in Blue Mountain Beach, so I decided to stop by and see how you were doing."

"Thank you, Hobbs, for thinking of me."

They both stood up. "I parked downstairs," he said.

"Then you should go out through the house." Claire led him through the great room and down the stairs to the entranceway below. A dusty green truck was parked behind Claire's car, and she recognized the Emerald Green Landscaping logo.

He climbed into the truck, then looked over at her. "Would you like to have dinner some night?"

Claire was taken aback. "I don't know. Would this be like a date?" She shook her head. "I'm not ready to date."

"How about we just be friends. You told me you were lonely. Maybe a night out would do you good."

"I don't know. My husband's only been dead a few months…" She ran her fingers through her hair, suddenly nervous. "And that hug, earlier. I'm sorry about that. I shouldn't have asked you to hug me."

"Just think about it. Here's my card. No pressure. We'd probably have lots to talk about. Okay?" His eyes searched hers.

She took the card. "Okay, I'll think about it. Thanks." Then she turned on her heel and went back inside. She closed the door securely and took the stairs two at a time. Upstairs, she pulled the glass door shut and turned on the security system. She didn't want anyone else walking into her house. A feeling of guilt flooded over her. How could she have entertained Hobbs, even consider having dinner with him, when Dax had only been gone a few months? Was her love for her husband so transitory? What kind of woman and wife was she?

Chapter 18

A few days later, Drakos called. Claire had spilled a glass of water on the floor and was cleaning up the mess. "Mrs. Simmons," the detective said.

"It's Claire. Just call me Claire."

He ignored the irritation in her voice. "The lab's gone through Dax's car. The interior was wiped clean."

"So, nothing?" Her voice sounded plaintive to her ears.

"Not nothing. The forensic team found a single thumb print on the inside of the trunk door. They're pretty convinced…I don't know if you really want to hear this."

"I do. I need to know everything."

She heard Drakos take a deep breath. "There's forensic evidence that the Chief's body was in the trunk, so whoever locked him in there left the print. It's only a thumb print, but it's enough to identify a known criminal."

Claire's heart beat faster. "Who is he? Are you arresting him?"

"We would if we could find him. His name is Louis Dubonnet. Since leaving prison, he's disappeared off the face of the earth. Supposedly, he was going from prison to his sister Mathilde's house in Pensacola, but now the two of them have disappeared. She's a massage therapist. They've been living up and down the Panhandle their entire lives, so we figure they're still here somewhere. We're looking into massage parlors."

"So, nothing," Claire said. Before he could answer, she hung up. The thought of Dax locked in the trunk of his car made her feel faint. Was he alive then? Or was he dead?

***

During the next couple of weeks, Claire retreated into loneliness. She didn't see Hobbs or anyone else. She stopped going to Zen meditation sessions and yoga. She got on the elliptical machine in the spare bedroom a couple of times a day and worked herself ragged, sweat pouring off of her. At night she tried meditating on her own on the upstairs deck. The rhythmic lapping of the waves on the shore lulled her into a hypnotic state, where she didn't have to think.

Early one morning, she drove to the Publix in Panama City Beach where she figured she wouldn't run into anyone she knew. As she went down the cereal aisle, she spotted Harrison Reed coming towards her. He was nicely dressed in a short-sleeved yellow dress shirt and dark pants. She turned her back to him, picked out a box of Cinnamon Toast Crunch and pretended to study the nutrition label.

"Excuse me," he said as he walked by. She moved over and looked up briefly, but he barely glanced at her. He was on the phone and pushing a cart containing orange juice, doughnuts and sweet rolls. "She'll do what I say. She'll be there. No worries," Harrison said, to whoever was on the other end.

After he'd gone by, Claire realized he probably wouldn't have recognized her anyway. He'd only met her once, and she'd been all dolled up that evening at La Crema in Rosemary Beach. Today she was wearing jeans, one of Dax's old tee-shirts and flip-flops. Her hair was in a messy ponytail and she hadn't bothered with make-up.

Something about this encounter shook her up, like St. Paul falling off his horse on the road to Damascus. What was she doing, scuttling around Publix, hiding out in the cereal aisle, dropping out of life? She thought back to Seijun's story about the two monks and the woman crossing the river. It hit her then, like a ton of bricks. She was carrying her unhappiness around like a heavy weight on her back. She had to shake it free. For a surreal moment, right there between the Cinnamon Toast Crunch and the Honey Bunches of Oats, she felt a curtain lift. She stood a little taller and pushed a lock of hair out of her face. With determination, she finished her shopping and left.

When she got home, she retrieved Lilly Rose Hamlin's email. By nine o'clock, she'd signed up for a real estate course that was part online and part in a classroom. Afterwards, she raced out the door and made it to a yoga class. She greeted Rhea and chatted with some of the ladies. When she got home, she washed her hair and blow-dried it. She put on make-up and clean clothes. Then she texted Hobbs.

Do you want to have a friendly dinner tonight?

Sure, where and what time?

How about 7 at the Old Florida Fish House in Seagrove Beach?

Great, see you at 7.

***

Claire arrived early. She took a seat at the bar and ordered a glass of wine. Moments later, Hobbs arrived. He looked around the restaurant somewhat frantically, then spotted her and grinned. His hair was wet, and he wore jeans and a blue shirt that set off his blue, blue eyes.

"Hey. Sorry I'm late. I rushed over. We had a late meeting at Bramble Bay. They keep changing their minds about what they want."

Claire gestured to a stool beside her. "Sit down and tell me all about it."

He took a moment to check her out. "You look nice. I like that dress."

Claire blushed. "This is a big night for me. I'm learning to be a new woman." She'd chosen a simple lime green sheath with gold beads and gold earrings. It set off the green in her eyes, which could also look more grey or blue depending on what she was wearing.

Hobbs sat down. "New woman?"

He ordered a glass of cabernet, and Claire told him about her experience in the grocery store. "It's weird, but something just switched in my psyche. I guess I've decided to re-enter the world."

"That's great. So, when do the real estate classes start?"

"The first session is Monday, but I've already downloaded the materials and I started studying this afternoon."

"You go, girl!"

"I'm actually kind of a nerd. I love sitting down at a desk with a couple of sharpened pencils, a nice new notebook and a big fat textbook." It was true. That afternoon, she had lost herself in the intricacies of Florida real estate law. Time flew by and she'd emerged content.

Hobbs looked thoughtful. "I did well academically, and I spent a lot of time designing on paper and on the computer, but the truth is I like being out in the field, working with my hands and digging in the dirt."

Claire nodded. "I've read that gardening is as good as Prozac for calming the soul."

"Unfortunately, these days I'm usually in the office giving directions rather than out planting begonias."

They spent a pleasant evening talking about a wide range of topics while they shared several sushi plates. For dessert, Hobbs ordered the deep-dish key lime pie and they shared the lusciousness as well as the bill. Claire insisted on going Dutch, and he didn't argue.

As they were getting ready to leave, Claire glanced toward the back of the dining room where a heavy-set waitress leaned over, consulting with a guest. The woman straightened and turned towards Claire as she jotted down the man's order on a pad. A cold shiver ran down Claire's spine. It was the woman with the red car, who'd decoyed her months ago on Lemon Cove Drive the day her house was robbed. She was sure of it. The woman's hair was red now, but Claire could see the flash of silver rings on her fingers.

The waitress hadn't seen her. Claire turned away and headed for the door at a fast clip. Hobbs followed her.

Outside, she rushed towards her car. Hobbs caught up with her and grabbed her arm. "Hey, what's going on? You look like you've seen a ghost."

"I've got to call Detective Drakos. We might have just gotten a break in my husband's murder case."

Chapter 19

Claire waited for Drakos in Hobbs's truck. She sat hunched over in the passenger seat, her fingers drumming on the dashboard and her foot bouncing up and down. Hobbs laid a hand on her shoulder. "They'll be here soon. Calm down."

She shrugged off his hand. What if the woman had seen her? Maybe she'd sneak out the back and disappear.

"Who was that woman you saw?" Hobbs asked.

"Remember I told you about the burglary several months ago?"

He nodded.

"That woman was a decoy to keep me from driving home while the burglars were in my house. She's dyed her hair a different color, but I recognized her anyway."

Five minutes later, a Sheriff's Department vehicle drove up. Claire and Hobbs watched as Drakos got out of the car with another officer and the two of them went into the restaurant. Ten minutes later, they came out with the woman. She was struggling in the officer's grip, yelling bloody murder. The officer shoved her into the back of the patrol car as Drakos surveyed the parking lot. He spotted Claire in the truck and gave her a thumbs-up, then got into the sheriff's vehicle and they sped away.

Finally, Claire relaxed. She turned to Hobbs, tears prickling in her eyes. "Sorry, I'm all wound up. Thanks for waiting with me."

"No problem. Will you be all right going home?"

"Sure. I probably won't sleep. I'll be waiting for Drakos to call. Maybe they'll be able to arrest Dax's killer tonight."

***

At home, Claire made sure all the windows and doors were locked tight. She enabled the security system and poured herself a glass of wine. She tried to calm down, but she couldn't sit still. She went upstairs and put on her pjs, then threw a load of towels into the washer. Back downstairs, she sat at the kitchen counter and opened her laptop. Could she study for a while? She opened Chapter 2 and read the first paragraph three times before she gave up.

She paced the great room, feeling edgy. Finally, at twelve-thirty, she texted Drakos: Any news? He called back minutes later. "We conducted an extensive interview with the woman in question."

"And?"

"She admitted she was paid to send a text when you appeared on Lemon Cove Drive. After that she was told to waylay you for several minutes."

"Who paid her—the burglars? Did she give you any names? Was she in on Dax's murder?"

Patiently, Drakos said, "She claims she never met the man. She was contacted through a friend of a friend. He told her he had a surprise for his wife, and he needed to set it up while the wife was gone. He paid this woman $400 to stand there in the road and waylay you."

"Four hundred dollars? That sounds fishy. How did they know I would leave to meet Alexia that day? Why would that woman trust this person she didn't know?"

"The woman says she just started working at the Old Florida Fish House. At the time of the burglary, she was out of a job and needed the money. She was paid half up front if she made herself available for the entire week. The day of the burglary, she got a text, drove over to Lemon Cove, and waited for you to arrive. When you came around the corner, she texted the guy back. Then she flagged you down and asked you for directions. When you took off, she texted him again."

Claire paced the room. "And she trusted this guy who called out of the blue? Enough to just do what he said, no questions? That's nuts."

"Claire, I think she's telling the truth."

Feeling frantic, Claire asked, "What about the phone number she texted to?"

"We're checking it. We've got her phone."

"Tell me she won't get off scot-free."

"We'll charge her as an accessory for now, but I don't think it will hold water. We still don't know if anything was stolen, right?"

Claire felt like bashing something. "That's true, but they trashed my house. That must count for something…breaking and entering." She clenched the phone. "How did she get the money, if she never met the guy?"

"He used Western Union."

"Does she think it was more than one guy?"

"She has no idea, Claire. If we find a valid phone number, it might give us a clue. But I'm betting the guy's phone was a burner."

Claire glanced at the kitchen clock. It was past one AM. Suddenly she felt exhausted. "Okay. Thanks for talking to me," she said, her voice low and tremulous.

"It's my job. I'll keep you up to date. And Claire, I won't give up." He paused, and she could hear voices in the background. "Good night," he said.

"Good night."

***

Claire slept very little that night. She kept seeing Dax lying on the beach. She tried to go to him, but she was pursued by a red-haired woman driving a Red Army tank. Claire kept running but she couldn't escape the massive vehicle barreling towards her.

In the morning, a black cloud of hopelessness descended on her again. She didn't want to fall all the way back into that dark pit of depression. She had to conquer these turbulent feelings. She felt divided into two personas, one pulling her down into darkness, the other fighting to stay in the light. She could feel the battle in her innermost soul.

She spent ten fruitless minutes trying to meditate. Then she gave up. After donning black running shorts and a blue tank top, she gulped down a cup of coffee and took off down the beach. Instead of going east, she went west towards Lemon Cove. The cove was actually one of the unique coastal dune lakes that are only found in a few places in the world. There was a well-maintained path around the lake. She hadn't run this way since Dax died. She had so many bad memories associated with the cove, but today she needed to shake herself up and test her nerve.

She spaced out as she ran and didn't become fully aware of her surroundings again until she was running past the Juniper place. It really did resemble a castle, with turrets and even crenelated walkways. All it needed was a moat. She smiled to herself. Such a monstrosity on the Gulf Coast was ludicrous.

A stern voice echoed from a loudspeaker. "Miss, please run down closer to the shore. You're above the high-water line."

Claire looked up and saw a guard gesturing at her. He had a semi-automatic rifle slung over his shoulder. Since the sand was hard under her feet, she was pretty sure she was close enough to the high-tide line, but she wasn't about to argue with this armed bulldog. She waved and ran closer to the shore. Then she heard another loud voice: "Come on, Mack, don't give the girl a hard time."

Claire looked up. This time, a white-haired man smiled down at her.

"Come on up here, honey," he said, gesturing. "We want to stay friendly with the locals."

Against her better judgement, Claire jogged closer to the castle.

"I'm Senator Juniper," the white-haired man said. "Sorry for Mack. He's just doing his job."

"Right, I understand." Claire shielded her eyes with her hand. The Senator was a good-looking man with crinkly blue eyes and a photogenic face. Claire had always thought he was handsome enough to play the role of Senator or President on TV. Trim and of medium stature, he radiated warmth and sincerity, but from what she'd learned, it was all an act. More than a few news articles had painted him as ruthless and immoral in his business dealings before he turned to politics. In Washington, he was known for wheeling and dealing with a small squad of dubious cronies.

He kept his gaze on her, and she sensed he was checking her out. "Are you one of our neighbors?"

"Yes, I live down the way." She gestured towards her house. Sweat was pouring down her face and between her breasts. She swiped a wrist across her forehead. It helped a little.

Senator Juniper smiled his gorgeous, toothy smile. "Listen, I'd love to get to know you. I'm planning on inviting people from the area for a cocktail party on the thirtieth. I would love to include you."

What a schmoozer. "That would be nice, but I'm not sure if I'm available. I'll have to check."

"May I ask your name?"

"Claire. Claire Simmons."

"Well, Miss Claire, please try to come."

"Thanks for the invitation. I better get going." She turned and ran off, heading for the low-tide water line. She was sure he was still watching her. She didn't know if she'd attend his little party. He kind of gave her the creeps. She didn't have to decide now, though. The cocktail party was nearly four weeks away.

Chapter 20

Claire spent the next few weeks studying day and night, as well as attending the live class sessions. The teacher was getting up there in years and peppered his lectures with second-tier jokes. The class dutifully laughed. Claire met a couple of nice women and they went out for a glass of wine after class. But mainly she taught herself and worked through the practice tests. After getting fingerprinted, she signed up for the exam and passed it easily. Armed with her real estate license, she was ready to contact Lilly Rose.

That afternoon she made the call. "Hi, Ms. Hamlin. This is Claire Simmons. I just passed the exam and I've got my sales associate license. I'm hoping you still have an opening for me. I'm eager to get to work."

There was a little moment of silence. Probably Lilly Rose had forgotten who she was. "Claire Simmons," Lilly said tentatively. "Yes, I remember now. Alexia's protégée."

That made Claire giggle. "Yes, that's me."

"Why don't you come into the office so we can talk? I'm busy today. How about tomorrow morning. Let's say nine o'clock. Would that work for you?"

"Yes, great, I'll see you tomorrow." But Lilly Rose had already hung up.

***

For her interview, Claire put on her black power suit, heels and a white silk blouse, and added a geometric-patterned yellow and black scarf. She blow-dried her hair and fussed with her make-up. She felt armed for her interview.

Lilly Rose Hamlin's office was in Rosemary Beach, a twenty-minute drive down 30A from Lemon Cove. Claire arrived right on time and parked in front of the agency. Looking at the building, she had an initial impression of reserved elegance. The woodwork around the storefront window was painted dove grey with white trim. The stylized bouquet of lilies and roses graced a corner of the window. Inside, Claire could make out a reception desk and several others, probably workstations.

A bell over the door gave a muted tinkling as she entered the office. The woman behind the reception desk stood up and smiled. She was tall, maybe Claire's age, dressed in flowing garments. High cheekbones and a wide mouth were set off by long, wavy chestnut hair. She stepped around the desk and came forward, hand out-stretched. She was wearing suede booties and jingling silver bracelets.

"Hello, I'm Ava. Welcome to the Lilly Rose Hamlin Agency. How can I be of service?" Her palm was damp, but her handshake was solid.

"I'm Claire Simmons. Here to see Ms. Hamlin."

Ava frowned and let go of Claire's hand. "Are you the new hire?"

"Maybe? I hope so," Claire said, smiling.

Ava's expression turned glacial, as she gestured outside. "You can't park right in front. That's reserved for clients. You better move your car. I'll tell Lilly Rose you're here."

So much for a friendly welcome. "Sorry," Claire said, and hurried outside to move her car as ordered. When she came back in, Ava gestured for her to follow and led her through the large, open room. It held several desks, many graced with vases of fresh flowers. The walls were pearl grey with white woodwork. Claire noted three tasteful paintings of the Emerald Coast.

Lilly Rose's office was in a separate room at the back. One wall was glass and looked out on the open office floor. When Claire entered the room, Lilly Rose stood and came over with a warm smile. She looked cool and elegant in a pale-yellow dress, pearls and white heels; her red hair pulled up in a sleek knot.

"Welcome, Claire. It's wonderful to see you again. Please, sit down." She gestured to a round glass table with a bouquet of yellow roses in the middle. Their sweet perfume filled the air. "What would you like to drink? Coffee? Tea? Water?"

"Just water, thank you."

Lilly Rose called out to Ava, who was swishing down the aisle between the desks, her flowing clothes moving like a cloud. "Ava, could you please bring us a glass of water and a black coffee? Thank you." She turned her attention to Claire. "Let's get down to business, shall we?"

The interview felt more like a conversation, though Claire listened more than she talked. She learned that for the first few weeks, she would basically act as a gofer for the entire office. She would be at the bidding of the other realtors while she was learning the ropes. Her duties would include manning the reception desk, answering the phone, making copies, conducting open-house showings, and helping out with advertising and marketing. They talked about money and Claire almost laughed at the pitiful salary. At one point when she was Marketing Director at Safetynaps, her salary had been in the high six figures. But she was starting out at the bottom in this industry and she didn't really know the ins and outs of the job.

"Keep your eyes and ears open. By observing how we conduct our affairs, you'll soon be ready to launch your own business." Lilly Rose sipped her coffee and looked at Claire over the rim of her cup, which was elegant bone china. Her own water had been served in a sparkling crystal tumbler. No plastic or Styrofoam here.

Claire smiled uncomfortably. "I'll do my best."

"What is the secret of succeeding in this business?" Lilly Rose asked.

Claire thought back to the lessons she had learned from Alexia when she was starting out selling Letízia purses and bags.

"I believe you need to listen to your customers. Really listen." She shifted in her chair and pushed a lock of hair behind her ear. "And I believe you need to form meaningful relationships. I guess I'm trying to say that you can't sell anything to anyone, if they don't feel you care about them."

Lilly Rose put down her cup and nodded. "Good answer. That's exactly what I believe." She reached over and shook Claire's hand. "Welcome to the agency." Then she stood and smoothed her skirt. "Are you ready to start?"

"Sure, ready and eager." Claire felt energized.

Focused on Lilly Rose during the interview, Claire had been mostly unaware of movement out in the main room. Now, several desks were occupied. Lilly Rose led her down the aisle and introduced her to two women and a man. Harrison Reed was not among them.

Claire immediately liked Barbara Larson, who looked to be in her fifties and wore her greying hair in an attractive bob. Her smile was genuine and extended to her sparkling grey eyes. She was dressed in a classic Talbot's outfit with slim pants and a tailored pink striped blouse.

At a nearby desk sat Consuelo Baker, a tall woman all dressed in black. Her dark hair was parted in the middle and pulled back in a bun at the nape of her neck. She wore round red-rimmed glasses and bright red lipstick. Claire thought she resembled a Spanish flamenco dancer. All she needed was a full, flouncy skirt and some castanets.

The man in the corner, Hal Jenson, was short and pudgy. Pronounced frown lines crossed his forehead below a receding hairline. He wore glasses with thick lenses, which gave him a myopic gaze. He was typing furiously on his laptop but paused just long enough to wave a hand at Claire in welcome. Then he turned back to his computer.

Claire had a lot to learn that first day. She needed to master the phone system, the printer and the copy machine. It would be her job to make copies of property brochures, advertising and sales documents.

Barbara agreed to help her understand the ins and outs of the machine. As they worked together, Barbara said, "I'm sorry for your loss. I know your husband passed several months ago."

"Thank you." Claire avoided Barbara's eyes, concentrating instead on writing down step-by-step instructions for fixing the finicky copy machine.

"I met your husband once, in Watercolor."

"Oh, yeah?" Claire said, without looking up.

"He was coming out of a house with a young woman. I forget her name…something starting with an S…Susan or Sharon or Sarah."

Claire blushed. "I don't know who that could be. He met so many people on a daily basis and he never talked much about work."

"Right," Barbara said.

Chapter 21

Claire was exhausted when she got home. She'd been on her feet a good part of the day. It felt heavenly to take off her suit and kick off her heels. She made an executive decision to wear flats or sandals from now on. Once she had clients and wanted to look snazzy, she'd put on some stilettos. But on the whole, she was happy with her day. It was good to have a new challenge and not be knocking around the house feeling depressed.

As she was pulling on some shorts, her phone rang. It was Hobbs. "Hey, Claire, how did it go?"

"I've got the job, but I am definitely the low man on the totem pole...lots to learn." She laughed.

"Do you want to do dinner? I could bring something over from Back Beach Barbecue."

"Would you? That would be great. I'm bushed."

"Anything special you'd like?"

"I love their whole menu. Surprise me." She was already salivating, and belatedly realized she'd skipped lunch that day.

"Good. I'll see you in a few."

While Claire waited for Hobbs to arrive, her phone rang again. She didn't recognize the number. At first, she didn't want to answer, but it could be someone looking to buy a house.

She picked up. "Hello?"

"Claire Simmons?"

"Yes."

"This is Senator Juniper's social assistant. I'm calling to encourage you to drop by the Senator's house-warming party this Saturday. Will you be able to attend?"

Claire stalled. "I forgot about the party...busy schedule, you know how it is." It was on the tip of her tongue to say she couldn't make it but then it occurred to her she might make some useful contacts. Besides, she was curious to see what the Senator's castle looked like on the inside. How often would someone like her get to see firsthand how the insanely rich lived? "Yes, I will attend."

"Great. See you then."

Vaguely, Claire wondered how the Senator had gotten her cell phone number. U.S Senators can probably get any information they want.

***

Hobbs arrived half an hour later, loaded down with bags. She handed him a beer as she unloaded the food. He'd brought Texas-style brisket, ribs, mac and cheese, baked beans, coleslaw and slices of key lime pie.

"Gosh, Hobbs, you went all out. We've got enough food for a week."

"I don't think so. I'm starved."

Claire had set the dining room table with festive placemats and napkins. She'd had a difficult moment as she placed the dishes and glasses on the table. Dax had always laughed when she insisted on eating at the table rather than at the kitchen island, their usual spot. He'd say she was pulling out the big guns and probably had ulterior motives. Usually after those special dinners they would tumble into bed and make mad crazy love. In no way was she looking for a sexual relationship with Hobbs. They had agreed to be friends.

The food was delicious, and Claire talked about her day and the people she'd met. It turned out Hobbs had met many of them at the Bramble Bay development.

"I really like Barbara, the older lady," Claire said. "She helped me a lot." She took a bite of the juicy brisket.

"Yes, she's nice." He raised his eyebrows. "What about Ava?"

Claire looked at him, trying to gauge his opinion. "Well…"

"She can be a total bitch," Hobbs said, and they both started laughing.

"Yup." She told him about her initial contact with Ava, how the woman had been friendly until she realized Claire might eventually be her rival.

"That's her all right. I've had run-ins with her," Hobbs said

"Do you know Consuelo Baker?"

"Yes, she's a big earner, I think. Her grandparents were born in Cuba and fled to Miami when Castro took over. So she's third generation, but sometimes you'd think she just got off the boat from Cuba. She married a Texan, Cyrus Baker. He's a major player in oil and natural gas. Big bucks." Hobbs picked up a rib and gnawed on the bone.

"Where do they live?"

"I think they've got a house in WaterSound, but he's not always here. I think he spends half the time in Texas or wherever."

Claire took a bite of mac and cheese and then put down her fork. "Hmm...I've got a lot to learn before I'm going to make any money."

"I'm sure you'll do great. It'll be a vertical climb." He gestured straight up with his rib bone, then cocked his head and smiled at her. "That's probably what Ava is worried about."

After they'd demolished most of the food, Hobbs helped her clear the table. While she put the leftovers in plastic containers and loaded the dishwasher, he wandered around the great room looking at the pictures. When she'd finished cleaning up, she noticed he wasn't in the room anymore. She looked out on the deck. No Hobbs. She went through the great room to the landing and called his name.

"I'm in here." He was in the office down the hall.

For no good reason, Claire was irritated he'd gone in there on his own. She'd been avoiding the office for days. "What are you doing in here?" she said as she entered the room.

Hobbs was inspecting the map of the Emerald Coast on the wall. He seemed oblivious to her tone. "What do these x's stand for?" He pointed to the marks Dax had made.

"I don't know. I used that map with pushpins, to indicate the shops and boutiques that carried Letízia products. I should probably take it down now."

Hobbs turned and looked at her. "Sorry, should I have asked permission to come in here?"

"No, no. I guess I'm annoyed because I don't like coming in here," she said.

He eyed her curiously, but she wasn't about to give him an explanation. She pushed two desk drawers closed that were pulled out.

They went back to the great room. Claire finished her glass of wine and Hobbs had another beer. They talked about this and that. "You should come out to Bramble Bay one of these days," Hobbs said. "I'd love to show you around."

"I'd like that. Maybe after work, I could drive out there."

When she started to yawn, he stood to leave. "Sorry, I need my beauty sleep," Claire said.

He grinned at her. "Don't think so. You're beautiful with or without sleep."

Claire blushed, feeling uncomfortable. She didn't want their friendship to turn into something else. She brought up the first change of subject she could think of. "Senator Juniper invited me to a party on Saturday. Would you like to come with me? I don't want to go alone."

"Really? Sure, what time?"

"It's cocktails. Let's go at seven."

Claire walked him downstairs, where she thanked him for the wonderful dinner and they hugged briefly. Once he'd left, she activated the security system and went up to bed. After she'd brushed her teeth and was under the covers, she let her mind go to what had been bothering her all day...what Barbara had said about meeting Dax. Who had Dax been with when he came out of a house in Watercolor? Who was the young woman whose name started with an S? Why had he kept some girl's underpants in the wall safe? Had Dax been having an affair? Was that why he'd been killed?

She tossed and turned for a long while until she managed to fall asleep.

Chapter 22

Drakos called every couple of days. He never had anything much to report, but he assured her he was still on the case. Claire thanked him for the call every time, but after she hung up, she had a feeling of hopelessness. He couldn't possibly be spending all day investigating Dax's death. After so long, it was probably on the back burner. Somewhere, she'd read that most cases went cold after twenty-four hours. How about after four months?

By now, Claire was into the swing of things at work. When she arrived at nine o'clock, she made coffee and arranged fresh pastries on a platter. The realtors rolled in closer to ten, when the office officially opened. In the afternoon, there was iced tea and cookies. Every four days, a box of fresh flowers arrived that Claire was expected to arrange in vases around the office. In addition, she answered the phone and welcomed clients when they arrived. If the customer didn't ask for someone in particular, Claire would take them to the next agent on the list. If that person was busy, it went down to the next person. It was a round robin system that they all abided by.

Claire became the copy queen and ran errands for agents or their clients. Most of the realtors were pleasant and helpful, but Ava continued to give her the cold shoulder. If Claire was free, Barbara included her in the process of closing a sale, and often gave tips about dealing with clients. Claire had studied much of this information but memorizing for a test was nothing like actually applying what she'd learned.

***

On Saturday, Hobbs arrived at six-fifty. Claire was dressed and ready to go. She'd decided to wear her little black dress with gold jewelry and strappy sandals, and she carried a cerise pashmina. Hobbs looked great in a sports coat, black slacks and black loafers. He'd cut his hair and it was neatly combed. Used to seeing him as a rugged outdoors man, Claire wasn't sure if she liked this more formal version. But he did look handsome. They decided to take her car, since his truck was pretty grimy.

Juniper's castle was all lit up like a birthday cake. There were cars parked all along Lemon Cove Drive. They decided to pull into a spot and walk the rest of the way. It turned out there was valet parking and they could have driven right up to the front. As they walked across the wide stone driveway, Claire looked up and noticed the cameras over the massive oak front doors and at the corners of the building. Clearly, Juniper didn't want any uninvited guests. Two well-muscled men in dark blue uniforms stood on either side of the door. They had earpieces and each wore a gun.

The guard on the left said, "Good evening, Ms. Simmons. Could we have the name of your guest?"

How did this guy know her name? Before she could introduce Hobbs, the guard said. "Sorry, Mr. Scranton. Welcome."

Claire and Hobbs looked at each other and then up at the cameras. Someone had done an instantaneous security check.

The guards pulled open the double front doors. Claire and Hobbs entered a high-ceilinged foyer with white marble floors and an enormous crystal chandelier. To the left, an elegant curving staircase carpeted in deep maroon led up to the floor above. Across the room were wide panels separated by gold wainscoting. A grey-bearded butler welcomed them by name and escorted them to one panel. He pushed a button and a door slid open. They entered a sleek elevator cabin. The butler accompanied them up two floors, where the elevator door opened onto another wide foyer. Ahead of them was an enormous ball room filled with guests, loud voices, music and laughter. A jazz band was playing in one corner and maids in black uniforms and white aprons were passing hors-d'oeuvres.

Their escort gestured for them to join the party. "Enjoy yourselves, Ms. Simmons and Mr. Scranton. Senator Juniper will be down shortly."

Once the elevator had gone back down, Hobbs said, "This place is something else. Did you see how fast that guy got my name? They must have face-recognition software."

"You're right. That must be how they knew my name, too. And what about the guns?"

"This place is a fortress and it's well-guarded." Hobbs looked around the room, then up at the ceiling. "There are cameras everywhere. Big Brother is watching us."

Claire reached over and slipped her arm through Hobbs's. There was something intimidating about the place. They moved into the great room and were quickly engulfed in the brouhaha of music and laughter. Hobbs snagged them each a champagne flute from a passing waiter and they clinked glasses.

"Here's to Senator Jupiter," Claire said.

"And to all his friends and acquaintances…of which he has many," Hobbs added, raising his eyebrows.

Claire laughed. They could barely hear each other with all the noise. "Let's head over there. It might be a little quieter." She gestured to the open French doors across the room.

They maneuvered their way around groups of people. Just as they approached the door, Claire felt a hand on her arm.

"Claire, what a wonderful surprise." Harrison Reed was standing there with Consuelo Baker and a tall Texan in cowboy boots and a light beige, Western-style suit. He was a handsome man with greying hair and strong features. This must be Consuelo's husband, that Hobbs had mentioned the other evening.

"Hey there, ya'll," Claire said. "Small world."

"Small world is right," Consuelo said. Her fitted red dress molded her upper body and flared below the knees. A red rose was tucked into the bun at the nape of her neck. She was lovely and absolutely looked like a flamenco dancer. Harrison was dressed in an elegant dark suit. They formed a handsome group.

"I didn't know you knew the Senator," Consuelo said.

"I don't. He invited me when I was jogging by his house a month ago."

The Texan's eyes swept over her. "Juniper likes to fill his parties with pretty girls."

Claire blushed. "Let me introduce my friend Hobbs Scranton."

"Oh, we know Hobbs." Consuelo gave him a big grin. "You clean up nicely."

"I'll take that as a compliment," Hobbs said.

Consuelo introduced her husband, Cyrus Baker. "He's almost never around, so you're lucky to catch him tonight," she said, with a hint of an edge to her voice.

Cyrus looked mildly irritated. He shook hands with Hobbs, then bent and kissed Claire's cheek. She could feel his hand on her rump. Just then, the band stopped playing. The crowd quieted instantly. There was a musical riff from the piano and Senator Juniper entered the room, with Lilly Rose on his arm. He wore a tux with a dark rose bowtie and cummerbund. Lilly Rose was in a strapless emerald green dress with twinkling diamonds at her throat, ears, and on her stiletto heels. Her red hair fell loose around her face. She was gorgeous. Claire figured she was at least forty-five, if not fifty, but tonight Lilly Rose looked twenty-five. How did she maintain that creamy white skin and fabulous body? Claire knew she worked out every morning before coming to the agency…but still.

The crowd made a wide circle around the couple. Senator Juniper turned his famous smile on them all.

"Welcome, my friends. Thank you for attending this party, which commemorates the completion of my beautiful Emerald Coast hideaway. As you likely ascertained when you drove up this evening, this house is built to withstand a Category 5 hurricane. It's a fortress against Mother Nature as well as unwanted peeping Toms."

Everyone laughed.

"Tonight, the house is open to my friends and acquaintances. Please feel free to wander around. There are attendants on each floor who can answer any questions you might have about the construction, décor or technology. Please enjoy the food and drink."

A waiter came up and passed Lilly Rose and the Senator a glass of champagne. Juniper raised his glass. "Thank you again for coming. Let's drink to my beautiful new home."

They all took a sip of the drinks they held and then conversation resumed as the jazz band struck up Brubeck's "Take Five". While Senator Juniper made his little speech, Claire had looked around at the crowd. There were several faces she recognized from the news: Senators, Congressmen, and big names from Silicon Valley as well as Hollywood actors. It was obvious that Juniper had tentacles reaching into a variety of realms. She wondered if he owed them all for helping to get him elected, or if it was the other way around and they were beholden to him. Shame on her, she should just accept them as his friends. The truth was, she didn't like the man and she didn't trust him. She really shouldn't be here tonight, celebrating the completion of his multimillion-dollar house. And where had he acquired the money to build this monstrosity?

Claire's face must have reflected her thoughts. Hobbs was smiling down at her. "Are you thinking what I'm thinking?" he said, sotto voce. "This guy is a piece of work." He gestured around the room. "And what about all these sycophants, paying him homage like he's a king. I thought we gave up royalty when we had the Revolution."

Claire grinned at him. "Sycophants. I like that word."

"Do you want to take the tour?" he asked.

"Sure, why not. But I want to grab something to eat first."

They each got a plate and helped themselves to mini crab cakes, sushi rolls, lobster vols-au-vent and asparagus wrapped in crispy phyllo. They took their plates outside to the wide patio that looked out over the Gulf, found a small unoccupied table, and sat down. It was a perfect night with a light breeze and a star-studded sky.

"I'm glad you asked me to accompany you. This is an amazing house," Hobbs said.

"I still don't get why he invited me. I mean, a lot of the other people here are big shots. I'm just a gofer in a real estate office."

"Yeah, I noticed several Florida bigwigs and members of the Walton County Board."

She nibbled at a California roll. "How about Tom Hanks and Jennifer Lawrence? I'm impressed at the people the Senator seems to know."

"Do you want another glass of bubbly?" Hobbs asked as he stood up.

"Yes, thanks."

He went back inside. Claire sighed and took a bite of the delicious lobster. She liked Hobbs, but she wished Dax was here. It would be wonderful to share the experience with him. Tears formed in her eyes. She dabbed at them with the corner of the tiny napkin she'd grabbed with the hors-d'oeuvres.

A hand rested on her shoulder. Startled, Claire looked up. "Oscar?" It was Oscar Snell, her dad's friend and golfing buddy.

Claire jumped up and gave him a hug. After holding her close for a minute, he backed off a step, his hands still on her shoulders. "How are you doing, honey?" Oscar was a rotund little man, with a big smile and not much hair, but right now he frowned as he searched her eyes.

"I'm actually doing pretty well. I just had a little moment of…of sadness." She smiled at him. "But tell me what you're doing here."

"I know the Senator. He was instrumental in helping me land a couple of military contracts. I was honored to be invited to this event. What about you?"

Claire couldn't remember what Oscar did. Was he an arms manufacturer? "I was jogging by this place one day. The Senator saw me and invited me to the party. I thought it was going to be a bunch of neighbors, but instead it's people from all over the country."

"Yes, he knows a lot of people. He's a good man, a really good man."

Claire nodded politely and gestured to an empty chair. "Won't you join us, Oscar?"

Hobbs came back just then with two flutes of champagne, and Claire introduced the two men. "Are you familiar with the Emerald Coast?" Hobbs asked.

"No, I've never been here in my life before today, but you know what? This is a great location. The beaches are pure white sand and there's all these restaurants and some good fishing. It's not that bad a drive from Atlanta. Today, I decided I'm going to buy a house around here."

Hobbs toasted him. "You're a man who knows what he wants."

Oscar chuckled. "I never dilly-dally around. I'm a decision-maker." He turned to Claire. "I'm glad you're here, Claire, because I was going to call you. I heard you'd joined the world of real estate. Well, I want you to find me a house and act as my realtor. I'd like to get the deal done in the next week. Prudy, my wife, has several houses in mind already. If you'll show them to me, I'll make a decision and we'll get the deal done."

Claire sat back, flabbergasted. Then she started to laugh, and so did Hobbs. Of all the crazy luck…this would be her first sale.

Chapter 23

That night when Claire got home, she began researching homes for the Snells. On Monday, she tapped on Lilly Rose's office door and asked if she could have a word.

Lilly Rose beckoned her in. "What's up, Claire?"

"A friend of my dad's is in town and he wants me to help him find a vacation home. I'd need to be out of the office for the next few days. Is that all right?"

A warm smile lit Lilly Rose's face. "Of course. Wonderful! This will be your first sale. Please don't hesitate to ask me if you need help."

"Thanks. I'm excited."

The smile dimmed and her eyes narrowed slightly. "By the way, I saw you at Senator Juniper's party."

"Yes, he invited me when I was jogging by his property one day."

"Did you meet a lot of people? It would have been a good place to make connections."

Claire felt as though Lilly Rose was appraising her. What did she want to hear? "Not too many, actually. I ended up talking to Mr. Snell, my dad's friend, most of the evening."

"Well, it sounds like that was a successful use of your time."

"Yes. And by the way, you looked lovely in that green dress."

"Thank you, Claire." Lilly Rose turned away, picked up a sheaf of papers and put on her glasses. Claire had been dismissed.

***

Claire and Oscar spent three days visiting seven to ten million-dollar houses up and down 30A. At first Oscar couldn't believe the cost of the beachfront real estate. "Damn, Claire. That's a lot of money for a house along the Redneck Riviera." He rubbed the top of his bald head.

Claire laughed. "Oscar, this is no longer the Redneck Riviera. It's the Emerald Coast, just like the Emerald Coast in Sardinia where all the film stars and royalty spend their holidays."

"If you say so. Prudy's got a couple of friends who've got houses down here. This is what she wants, and it has to be on the Gulf." He didn't look totally convinced.

Claire had never met Prudence Snell, but she'd heard her mom talk about the woman. Prudy ran the women's golf league as well as the bridge group at the club, and apparently ruled the roost.

During their search, Oscar walked straight through the rooms, hands clasped behind his back as he glanced from left to right. Claire hustled along behind him. Sometimes he made a snap decision and nixed the house because of the kitchen layout or the size of the pool or the view from the master bedroom. Sometimes he went back and enumerated on his phone the good points and bad points. Then he called Prudy and told her what he saw and what he thought. She would be doing a virtual tour of the same house back in Atlanta, and they'd compare notes and argue. Sometimes, Claire put in her two cents' worth.

Eventually, it boiled down to three houses. That night Claire and Oscar went to Restaurant Paradis in Rosemary Beach. Between the tuna tartare and the veal chop marsala, they made a decision. Oscar had Prudy on speaker phone, and they discussed the ins and outs of each house. The winner was a stately yet comfortable house in Seacrest, with five bedrooms and a bunkroom, six bathrooms, and a fabulous kitchen with Sub-Zero appliances. There was also a walk-in wine-cellar and an amazing game room, and spectacular views from decks on every floor. Oscar didn't blink at the ten-million-dollar price tag. He wanted to make Prudy happy, but she wasn't sure if he was truly in love with the Emerald Coast. Once they'd made their decision, Oscar and Prudy began to discuss color schemes, which bedrooms to make over for their kids and grandkids, and whether they should spend Christmas in Florida that year.

Oscar was paying cash for the house, and the closing took place a few weeks later. He returned briefly and left right afterwards. "I've wasted way too much time on this house deal. But it's been a pleasure working with you, Claire. I think you'll do great in this industry."

"Thank you, Oscar. Say hello to Prudy. I hope we'll meet one of these days."

After he left, Barbara gave her a hug. Consuelo gave her a pat on the back. Hal high-fived her and Ava smiled vaguely.

When Claire got home, she felt lonely. If only Dax were there to celebrate with her. She tried calling Olivia to see if she was available for dinner, but there was no answer, so she left a voicemail. Olivia called back at six—she was in Tallahassee and wouldn't be back for several days. Claire tried calling her parents next, but they didn't pick up. She went upstairs and threw herself on the bed, fighting not to cry. Then the phone rang. It was Hobbs.

"How did it go?"

Claire sniffled before answering. "Great. I'm now officially a realtor."

"We should celebrate. How about dinner at Café 30-A?"

She didn't hesitate. "I'd like that. Thanks, Hobbs."

"I'll pick you up at seven."

Claire showered and changed into black leggings and a rose-colored tunic. She was ready when he arrived. At Café 30-A, they split the roasted red beet salad and followed it up with cioppino, paired with a crisp white wine.

Hobbs raised his glass. "You're on your way, Claire. Here's to your continued success."

"Thank you, my friend." Claire smiled, but she could feel those damn tears in her eyes again. She looked at her salad plate, trying to calm down.

Hobbs set down his glass and speared a crunchy pecan. He gave her a moment to regain control. "When are you going to come out to Bramble Bay? Lilly Rose might have you selling out there one of these days."

Claire thought about that. "You're right. If I join the roster of active agents, I will probably be expected to do a stint out there. I should become familiar with the houses, the layout…and most importantly, the landscaping." Her eyes twinkled.

"Why don't you come out tomorrow? I can show you around."

"It's a deal. I'd love to do that."

When Hobbs dropped her off back at the house, she thanked him again for dinner and celebrating with her. She gave him a sisterly hug and hopped out of the truck. He waited for her to go inside, and she waved as he drove off.

Chapter 24

Claire arrived at Bramble Bay at three-thirty. Things were slow at the agency and Barbara said she would take care of the phones if Claire left early. A couple of other agents were busy at their desks and could handle any walk-ins.

Claire drove over to Highway 98 and then down to the entranceway to the Bramble Bay Estates. "Wow," she murmured as she turned into the development. At the entrance, a waterfall tumbled down over massive rock formations into a pool surrounded by lush green plants and colorful flowers. It was exquisite and probably designed by Hobbs. Claire drove over a bridge and followed the road that curved around through a golf course and wooded areas. Majestic palm trees swayed in the breeze, over vibrant flowerbeds. Eventually, the road opened out to a village center. There were several shops around a square and a bubbling fountain. Not all the storefronts were occupied yet.

Claire saw a sign directing her to the sales office. She continued along the road, following the arrows. Newly built houses were set back from the road. Some of them seemed to be inhabited, with cars in the driveway and curtains in the windows. She came to an intersection and turned left toward the sales office. Across the street, a construction crew was working. Claire swung into a parking spot and got out of her car.

As she walked up the steps to the sales office porch, Harrison Reed came out to greet her. "Hello, Claire. I didn't know you were coming out here today. Great to see you." He held out his hand, and she shook it briefly. He looked impeccable as always, in a blue-checked short-sleeved shirt, blue and grey patterned tie, jeans and black leather sneakers.

"I wanted to check out Bramble Bay. I felt I should know what the homes and area are like."

"I'd be glad to show you around. Things are quiet here today."

"That was true at the Rosemary office as well. That's why I came out." She hesitated. "Hobbs—Mr. Scranton—already offered to show me the place, so I thought…"

"How about I get you started? Hobbs can easily catch up when he's ready."

"All right. Thanks."

Harrison held the door open and showed her into the sales office, which was actually one of the models. First, he took her over to a miniature of the entire development. "These houses in red have been completed, sold, and are lived in. Those in yellow are under construction, and these in blue haven't been started yet. The golf course stretches through this area. Here's the family center, swimming pool and tennis courts. All this green area is forest. The yellow lines are bike and hiking paths that run throughout the property, the meandering blue line is the kayak and canoe stream. See how it flows out to this lake?" His long, thin finger moved over the glass-covered case. Claire noted his nicely manicured nails.

"This is impressive," she said, and meant it. "How have sales been?"

"It's going well. Since Hurricane Michael, many people don't want to be on the Gulf. Living here, you can enjoy everything the Emerald Coast has to offer while being at a reasonable distance from the flood threat of a chance hurricane. From here it's a mere three miles to the beaches and 30A. It's also a hop, skip and a jump to Pier Park and Grand Boulevard for shopping."

"What about restaurants or shopping in the development itself?"

He gestured toward another portion of the diorama. "Eventually, this area here in the town center will house a breakfast and lunch café. There will also be a restaurant in the club house. See this spot here? This will be a shop for sundries…you know, milk, eggs, soap, stuff like that."

"Looks fabulous. Could I visit some of the model homes?" Claire asked.

"Sure. Let me give you the brochures and map. It would be good to study all this before you join the sales staff."

He gathered some glossy fliers and a map of the development. Together, they went back outside. "By the way, I didn't get to congratulate you on that first sale. That was a coup. It was the biggest sale of the month so far."

Claire shrugged. "I can't take credit for being an especially talented agent. The buyer was a friend of my dad."

"Nonetheless, you made it happen." He took her arm and smiled down at her.

She felt a happy shiver and beamed up at him. They went around the corner and up the brick walkway to the first house. Geraniums in pots graced the porch, along with a swing covered in bright-colored cushions. Two deck chairs with matching cushions stood on the other side of the front door.

Harrison ushered her into the house. They stood in an attractive foyer, with a living room off to the left and a den to the right. He led her into the living room and kept on talking as she looked around. "Are you aware that these are all smart houses?"

"What does that mean, exactly?"

"It's a home with an automation system that controls lighting, climate, entertainment, appliances and security systems."

"So, you can basically control everything with your phone?"

"Yes. Each house also has solar panels with a Tesla battery."

Claire frowned. "A Tesla battery? Isn't that for a car? What does it do in a house?"

"The Tesla battery stores the sun's energy captured by the solar panels. If there's a storm and the electricity goes out, the battery kicks in and keeps your lights on and the air conditioning running."

Her eyes widened. "Very cool. Another safety measure for when the next hurricane hits."

"Right, and in addition a homeowner can sell excess energy to the electric grid. It's a win-win."

The living room was attractively decorated in tones of beige, white, and light green. This model was the biggest, Harrison told her, with five bedrooms and a large kitchen. He explained additional features as they walked through the house, and then they went on to visit three other homes. Each one was beautifully decorated and included a pool and an outdoor kitchen. The plantings were attractive as well, probably Hobbs's doing. Several times, Harrison took Claire's arm, or leaned in close. She felt a little unnerved—he seemed a little too touchy-feely for their first time one-on-one—but she wasn't sure what to say, so she let it pass.

As they came out of the smallest cottage, an empty-nester home, Harrison stopped on the porch. He held her shoulders and smiled down at her. "Claire, I've really enjoyed talking to you. I wonder if you would like to go out for dinner one of these nights. I'd love to get to know you better."

Claire smiled uncomfortably at him, but before she could answer, someone called her name. She looked across the road and saw Hobbs waving at her. He was shouting something, but a bulldozer behind him, digging up the yard of an unfinished house, made it hard to hear. He gestured for her to come over.

Claire raised her eyebrows at Harrison. "Let's see what he wants." She started across the street, Harrison followed behind her. Hobbs's dark green uniform was covered with dirt, and patches of sweat showed under his arms and on his chest. He was wearing a hardhat and perspiration ran down his face. He looked from Harrison to Claire, his expression cool.

What was that about? "Hi Hobbs. You were right. These are lovely homes here at Bramble Bay. Harrison very kindly showed me around, since you weren't free yet."

Harrison was squinting at the bulldozer. "What's going on?"

Hobbs shrugged. "There's a drainage problem. I said we'd take a look."

The bulldozer's hydraulic arm plunged the bucket into the soil. The driver in the cab waved at them. As they watched, the arm lifted, and the bucket came up full of sandy soil dripping with water. But that wasn't all.

Claire screamed. A body was dangling over the bucket's edge...a body with long, dark hair.

Part II

Chapter 25

Claire kept screaming. She was aware of Hobbs and Harrison beside her. Both men's faces were white with shock. Then Hobbs ran towards the gaping hole the bulldozer had made. Harrison took Claire's arm and pulled her towards the real estate office across the street. She let herself be led. She didn't need to look at that pale body dripping with water and sand. The image was fixed in her brain.

As she walked into the office, the frigid air conditioning hit her like a wall of ice. Despite the heat and the battering afternoon sun outside, Claire started shivering. Harrison was perspiring heavily. He loosened his tie and grabbed some tissues from a box to wipe his face. Then he walked her across the room to a couple of armchairs. Claire sank into one. She rubbed her upper arms with her hands and took deep breaths, struggling to calm down. A moment later, Harrison returned with bottles of water, one for her and one for himself. Feeling a little woozy, she opened the bottle and gratefully gulped the water down.

Harrison sat across from her in the other armchair. "Man, that was one hell of a shock." He was still sweating.

"Yeah," Claire murmured.

"Are you all right?" He studied her with concern, then wiped his forehead with a balled-up tissue.

"I'm just…shocked, that's the right word for sure. I mean, this is the second dead body I've seen in the last few months."

He cleared his throat. "I heard about your husband. I'm sorry for your loss."

Claire looked down at her hands and nodded. She knitted her fingers in her lap.

They were quiet for a moment. Then Claire said, "How did that woman get buried there? Wouldn't someone have seen it? The…the grave being dug, I mean."

Harrison shook his head. His face looked grey. "I have no idea. It could have happened anytime. They've been digging and planting around here for months."

Claire heard police sirens, in the distance. Moments later, several cruisers pulled to a stop outside the sales office. As Claire watched through the window, an ambulance pulled in beside them. The paramedics joined the officers and walked towards the bulldozer on the far side of the road.

She glanced at Harrison. "Do you think we need to stick around? I'd like to leave."

"Maybe they'll want to question us." Harrison wiped his forehead again. He was still ghostly pale.

"Why? I mean, we didn't see anything except a…a…a body." As Claire stumbled over her words, a shiver of horror ran down her spine. Quickly, she stood and headed towards the door. "I'm leaving. They don't need to talk to me. I don't know anything. I've never been here before." She pulled open the door and hurried across the porch and down the stairs towards her car.

She opened the driver's-side door, threw in her purse and got behind the steering wheel. Roughly, she backed out and turned towards the entrance road, but a patrol car blocked her path. An officer got out, came over, and stepped in front of her vehicle. She waved at him to get out of the way, but he didn't budge.

Claire rolled down the window. "I've got to go. Please get out of the way."

"Sorry, miss. No one's leaving until they've been debriefed."

Claire banged her hand on the steering wheel. Her voice rose. "I do not need to be debriefed. I don't know anything. I've never been here before." She leaned on the horn, and the officer actually looked frightened. If Claire hadn't been so angry, she might have laughed. This was ludicrous. Why did anyone need to talk to her? Her throat choked up and she felt tears coming. Then she saw Drakos standing beside her car.

She leaned out the window and shouted at him. "Are you in charge here? Why can't I leave?"

He sighed and looked heavenward. "You of all people know we need to interview everyone present when the body was discovered. You might have valuable information and not know it."

Claire shook her head. "Detective Drakos, I saw a body dangling from the bucket of that bulldozer over there. I screamed and turned away. This was my first-time visiting Bramble Bay." She punctuated her speech by honking her horn one more time. "That is the extent of my information. May I please leave?"

He stayed silent a moment, as if considering it. "Okay, you can go. But I might be calling you."

"You know my number." Claire rolled up her window in dismissal.

The officer got back in the patrol car and cleared the path for her. As Claire drove off, she saw Harrison in her rearview mirror, leaning on the porch railing, holding his phone as if he was texting a mile a minute. Across the tarmac, Drakos was talking to Hobbs. Hobbs was gesturing frantically, flanked by two officers. The sight deepened her distress. They can't possibly think he had anything to do with that body, can they?

***

At home, Claire dropped her dress on the closet floor and pulled on her running clothes. Then she left the house and took off down the beach at a fast clip. She needed to clear her head of that dead body hanging from the blade of the bulldozer. Would she ever be able to get over it? The image was imprinted on her brain. She picked up her pace.

She ran down beyond the Grayton Beach camping grounds. On the way back she slowed her pace and allowed herself to look at the beauty before her. The sun was setting, painting the sky a panoply of colors. The Gulf shimmered in the evening light and the sand glowed white as powdered sugar. She slowed to a walk and took deep breaths. Life was too precious to get so upset about being interviewed by the police, even with the shock of a dead body turning up. She felt ashamed of herself. Next time, she saw Drakos, she would apologize.

At home, she activated the security system and closed the curtains. Then she took a shower. Downstairs, clad in a cotton nightgown, she poured a glass of wine. A slice of Brie in the fridge looked tempting. She put the cheese on a plate along with some crackers and an apple, then carried this simple meal upstairs to her boudoir. As she did every night, she checked the lock on the sliding glass door that led out to the upstairs deck. Then she locked the bedroom door.

As she ate, she went through her emails and texts. She still received messages from former clients for Letízia, even though she had notified all of them that she no longer worked for the company. Morgan had sent pictures of the baby. Harper was adorable. Olivia had texted, suggesting dinner the following week when she would be back in town. There was a text from Hobbs asking her how she was. She responded that she was all right and would rather not communicate right now. The last text was from Lilly Rose. She wanted to meet with Claire in the morning. She'd probably heard about the body in Bramble Bay and wanted to discuss it. Feeling anxious, Claire finished her glass of wine and went to bed.

The night was long. She kept waking from nightmares of a Barbie doll suspended from a hook dangling from a crane. The plastic figure was dripping blood.

Chapter 26

The next morning as Claire was finishing a cup of coffee, her phone rang. She didn't recognize the number, but it had an Atlanta area code. She took a chance and answered.

"Hello, Claire? This is Lincoln Morehouse. You don't know me, but I'm a friend of Oscar Snell. He gave me your number. Said you were a charming lady and a great real estate agent."

Claire laughed. "Oscar is the charmer. And he's giving me a lot of undeserved credit."

The deep voice continued. "My wife and I are here in the Panhandle. We're staying at the Watercolor Inn. We would like to buy a house here in Watercolor. We've picked out a couple we're interested in. Could you help us out?"

Claire couldn't believe her luck. "I would love to help you find the perfect house. Do you have the addresses of the properties you'd like to look at?"

"Yes, my wife wrote them down while we drove around. Here, I'll pass her the phone."

Claire grabbed a pencil and the notepad she kept in the kitchen. A woman's warm, cheery voice came on the line. "Hey there, Miss Claire. This is Rhonda. How are you, honey?"

Claire smiled. "I'm just fine, Rhonda. It looks like we're going to get to know each other. I'm looking forward to it."

Rhonda prattled away, eventually giving Claire the addresses of four houses they had seen for sale online. They arranged that Claire would arrive at eleven-thirty at the Watercolor Inn. The three of them would have lunch and then visit the houses on the Morehouses' list.

Claire hung up and pumped her hand in the air. What fabulous luck. God bless Oscar. She jumped off the kitchen stool and did a little pirouette. Then she skipped to the stairs. Today she would wear the new navy jumpsuit she'd bought online; it was elegant and comfortable.

On the way to Rosemary Beach, Hobbs called. "Hey, just wanted to see how you are after yesterday."

"Listen, Hobbs, thanks for your concern, but I'm trying to forget. I don't want to talk about it."

"I get you. I won't bring it up."

"Here's some good news. I just got a call from a couple who want to check out some houses in Watercolor. They're friends of Oscar's. Talk about lucky."

"That's great."

Abruptly, Claire realized how self-centered she was being. "Sorry, Hobbs. I'm a bit obtuse. How are you doing? You were as shocked as me."

"I guess I'd just as soon forget about that dead girl, too. But I'm going to Bramble Bay today and I'm going to have to figure out when she was buried. This was murder, and I feel kind of responsible."

"You're not responsible."

"Somebody buried that body after I did the planting of those bushes and the palm tree. I should have noticed if the earth had been disturbed later."

"No way would you have noticed that. Forget it."

He sounded worried. "I'd still like to know who thought they could hide a body in Bramble Bay. It's got to be someone familiar with the development. Like maybe one of my workers?"

"I'm telling you, Hobbs, don't let this eat you up. I know about that."

"Right. I know you do." He cleared his throat. "Well, I'm almost on site. Talk soon."

"Thanks for checking up on me. Be strong," Claire said, but Hobbs had hung up.

***

When Claire arrived at the office, Lilly Rose wasn't there. Consuelo said she'd been suddenly called away. That was a relief because Claire had lots to do. By noon, she had the information and the codes to get into five houses in Watercolor. Along with the ones Rhonda had mentioned, she found another that looked promising. She arrived at the Watercolor Inn and met the Morehouses in the Fish Out of Water restaurant. FOOW, as it was known by locals, had great food and a fabulous view of the Gulf.

The couple were outside at a corner table. Lincoln was tall and distinguished looking, clean-shaven with neatly cut salt and pepper hair. His grey eyes scrutinized her from behind black-rimmed glasses. Claire got the feeling he didn't miss much. Rhonda was petite, blond and blue-eyed, with a warm and sincere smile. She was dressed to the nines in a black and white designer dress and python-print sling-back shoes. Her jewelry was a perfect match.

The waiter arrived and Claire ordered the blackened grouper tacos. Rhonda chose the Coastal Blue Farm salad and Lincoln went for the shrimp basket. As they waited for the food, Claire learned a little about the two of them.

Lincoln was partner in a law firm and a marathon runner. He'd qualified for the New York and Boston races. Claire mentioned the half-marathon race in Seaside that benefited the Seaside School. "It takes place in February. That weekend there's also a Taste of the Race event with great food, put on by Emeril Lagasse."

"I'll think about it," Lincoln said, though without much enthusiasm. Maybe a half marathon was beneath him, Claire thought.

Rhonda discussed several charities that occupied her time. When she mentioned that she ran the Women's League for the hospital in their town, Claire told her about the Girls' Getaway Weekend that took place in Rosemary Beach over Super Bowl Weekend. "It's a lot of fun and a fundraiser for the Sacred Heart Hospital on the Emerald Coast."

"My oh my, that's a clever idea for raising money." Rhonda pulled out her phone and tapped in a note to herself.

"You might even think about coming down for the weekend. You'd meet a lot of interesting women of all ages," Claire said.

"I might just do that. I'd like to get to know some locals."

After their orders arrived, Lincoln turned the conversation back to the houses. Claire had boned up on each of the properties and was able to provide information on each house. After lunch, they got into Lincoln's car and visited the properties. Compared to house-showing with Oscar, this was an entirely different process. Rhonda needed to stop in every room and open every cupboard and closet. She took notes and even went back to several rooms to check on window placement and views. Lincoln was less demanding and amazingly patient with his wife.

As they stood on the porch of the last house, Lincoln asked Claire about the body that had been found the day before in Bramble Bay. He'd been studying his phone and seen a story about it on his newsfeed.

"It must've looked pretty gruesome, with the body hanging out of the bucket like that." He shook his head. "There's a lot of evil in this world."

Claire avoided his gaze. "I'm afraid I missed that. I didn't have time to watch TV or read the news on my computer this morning," She didn't want to tell the Morehouses she was present at that horrible scene.

The Morehouses said they wanted to talk and would get back to Claire. Back at the inn, she got into her car and started home. She felt a little iffy about the afternoon. Maybe Rhonda hadn't found the perfect house or maybe Lincoln would nix them all. As she drove, she thought about the homes they had visited. All of them were large, with five or six bedrooms, spacious living rooms, designer kitchens and bubbling pools. She was glad to be wandering through the empty rooms with the Morehouses. At this time of year, most houses in Watercolor were vacant. The thought of visiting them alone was disturbing.

Chapter 27

At home, Claire suited up and went for a run. Again, she went east. She didn't want to run by Senator Juniper's castle, with its army of security guards. As she ran, she thought about her day. Maybe the Morehouses wouldn't buy, but it had been good to interact with them and forget about the body discovered yesterday. She needed to keep busy and look forward, not backward.

After her run, she took a shower and put on sleep-shorts and a tee-shirt. As she poured herself a glass of wine, her phone rang. She rushed to pick it up, hoping it would be Lincoln Morehouse, but it was Detective Drakos. He was downstairs and wanted to come up and talk. Instinctively, she felt bad vibes from his tone of voice. She suppressed her own feelings and said, "Sure, come on up. I'll be down in a jiff." Quickly, she pulled on a sweatshirt.

Downstairs, she disarmed the security system and opened the double locks on the door. Drakos looked tired and disheveled. His shirt was rumpled, his tie askew and his khakis looked as though he'd slept in them for a week. He probably hadn't been home since yesterday. He had dark circles under his eyes and his hair looked greasy.

"Hello, Claire. I've got some questions and some news."

"Good. Come in." She turned and ran up the stairs. He trudged along behind. When they reached the great room and kitchen area, she said, "Can I get you a glass of wine?"

He barked a laugh. "No thanks, alcohol would probably put me to sleep and I'd have to crash on your sofa."

He accepted a glass of iced tea and they sat down at the kitchen island. Claire sipped her wine and waited. His presence made her nervous. He took a long drink, put down the glass and turned to look her in the eye. "The body uncovered in Bramble Bay is the body of Samantha Marshall. Did you know her?"

Claire cocked her head. "No, I've never heard the name."

"She was a journalist for The Emerald Times." Drakos concentrated on his glass, turning it in his big hands. "Did Dax know her?"

"I don't know. I'm pretty sure he never mentioned her." Claire took a longer sip of wine. She noted a strong smell of sweat. Drakos needed a shower.

"I had to ask that, Claire. I'm wondering if there's a connection between these two murders."

"Why would there be a connection?"

"It's something I need to check out."

Claire finished her wine, reached for the bottle, and refilled her glass.

He eyed her from under his heavy lids. "I've got some other information."

"Oh?" She took a gulp and then moved the glass away.

"The county officer working the missing persons unit was away for several months. She went north to stay with her mother."

Claire raised her eyebrows. Where was this going?

Drakos continued, "Her name is Mary, she was expecting twins and had to stay in bed all day before they were born. You probably know about that. Some special condition?"

Claire suppressed her irritation. "I don't know a thing about pregnancy." A couple of weeks don't count, she thought.

"Anyway, she came back a couple of days ago. Yesterday, she contacted me because she knew I was investigating the Chief's murder. She told me Dax had been in to see her some days before she left. He consulted her about some missing girls." Drakos looked down into his iced tea. "Did he talk to you about this at all?"

"About missing girls? No." Claire's foot bounced up and down.

"These are girls who disappeared from the Emerald Coast, but who weren't initially reported missing. "

Claire ran her fingers through her hair. "What do you mean?"

"Two girls vanished from their jobs and their apartments, but their disappearance seemed to be planned. So no one around here reported them missing.

It was a relative who contacted the police weeks later."

"Dax was investigating these girls?"

"Maybe. At least he quizzed Mary about them sometime before he was killed." Drakos finished his iced tea, got up, went around the island and rinsed his glass in the sink.

"Was this Samantha Marshall one of them?" Claire asked.

"No. She was reported missing the first day she didn't show up for work."

"By her boss at the Times?"

"Yes, and a couple of friends. She was supposed to have dinner with them and never showed."

"How did she die?"

"The ME will get back to me after the autopsy, but it looked as though she'd been strangled."

A wave of nausea broke over Claire. She covered her face with her hands.

"Claire, are you all right?"

Claire rubbed her eyes and looked up. Drakos stood across the kitchen island from her, bracing himself against the counter with his big hands. His paunch bulged over the edge. "So why do you think her death is linked to Dax?" she asked.

"I try to cover all the angles."

"When did she go missing?"

"She disappeared right after Dax was killed."

Claire thought about that. She had been living in a fog back then. She wouldn't have noticed any news story about this woman, Samantha's disappearance. Thinking about missing girls, she suddenly remembered those panties in the safe.

Claire stood abruptly. "I don't know anything about Samantha Marshall or any other missing girls, but I think I've got a piece of evidence." She hopped down from the stool and beckoned for him to follow. In the office, she took down the painting of Rosemary Beach and punched in the code for the safe. She opened the door, reached deep inside, and pulled out the evidence bag containing the pair of pink panties. She held it out to Drakos by her thumb and forefinger. "Here, I found these when I was going through things, not long after Dax was killed."

Drakos took the baggie and inspected it. "Did you find anything else?"

"No. Do you think this is what those burglars were looking for when they ransacked the house?"

"I don't know. I'll have to think about that." He locked eyes with her. "Why didn't you hand these over months ago?"

She walked over to the window and looked out with her back to him. "At first, I tried to forget about them. Then I didn't tell you because I was worried..." Tears stung her eyes. "I thought Dax might have been having an affair. I thought these panties might belong to a girlfriend." She swallowed past a lump in her throat. "I'm ashamed I didn't trust Dax. And I'm sorry I didn't tell you about them earlier."

Drakos sighed heavily. "I'll get these to the lab. Maybe we can figure out who they belonged to. And Claire, don't beat yourself up. I'll take it from here."

After Drakos left, Claire went back to the kitchen. She took out a Strawberry Fields salad pack and dumped it in a bowl, then added the spicy nuts and poppy seed dressing. She sat down at the counter and googled Samantha Marshall on her laptop as she ate. The Emerald Times had a story about her, as did the Northwest Florida Daily News, the Panama City News Herald, and local TV stations. Someone, probably a construction worker or one of Hobbs's employees, had taken a photo of the bulldozer and the body hanging off the bucket's edge. Since everyone had a phone nowadays, images of the most gruesome scenes popped up instantly online. She quickly scrolled past the photo and read the story.

Apparently, Samantha had disappeared four months ago. Her boss at the Times said Samantha was a talented writer and a bulldog when it came to a story. "She never let it go, until she uncovered the truth," he was quoted as saying. Reading further, Claire learned that Samantha was responsible for uncovering the restaurant wine caper and had investigated the fraud connected to construction on the Highway 98 bridge. Her friends said she was caring and supportive. The article was followed by a slew of comments reiterating Samantha's kind and caring nature.

Claire spent some time looking at pictures of the dead girl. Samantha had been beautiful, with dark eyes and an infectious smile. In most of the snapshots, she wore jeans, tee shirts, and flip-flops. She had long, dark brown hair and a thin, taut body.

Claire's phone rang. It was Rhonda Morehouse, who told her they wanted to buy the house on Western Lake Drive. Rhonda made an offer of three million, one hundred thousand. Claire clicked away from the news story about Samantha and worked up a contract in a new window, and then called the realtor handling the Western Lake house.

It was a long evening. The owners counter-offered at three million four. Rhonda came back at three million, one-fifty. Eventually they agreed at three million two. By the time the negotiating was over,

Claire fell into bed exhausted and reasonably happy. It wasn't until five in the morning that Samantha Marshall surged into her dreams and she awoke drenched in sweat.

***

Claire arrived at the office at eight AM. She figured she'd be the only one there, and she wanted to work on the details of the Morehouse deal in peace and quiet. To her surprise, Barbara was already at her desk, dressed in slacks and a mauve knit top. She looked neat and professional, as always.

She eyed Claire over her granny glasses and then stood. "Good morning. You're here early."

Claire grinned at her. "Guess what! I sold another house last night."

"That's wonderful! Pretty soon you'll be the top earner."

"I'm so grateful for all the help you've given me."

Barbara came around her desk toward Claire. "I'm glad we're alone. I wanted to talk to you. I understand you were there when they uncovered the body out at Bramble Bay."

Claire grimaced at the memory. "Right, but I'd rather not talk about it. It was horrible."

"I understand." Barbara looked anxious and had lost her usual cool veneer. When she continued, Claire had the sense she was carefully choosing her words. "Remember I told you I'd met your husband?"

"Right, you told me he was coming out of a house with someone." Claire placed her purse and her briefcase on her desk, then looked over at Barbara.

"Well, the woman he was with…remember I said her name started with an S."

Claire nodded.

"It was that woman they found in Bramble Bay. Samantha Marshall."

Claire wrapped her arms around her torso. Suddenly, she felt cold.

Barbara was still talking. "Do you think I should tell the police?"

Not trusting her voice, Claire nodded. Drakos had been right. In death—and apparently in life—Samantha and Dax were intertwined.

Chapter 28

Claire put a call in to Drakos and passed the phone to Barbara. He asked her to come into the station to give a statement. Before hanging up, Barbara passed the phone back to Claire.

"I guess you were right," Claire told him. "Dax and Samantha Marshall were involved somehow."

"Claire, we don't know anything yet. Don't make unfounded assumptions," Drakos said.

She snorted. "That's a joke, coming from you."

***

By afternoon, Claire had contacted the title company and set a date for the closing. Like Oscar, the Morehouses were paying in cash. Where do people get money like that, Claire wondered.

A short while later, she told Lilly Rose she didn't feel well and would be heading home. Lilly Rose looked sympathetic. "Sure. Go home and relax. You had a big shock the other day and you need to take care of yourself."

But Claire didn't head home. She needed to know more about Samantha Marshall. Who exactly was this woman? What was her relationship with Dax? Had they been having an affair or working on a case? She needed to know, or she would go nuts. In the car, Claire googled The Emerald Times. The editor's name was Joe Brinell, and the office was in Panama City. At this hour, it would be a quick trip through Panama City Beach and over the bridge.

Thirty minutes later, she surveyed the torn-up buildings and overturned trees as she drove through Panama City. The town had been hard hit by Hurricane Michael. But the destruction here was nothing like the devastation in Mexico City Beach. She and Dax had driven over there shortly after the hurricane and had helped distribute food, water and household supplies. Dax had spent weekends afterwards helping to rebuild wrecked homes and businesses.

The Emerald Times office was off 23rd street. The plain brick building had been saved from the ravages of the hurricane, in marked contrast to the forest of upturned palm trees in the empty lot to the south. Claire parked and surveyed the building. What was she going to ask Mr. Brinell? Surely, he would know if Samantha Marshall was researching missing girls. Maybe Dax had turned up at the office and they'd all had a chat. With a sense of determination, she got out of the car and approached the glass door that bore the newspaper's name. She pushed the door open and went in, momentarily blinded as she left the bright sunshine and entered the darkened interior.

Her eyes adjusted rapidly, and she took in her surroundings. In front of her was a waist-high scratched wooden counter. Behind it sat a nymph of a girl. She had a pixie face with a small pointed chin and great big dark eyes. She wore her hair in handlebar ponytails. She was typing on a computer and took a minute to register Claire's silhouette delineated in the doorway.

"Hey there," the girl finally said. "Welcome to the Times. What can I do for you? Is it about advertising? If it is, you'll have to talk to George. He handles all that and he's not here. He actually works from home. If you want to subscribe, I'm the girl for you." She delivered this monologue without taking a breath. At the end of it, she smiled, and her face lit up like fireworks on the fourth of July.

Claire couldn't help but like her. "Hi, I'm Claire Simmons."

"My name's Poppy. What can I help you with?"

Poppy. What a perfect name for this girl. "I'd like to talk to Joe Brinell. Is he in?"

"Yeah, he's back there. Go on ahead." Poppy gestured to a doorway at the back, behind the counter, and yelled, "Joe, someone to see you."

A gruff voice responded, "Send her back."

Claire smiled at Poppy and walked through the doorway to a huge, open room that held several large tables and a bank of computers. She looked around. No presses or anything like that. She guessed they didn't print the newspaper here. Maybe it was outsourced?

In one corner was a massive desk piled high with papers, coffee cups, fast-food bags and Coke cans. Behind it sat a walrus of a man with a drooping moustache and a shiny bald head. He made an effort to stand, bracing himself on the edge of the desk. Tall and massive, he must have weighed three hundred and fifty pounds.

He held out his hand. "Joe Brinell." His eyes seemed to be evaluating her.

She shook hands with him. "Hi, I'm Claire Simmons."

"I heard you say that. Are you the Chief's wife?"

"Yes. Yes, I am." Claire hadn't expected that.

"Sorry for your loss. I met the Chief several times. He seemed like a nice guy." Joe hobbled around and swept some papers off a chair beside his desk. "Sit down." He limped back to his padded office chair and fell heavily into it. "Why are you here? Is it about Samantha?"

Talk about being direct. Claire was momentarily taken aback. "Well, yes, it is."

"Detective Drakos has already been here. He talked to Poppy. He talked to me. He wanted to know what Samantha was working on. He also told us Samantha had been in touch with your husband."

Claire took a deep breath. "I guess I want to know the same things."

"Here's what I told Drakos. I have no idea what Samantha might have been working on. Drakos mentioned missing girls. I know nothing about any missing girls." He leaned forward. "Samantha covered the stories I asked her to cover. But she always had her ear to the ground. Some of her best work was articles she developed on the side. Before she ever came to me, she had the story researched and evaluated. Then we discussed it together and planned the spin."

"Did my husband come here to meet with her?"

"I never saw him here. I might have met him at a Rotary or a county board meeting. I never saw him with Samantha."

The next question had to be asked even if the answer might make her very unhappy. Claire knitted her fingers in her lap. "Do you think they were having an affair?"

His droopy eyes were soft with kindness. "Miss Claire, I don't know about Sam's love life. She didn't share her personal life with me. I think she had a boyfriend." He scratched his head. "Maybe Poppy knows something, or her roommate does. With me, Samantha was strictly business." He fiddled with a pen. His fingers were pudgy and there was ink under his nails. Then he said, his voice low, "But I do miss Sam. She was a beacon in the storm."

Claire sighed, and stood. "Thanks for talking to me."

As she turned away, he said, "If I were you, I would leave this to Drakos and his team. We know your husband and Samantha were both murdered. Stay away and let the police do their job."

Claire nodded and took her leave. In the outer office, Poppy was typing, but as soon as she spotted Claire, she stopped and held up a finger. Then she slid down from her stool, came around to the front of the counter and pulled open the door, beckoning Claire to follow her. They stepped outside together.

"Joe is right, you should probably leave well enough alone," Poppy said.

"Right, I know, but I just want some answers."

"Well, for what it's worth, I'm sure Samantha wasn't having an affair with your husband. She's been dating this guy for a couple of years. Maybe you should talk to him. It might make you feel better."

"I'd like that. What's his name?"

"Hank. Hank Robbins. He's a fisherman. He runs charters. I think he keeps his boat at the St. Andrew's Marina. Ask around. I bet somebody will know him. I think he lives on his boat."

"Thanks, Poppy. I'm sorry about Samantha. It sounds like she was a good friend."

Poppy's eyes filled with tears. "Yeah, she was like a big sister." Abruptly, she turned away and went back into the newspaper office.

Chapter 29

When Claire got back to the car, her phone rang. She looked at the screen. It was Drakos. She didn't want to talk to him. Not now. He would probably ask her what she was up to, and she'd have a hard time lying. Better to avoid him. She put St. Andrew's Marina in her GPS and saw it was an easy drive down Beck Avenue. As she drove, she thought about what she would say to Hank Robbins.

She wanted to know if he knew what Samantha was working on; if Samantha had ever mentioned Dax. Did Hank know Dax? Maybe Dax had been on his boat. After months of inertia, maybe she would learn something useful.

Claire reached the marina and found a parking spot. She turned off the engine and googled Hank Robbins. A picture of a fishing boat and a man holding a giant fish appeared on the screen. The website advertised day trips for six, eight, or ten hours. She noted the phone number and punched it in, but no one picked up. She decided not to leave a voicemail.

She grabbed her bag and got out of the car. The late afternoon sun glinted off the boats in the harbor. She needed to find Hank and interview him before it got dark. Across the way, she saw two men working on the deck of a boat. She jogged over. "Hello," she called out.

One of the men looked up.

"Hi, I'm looking for Hank Robbins. Do you know him?"

The man shouted back, "Yeah, everyone knows Hank."

"Do you know where I could find him?"

The two men eyed each other. Then the other guy said, "He's in slip forty-two. Head over that-a-way." He gestured to the right.

Claire thanked him and found her way to slip forty-two. As she approached, she saw two grey-haired couples getting off a shiny, white boat. They waved at a man on the deck and called, "Thanks again, great trip." Claire waited for them to pass before approaching the man on the boat. She assumed he was Hank Robbins.

He stared at her. He was a sturdy man, about five-foot ten. He projected strength and authority. "Hey, can I help you? Are you lost?"

She realized she didn't look anything like a seafaring maiden…far from it. She knew nothing about boats or fishing. "Hi, are you Hank Robbins?"

"At your service."

Claire stepped closer. "I wonder if I could talk to you for a few minutes?"

He stepped back, frowning. "I've got a lot to do right now. Got to clean up the boat. Get it ready for tomorrow. It better be quick." He pushed back a shock of straight, dark hair and eyed her suspiciously.

"It's about Samantha Marshall."

Hank's eyes, deep set and intent, flashed with anger. "I already talked to the police. The subject is closed." He turned his back on her and picked up a couple of beer bottles. Then he glared at her over his shoulder. "Who in the hell are you?"

"I'm Claire Simmons. My husband was killed, too. I think he was a friend of Samantha's."

Hank looked around as though he thought they were being observed. He gestured to her. Lowering his voice, he said, "Okay, come aboard,"

Claire stepped across the little gangway. Hank put out his hand. She grasped it and hopped into the boat. It rocked slightly and she laughed nervously. "I'm not a boat person."

"Why don't you come down below. We'll talk there." Again, he nervously surveyed the area. Then he led her down a short flight of stairs to a neat wood-paneled room. There was a small kitchen area, an oblong table set before a long bench. Across from it was another cushioned bench that served as a sofa.

Claire felt a little claustrophobic in the small space. Hank cocked his head, studying her. "Can I get you something to drink?"

"No thank you, I'm fine."

He gestured to the bench. "Sit down and tell me what you want to know."

Claire sat. Hank grabbed a beer from the fridge and popped the cap, then took a long swig. "I never drink when I've got a charter group. But afterwards, I usually need a beer," he grinned.

Claire smiled. "I've changed my mind. I'll have a beer too."

Hank got one out for her, popped the cap and handed it to her. "So, why did you come here looking for me?"

Claire took a swallow of beer to fortify herself. "I just learned this morning that my husband, Chief Dax Simmons, was seen with Samantha days before Dax was killed. I went to talk to Joe Brinell at The Emerald Times, and Poppy suggested I talk to you."

"Poppy sent you over?" He chuckled. "I like Poppy, but she should mind her own business." He sat on the bench behind the table and propped his elbows on the smooth, shiny surface.

"Detective Drakos must have told you about finding Samantha's body. I was there." She blanched. "It was terrible."

Hank looked at her. His deep-set eyes resembled dark pools. Then he looked down and studied the label on the beer bottle. "Yeah, it must have been." With sudden violence, he banged the bottle so hard on the table that Claire thought the glass would break. "Who in the fuck did this to Sam? If I could find them, I'd kill 'em." He roared the last few words like an angry lion.

Claire shrank against the padded backrest. "We need to find out," she said after a moment.

Hank drank down the rest of the beer, got up and got another. "Let's go up on deck. I need air." Claire felt the same way.

Up on deck there was a light breeze. The water lapped gently against the hull of the boat. The sun's last rays glowed pink and orange. Hank picked up some binoculars and surveyed the marina, doing a full three hundred and sixty degrees. Then he sat down under the canopy over the fishing deck, putting himself in semi-darkness.

"You seem nervous," Claire said tentatively.

"Someone's been watching me. Not all the time. I just have this sixth sense that there's someone out there...ever since Sam disappeared."

Claire looked around the marina. It was getting too dark to make out much. "Were you robbed? After she disappeared, I mean."

"I think someone came onboard when I was out at a party on another boat. Nothing was taken, but I could tell someone had opened cupboards, looked through my stuff. You know, things were moved around."

"After Dax, my husband...after he was killed, someone ransacked my house."

Hank leaned forward. "Who do you think did it?"

"I have no idea. The Sheriff's Department went through the house for fingerprints and canvassed the neighbors. No one saw anything." Claire took a breath. "So did Samantha ever talk about Dax?"

"No. But Sam never talked about what she was working on. She had this thing about complete secrecy until she nailed the story down."

"Dax was working alone, too. I learned recently that it might have had to do with missing girls. Did Samantha…did Sam ever talk about missing persons?"

"No. We talked about lots of other stuff. Sam was an idea freak." Claire could hear the warmth in his voice. "One day it was about saving sea turtles. The next, she was into medieval history and followed the Medievalists site on Twitter. I learned about the difference between Monet and Manet from Sam. Hell, she loved learning. She wanted to explore new ideas and old philosophies…everything from the harnessing of wave energy to Seneca's stoicism."

"She sounds like a fascinating person."

"She was good at making connections." He sighed. "Sam had a great sense of humor. She'd laugh this fabulous deep belly laugh…and she was beautiful…but she didn't realize it. I mean, she always wore tee-shirts and jeans. No make-up, no artifice. What you saw was what you got." His voice shook with emotion.

Claire couldn't see him very well in the dark, but she could tell Hank had truly loved Samantha Marshall. She waited a moment. Then she said, "So you have no idea what she might have been working on that could have gotten her killed."

"No, no idea."

"Nothing about missing girls?"

"I said no. Give it up." He sounded irritated.

"I'm just trying to find out why my husband was killed, that's all," Claire shot back.

Hank sighed. "Okay, sorry, I get it."

"One more question," she said, more gently this time. "Where did Sam keep a record of her research? On her computer?"

He cocked his head. "She wrote on her computer, but she kept notes in a notebook. A red five-by-seven notebook she could put in her purse. Sometimes she'd get an idea, and out would come the notebook. She had an organized system of keeping notes."

"Do you know where her notebook is?" Claire asked.

"No clue. Heck, maybe that's what these guys were looking for when they went through my boat."

What were they looking for at my house? Claire wondered.

Hank stood. "Are you hungry?"

Claire realized she hadn't had lunch. "Yeah, I'm starving."

"Okay, come on down and I'll serve you up some of my famous chili."

They went down below. Hank removed a plastic container from the mini fridge, dished chili into two bowls and placed them in the microwave. Along with a bag of tortilla chips, he set containers of grated cheddar, chopped onions and sour cream on the table and got out two more bottles of beer. When the chili was heated, they sat at the table side by side and began to eat. The overhead light enclosed them in its warm glow. A companionable silence reigned.

"Where did Samantha live?" Claire asked after a while, as she sprinkled cheese on the chili.

"She shared a little house with another girl here in Panama City. Luckily, it wasn't touched by the hurricane."

"Could you give me the address? I'd like to go over there and talk to her roommate."

"Sure. The roommate's name is Abby. She's like the exact opposite of Sam…very quiet, introverted and not too swift."

He took a swallow of beer. Then he said, "I've been thinking. You asked me what Sam and I discussed the last few weeks before she disappeared."

Claire nodded as she scooped some chili with a corn chip.

"I was just remembering that we were sitting right here, and Sam brought up politics."

Claire put down the loaded chip. "And?"

"She was talking about congressmen and senators and what states they represented. Stuff like that."

"Did she mention Senator Juniper, by any chance?

Hank shoveled chili onto his spoon. "Yeah, I think I remember that name."

Chapter 30

After dinner, Hank accompanied Claire to her car. He apologized as she opened her door. "Sorry if I was a jerk. This latest news has opened a festering wound...I can't get over the fact that Sam is gone. I guess, all this time, I just hoped she would return."

"I understand. Right now, the pain is fresh." She reached out to shake hands, but he pulled her into a hug.

"Take care of yourself, Claire. Keep in touch. Contact me if you learn anything." He stepped away. His eyes glimmered with tears.

"Yes, you too. If you think of anything that would help my investigation."

As Claire pulled onto Beck Avenue, she noticed another car's headlights flash on behind her. The vehicle followed her all the way to Highway 98. She kept looking in the rearview mirror. Was she being overly suspicious? Hank had made her nervous with his talk about being watched. When she turned on to 98, the car followed along behind her. Come on, Claire, you're being paranoid. With the traffic on 98 she couldn't differentiate one car from another. The car's headlights blended in with all the other headlights traveling behind her.

When she turned onto 283 towards Grayton Beach, no one followed her. She sighed with relief. Nonetheless, when she got home, after activating the security system, she went around and checked the doors and windows.

In bed, Claire went over what she'd learned in the last twenty-four hours. Dax had been investigating the disappearance of local girls. Then he'd been killed. Samantha had been seen with Dax. Then she'd been killed. Therefore, they must have been working together. It was like a simple, logical equation. She decided to stop by the Sheriff's Department in the morning, before work, and talk to Mary in Missing Persons. After work, she would drive to Panama City again and visit Abby. Hank had given her the address. Little by little, she would do her own investigation. She would be doing something positive for Dax.

***

Officer Nilsson was manning the front desk when Claire reached the Sheriff's Department at eight-thirty the next morning. He welcomed her with a friendly wave.

"I'm here to see Mary in Missing Persons," she told him. "Could you direct me to her office?"

"Sure, ma'am. Let me buzz you in. Her office is down that hallway, turn to your left. It's the second door on the right."

Claire followed Nilsson's directions. The second door on the right was open. Inside, a high counter prevented further access into the room. File cabinets lined the back wall. To the right was a long counter holding printers, a fax machine and other equipment. To the left was a whiteboard. A series of photos was affixed to the board with colorful magnets. Underneath the pictures, names were neatly printed along with bullet points of information. In the middle of the room, two desks faced each other. At one desk, a woman was typing on a computer keyboard. She was wearing a headpiece and was talking to someone. She spotted Claire, smiled, and waved. As Claire waited for the woman to finish her conversation, she looked at the photos. There were two pictures of young women, a photo of a small boy and one of an elderly woman. Were all these people currently missing? It was a disturbing thought.

The woman finished her call. She took off her headset, got up and came over to the counter. She was short and sturdily built. Curly ginger hair framed a round, freckled face. She was in uniform: dark blue, short-sleeved tailored shirt and blue pants. Around her waist was a duty belt with holster and gun. Claire noted her name on the name tag: Mary O'Sullivan.

Mary studied Claire through tired blue eyes. "How can I help you?" she asked.

"I'm Claire Simmons. I'm—"

Sadness crossed Mary's face. "Oh, Mrs. Simmons, I'm so sorry for your loss."

That phrase again. Still, she meant well. "Thank you, Mary."

"How are you getting along? It must be hard." Mary teared up. "I don't know what I'd do without my Joe."

"It is hard, but I'm doing all right. I'm actually here to see if you can help me."

"Sure, anything I can do."

"I understand Dax came here to see you some time before he was killed. Can you tell me what he wanted to know?"

"Yeah, sure. I remember it pretty well, because right after he was here, I had to leave. I was pregnant, and my doctor prescribed total bedrest. So I moved in with my mom and dad up in Birmingham and they took care of me until I gave birth. I had twin girls." She beamed.

"Congratulations," Claire said.

"Thanks. I love them like mad, but I'm not getting much sleep." She pushed a curly lock of hair out of her face.

Claire smiled with empathy. "I can imagine."

"Anyway, I was gone when Chief Simmons was murdered. It wasn't until I came back to work that I told Detective Drakos about the conversation we had."

"Tell me about it."

"Why don't you come around back here." Mary lifted one end of the counter and Claire slipped through the opening. Mary pointed to a chair beside her desk. Claire sat down.

"Would you like some coffee?" Mary was hovering.

"No, thanks. I've got to get to work after I talk to you. I don't have much time."

Mary sat down. Now she was all business. "Chief Simmons came in one morning to ask me about two missing girls. He said he had received a tip. I opened the database and checked the names, but neither one of them appeared in our list of missing persons."

"That's weird."

"That's what we thought. The women left their jobs and their homes, and just vanished. Lauren Reynolds and Tammy Schulz, those were their names."

"So why weren't they reported missing?"

Mary frowned in thought. "As I understand it, they each texted their employer saying they had to return home for a family emergency. Lauren shared an apartment with a friend, and she texted the friend that her mom was ill. She apologized for leaving without warning. Then she asked her friend to take anything of hers she wanted and to throw the rest away."

"And the roommate didn't think this was odd?"

"Apparently, she was glad to have Lauren's clothes and shoes. They were about the same size."

"What about the other girl? Tammy, you said?"

"Yes, Tammy Schulz. Wait a minute, let me check the database." Mary typed in the name and read from the notes. "Her roommates said she was kind of a loner, barely communicated with them. When Tammy left town, she texted them to dump her stuff or sell it on eBay."

"Has someone been investigating their disappearance since then?"

"No…the Chief told me not to mention it to anyone. But after he passed, I thought it was important to tell Detective Drakos, since he's investigating the Chief's murder." Mary nibbled on her bottom lip.

Claire sat there, digesting this information. "And Dax never told you where he got the tip?"

"No, he didn't divulge that information." Mary sat back and looked past Claire to the whiteboard behind her. "We have a picture of each girl, sent digitally by their family when Detective Drakos contacted them. Lauren Reynolds is the fourth one in from the right. Tammy's picture is next to hers."

Claire got up and went to the whiteboard. The picture of Lauren Reynolds showed a tall willowy blond. She looked dressed for the prom in a long silver-blue gown. Under the picture was a short description including Lauren's height, weight, coloring and the approximate date of her disappearance. Tammy Schulz was petite, with dark hair and wide-set eyes. Under her picture was the same information. The two women had disappeared within a few weeks of each other.

Claire looked back at Mary. "Why didn't the parents contact the police when they hadn't heard from their daughters in a while?"

Mary shrugged. "Apparently, Lauren never knew her dad. Her mother was against her move down to Florida, and they were on the outs. So when Lauren left Pittsburgh and moved down here, she never called her mom."

"What about Tammy?"

"She was raised by her aunt. The aunt sent us that picture. She told Detective Drakos she kicked Tammy out once she turned eighteen. That was how it was in her family, and the aunt said Tammy was old enough to take care of herself."

"So both of these young women were on their own." Claire ran her hand through her hair in frustration. "What about Samantha Marshall? She's the woman found dead out at Bramble Bay."

Mary blanched. "Gosh, wasn't that terrible. Everyone here has been talking about how a bulldozer dug up her body."

Claire tried to maintain her cool. "Do you have information in your database about her disappearance?"

Mary turned to the computer, typed and scrolled. "Got it. Samantha was reported missing by her boss and her boyfriend. She left the newspaper office in the morning, saying she had an appointment, and never returned. No one knew where she went or who she was meeting. That evening she'd planned on having dinner with some friends, but never showed up."

Claire stood abruptly. "Thanks for talking to me. Good luck with your twins. I'm sure they're a handful." As Claire walked back down the hallway, she tried to recall where she'd heard a similar story. Had Dax talked about missing girls? She couldn't remember.

Chapter 31

Hobbs called as she was pulling into a parking place in Rosemary Beach. "Hey, Claire. How are you? I've been worrying about you."

"I'm all right. How about you?"

He paused. "I've been trying to figure out how, why and when that body was buried. Drakos drilled me for a couple of hours. We went through my landscape schedule over and over. Then he wanted to know if I knew Samantha Marshall. It's hard to prove you've never met someone." Hobbs sounded frustrated.

"He didn't think you were involved, did he?"

"I hope not. But he probably thought I had the means to do it."

"That's nuts," Claire said.

"He's got detectives talking to all the gardeners working for me and the construction workers; but I don't think they had anything to do with it."

"Neither do I. This is much bigger than that."

"What do you mean?"

Claire didn't want to tell him what she'd learned about missing girls from Drakos, Hank and Mary. For now, she wanted to keep her investigation to herself. "Samantha was known to do in-depth investigations that rubbed people the wrong way, particularly people in power. She must have been onto something major."

"And they wanted her out of the way," Hobbs said.

"Listen, Hobbs, I'm at work. I've got to go in."

"Okay, do you want to have dinner tomorrow night?"

"Sure. Where?" Claire asked.

"How about the Grayton Seafood Company? Seven o'clock."

"Wonderful. See you then."

***

Claire was busy that day; lots of phone calls and walk-ins. She spent time with a young couple who were moving down to the area. The husband was a surgeon and would be working at Sacred Heart Hospital. The wife didn't seem too keen about the move. She considered the Emerald Coast a vacation spot, but not an appropriate place to raise three young children.

"Where will I make friends? It's not like living in the suburbs in Omaha, near my family and all kinds of folks I know. I'll be totally alone. What about the schools? I definitely am dreading this move," Anne Johnson said.

Bill Johnson seemed annoyed and amused by his wife. They spent an hour discussing where they wanted to live. Claire found several houses that met their expectations. At the same time, she talked about the Seaside Neighborhood School and local activities for children and their parents. "Believe it or not, there's a healthy number of families who live here year-round. You're going to make lots of friends through your kids. And...there will be no snow days."

Anne laughed and Bill beamed with pleasure. Claire set up appointments to see more houses the following morning.

At three o'clock she had a meeting with Lilly Rose. It had been planned in advance and was to be a monthly evaluation.

As she entered the office, Lilly Rose asked her to shut the door. The heavy smell of the yellow roses perfumed the room. Lilly Rose worked in a permanent garden, Claire thought as she sat down across from her boss.

"Congratulations on your two big sales," Lilly Rose said. "You're an asset to the agency already."

"Thank you. I've been incredibly lucky."

"Well, I think you've got the knack. I saw you out there today. That couple came in looking miserable, and they left all smiles."

"The wife didn't want to move down here. She needed a lot of convincing." Claire laughed. "We're going house hunting tomorrow morning."

"Good." Lilly Rose cleared her throat. "How are you doing since that horrible experience last week?"

"I'm trying to forget all about it."

"That's the best thing to do. You can't dwell on the past."

"How's Harrison? I haven't seen him since that day."

"He's working permanently out at Bramble Bay. We need to work especially hard to dispel the image of Bramble Bay as the site of a murder. Harrison sold two houses yesterday that are still under construction. He's a wizard."

"That's great. Tomorrow I'm taking that couple, the Johnsons, out there. Bramble Bay has the feeling of a neighborhood and that might attract them."

"Excellent."

Claire was ready to stand up and leave, but Lilly Rose wasn't finished. "What do you do for fun, Claire?" she asked, a smile hovering on her lips.

"Fun?" Claire was taken aback. "Well...I have dinner with friends, yoga, running."

"Do you like to party?" This question seemed out of character. In a severe black suit and a meticulous white silk shirt, Lilly Rose didn't look much like a party girl herself.

"I'm not really...I mean...I like to have a good time, but I'm not into drugs or getting wildly drunk, if that's what you mean?" Claire swallowed. "I do like to dance, though," she added.

"How about quiet get-togethers?"

Thank heavens, she hadn't stuck her foot in it. "Yeah, that's probably more my thing."

"Maybe we can organize a little party some time."

"Yes, that would be nice."

Lilly Rose turned to her computer. Claire had been dismissed.

***

Claire spent a good part of the afternoon setting up showings of various houses for the Johnsons. At five o'clock, she left the agency and headed back towards Panama City, intending to stop by and visit Abby, Samantha Marshall's roommate. The traffic was heavy going over the bridge, and the trip took her nearly an hour.

Eventually she arrived at Abby's address. Some of the houses on the quiet street looked to be in pretty good shape, but the roofs of several others were covered with the familiar bright blue tarp. Undoubtedly, they had lost all or part of the roof in the hurricane.

Samantha and Abby's house seemed to have escaped the ravages of the storm. It was painted salmon pink and had a small front porch. Claire parked, got out, and walked up the steps to the door. She hadn't called ahead, so she wasn't sure if Abby would be there. Hank had told her Abby was a homebody, though, so Claire figured she would probably be home by six at night. Claire rang the bell. She heard a shuffling sound behind the door. Then a suspicious voice said, "What do you want?"

"Hi, I'm Claire Simmons. I'm here to talk to you about Samantha Marshall."

"I don't have anything to say."

"I talked to Hank, yesterday. He gave me your address."

A small silence fell. Then: "Why did he do that?"

Claire could understand Abby's reluctance to talk to her. "My husband was killed, and he was working with Samantha."

"Your husband? Who was he?"

"Chief Daxton Simmons. He died several months ago."

Another silence. Claire guessed Abby was thinking this over. Then Abby said, "Okay."

Several bolts and deadbolts clicked. Like Claire, Abby was living in a fortified castle. Finally, the door opened. Claire saw a tall, skinny woman with long dark hair parted in the middle. She was wearing a floral-print midi dress and her feet were bare. Dark brown eyes glared at Claire with suspicion and maybe a speck of fear.

"I don't really know anything about Samantha's life," Abby said.

"Can I come in?"

Abby looked up and down the street and then back at Claire. "Yes. Hurry."

When Claire had crossed the threshold, Abby slammed the door behind her and turned the bolts. What was she afraid of? It made Claire think of Hank, convinced someone was watching him…and also of herself.

She looked around at the small, cozy living room where she stood. A beige sofa decorated with two embroidered cushions sat against one wall. Above it, an exquisite framed quilt depicted fish darting through turquoise water. A crocheted throw lay across an armchair a few feet away. Everywhere Claire looked, there were clever pieces of handiwork. She turned to Abby. "Wow! Did you make all these beautiful creations?"

Abby blushed and looked down at her feet.

"You're truly an artist." Claire walked over for a better look at the quilt. Then she picked up a cushion and examined the delicate stitched design of blue irises on a green background. This was definitely not Claire's style, but she admired each individual craft.

Abruptly, Abby asked, "Would you like some pink lemonade?"

"Sure, thanks. Do you mind if I look around?"

Abby nodded. "Go ahead."

Above the TV was a series of framed needlepoint designs of birds. They were delightful, and Claire marveled at the precision of the work. When Abby came back, they sat on each end of the sofa. The coffee table held hand-painted wooden coasters. A bouquet of silk flowers bloomed in a painted glass vase. Each item Claire admired was exquisite, but all together they were overwhelming. Claire wondered how Samantha had fit into this craft-crazy room.

Abby brought over a round basket and took out some knitting needles and bright red yarn. A partially finished garment hung from one of the needles.

"What are you knitting?" Claire asked.

"It's a baby sweater for my sister's little boy. He'll be one year old this Christmas."

"She must really appreciate you."

"She can always count on me for a sweater." Abby smiled with self-satisfaction.

Claire sipped the lemonade. It tasted like Kool-Aid.

She put down her glass and smiled encouragingly at Abby. "I came here to find out anything you might know about Samantha. I'm wondering if she talked to you about her work."

"Samantha and I didn't talk much. I work at the Dollar Store and I talk all day. I don't want to talk at home. I just like to relax and work on a project."

"So, she didn't tell you anything about her investigations?"

"No. I think she liked it that we didn't talk. She would go up to her room and type on the computer or talk on the phone. She had her own life and I had mine."

"Did you eat meals together?"

"No, we shared the fridge, but she had practically nothing in there. She didn't eat here much."

"Did you share the rent?"

The knitting needles clicked away. Abby's eyes stayed glued to the complicated pattern. "I own this house. My parents left it to me. Samantha was my tenant. She paid me right on time each month."

Claire sipped more of the fake lemonade. "You're sure she never mentioned anything, even briefly?"

"Like I said, we didn't talk. Only when necessary."

Click, click, click.

"You heard about her death, right?"

"Yes. Everyone at the store was talking about it." Abby kept knitting.

"It was pretty terrible," Claire said.

"She involved herself in other people's business. Not a good idea." Abby raised her eyebrows in disapproval.

So much for Samantha, Claire thought. She cleared her throat. "Could I take a peek in her room?"

"Sure, go ahead. It's right up those stairs. She had a bedroom and a little study."

Claire set the glass of lemonade on the coaster and stood up.

Abby said, "I put everything back the way it was after the robbery."

Claire stopped in her tracks. "Robbery?"

"Yes. I was robbed a few days after Samantha disappeared. They tossed everything around. It was a mess. Now I have better locks."

Chapter 32

As it turned out, Abby had never called the police. "I didn't want them pawing through my things. I mean, they could steal something, too. You can't really trust the police. They came here after Samantha disappeared and looked around. That boss of hers, Joe, sent them here. They made me nervous."

"So, no one knew about the robbery?" Claire needed further clarification.

"No. I didn't want anyone else in here. The next day I had the locksmith come and he put on these super locks." Abby was knitting at a rapid rate.

"What was stolen?" Claire asked.

"Nothing that I could tell. They didn't want my TV. It's too old. The police had already taken Samantha's computer. I don't really know what she had in the way of valuables." Click, click, click.

"By any chance did Detective Drakos come here yesterday?"

"Yes, he was here with another guy. They went upstairs and looked around."

"Did they take anything?"

"I don't know."

Claire figured there wouldn't be anything left if the robbers and Drakos had already gone through Samantha's things. Nonetheless, she went upstairs and spent time going through the drawers and the closet. Samantha's clothes and shoes were still there. She looked under the mattress and checked for loose floorboards. In the little den, she went through the desk, and even turned the armchair upside-down looking for hidden compartments. Hank had said Samantha wrote notes in a red notebook. But there were no notebooks, or pieces of paper with notes or lists or anything.

Back downstairs, Abby was still knitting. "How did your husband die?" she asked.

"He was drugged and drowned."

Click, click, click. "By the same evil men as killed Sam?"

"Maybe. That's what I want to find out." Distractedly, Claire reached down for the lemonade glass and sipped a bit more of the sugary liquid. There was nothing else to learn here. "I guess I'll go now. Thanks for the lemonade."

Abby had stopped knitting. A knot appeared between her brows and she seemed to be debating something. Then she said, "Samantha won't be coming back."

Claire nodded.

"I've got something of hers. The last time I saw her, she told me to keep it until she got back. I keep it in this basket." Abby pulled out a fat skein of red yarn. Carefully, she extracted a red notebook from between the bunched strands.

Claire drew in a sharp breath. "Could I have it? Samantha won't need it anymore."

Abby scrunched up her face. The question seemed to trouble her. "I guess so. You're right, Samantha doesn't need it wherever she's gone."

Claire took the notebook, tucked it in her purse, and said goodbye. Once she was outside, Abby slammed the door shut behind her, and Claire could hear the turning of the locks. She looked up and down the street. Abby's fears were infectious, like a virus. She rushed to her car, slid in, and locked the doors.

As she drove back to Lemon Cove, she wondered why Samantha had lived with Abby. Surely, she could have found another bright, intelligent girl to share a house or an apartment. On the other hand, the rent was probably low, and the offices of The Emerald Times were close by. Maybe she wanted to live with someone who would leave her alone.

Claire wanted to pull over and look through the notebook, but she needed to get home. It was getting late and she had an inkling that this little red notebook might provide answers to Dax and Samantha's deaths. Nervously, she glanced in the rearview mirror. Was someone following her? She thought about Hank and Abby, who were both convinced they were being watched.

She had learned a lot that day. Dax and Samantha had been investigating the disappearance of Tammy Schulz and Lauren Reynolds and were probably killed because of what they had learned. She imagined Drakos had come to the same conclusion. Should she leave all this to him, or should she continue asking questions? Didn't she owe it to Dax to do everything she could to uncover his murderer? She didn't want to give up. Not yet.

At home, she locked the doors and activated the security system. After pouring herself a glass of wine, she settled down in the boudoir and opened the red notebook. The entries were in chronological order with the date and time at the top, then the name of the person interviewed, followed by the information gleaned in bullet point format. Samantha had interviewed Lauren's employer and also the roommate, Sarah Kendall. Sarah reported that Lauren didn't share much with the people in her life. She had moved down to the Panhandle from Pittsburgh. Sarah said Lauren was quiet and naïve when she first moved in. She was blown away by the beautiful houses, the expensive boutiques and chic restaurants. She'd never seen the Gulf of Mexico and had never eaten shrimp. Lauren worked at Vanilla Sugar, a candy, fudge and ice cream shop along 30A. Until a few weeks before she disappeared, Lauren had been a dependable employee and a fun roommate. Then things changed. She started staying out late, spent money on new clothes and became secretive. Sarah thought Lauren had met a guy and was spending all her time with him. Before she changed, they'd gone out together in the evenings or hung out at the beach. But suddenly Lauren was no longer available. Sarah said things were uncomfortable between them and they'd basically stopped talking.

At Vanilla Sugar, no one seemed to be particularly close to Lauren. One girl said she thought Lauren had started taking drugs or smoking pot. Another one thought she was partying every night. A guy said, "This girl made a one-eighty. One day she was shy and dorky, and the next day she was this sexy siren."

Claire finished her wine and thought about what she'd read. Lauren had definitely become somebody totally different. Claire wondered if she should interview some of these people herself. But would she learn any more than Samantha had, as an experienced journalist?

It was getting late and Claire hadn't had dinner. She carried the wine and the notebook downstairs. She needed to eat something. Pasta would do the trick. As she heated water for noodles, she sautéed some cherry tomatoes and garlic in olive oil. She slid angel hair pasta into the boiling water and added a few tablespoons of pesto to the tomatoes. When the pasta was al dente, she used a spider to add it to the tomato mixture. Voilà…dinner was ready in under fifteen minutes.

As she ate, she read Samantha's notes about Tammy Schulz. The story was similar to Lauren's. Tammy had come down to the

Emerald Coast from Michigan. She'd shared an apartment with two girls. Neither one of them knew about her background. They found her annoying; she didn't pick up after herself in the kitchen and left the bathroom a mess. When she skipped town, they thought good riddance. Initially, they were irritated that she left all her stuff for them to deal with, but they ended up making money selling her clothes online on thredUp. Samantha had mentioned that the two girls seemed jealous of Tammy because she had started dating someone and suddenly had money to buy clothes, make-up and jewelry not long before she vanished.

Claire twirled the last strands of pasta on her fork and thought about these mysterious disappearances. The stories were remarkably similar. Where had these girls gone? Had they made the decision on their own or had they been coerced?

Impulsively, Claire turned the page. In big block letters, the name RUBY BRANSON was printed, along with the words: THE LIST. Where had Claire heard that name? She closed her eyes, trying to remember. Had Dax mentioned Ruby Branson? She shook her head in frustration. It wasn't until she was brushing her teeth later on that it came to her.

Ruby Branson had been Aunt Irma's tenant. Claire remembered reading her name on the bottle of Valium in the bathroom when she'd slept over at Irma's after the break-in. Aunt Irma had complained because Ruby suddenly "up and left."

Chapter 33

The next morning, Claire attended an early yoga session. At home she showered and dressed quickly in a sea-green tunic and black leggings. She arrived at Aunt Irma's house by eight-thirty. They would have time to chat before Claire needed to be in Rosemary Beach.

She knocked on the screen door. As usual, the front door was open.

"Is that you, Louise? Come on in," Aunt Irma yelled from the kitchen.

"Hey, Aunt Irma. it's Claire."

"Come on in, honey."

As usual, the kitchen smelled delightfully of chocolate and spices. Aunt Irma was taking something out of the oven. "You arrived just in time for banana chocolate-chip bread. You've got to have a piece. It's yummy."

Claire laughed. "I'm sure it's delicious."

"Coffee?"

"Yes, please. But I didn't come over here to eat. I just wanted to ask you a couple of questions."

"Sure thing. But eat, too." Irma glanced over her shoulder at Claire. "You look too skinny to me."

Two minutes later, Claire had a cup of fragrant coffee and a thick slice of the bread. The chocolate chips were still gooey, and the bread was redolent of cardamom and cinnamon. She took a generous bite and groaned with pleasure. "This is so good."

Aunt Irma sat across from her and smiled smugly. "So, what was so important to show up at eight thirty in the morning?"

Claire patted her mouth with a napkin. "I want to ask you about Ruby Branson, the girl who lived here for a few months."

Aunt Irma frowned. "Why? She's long gone."

"Tell me about her. Tell me what happened before she disappeared."

"Land sakes, I barely remember the girl." Aunt Irma sipped her coffee.

"Did she tell you about her family, or about her friends, or her job?"

"She didn't tell me much. I think she thought I was just some old lady. It wasn't like when Amy lived with me and we watched 'Wheel of Fortune' together or cooked a pot of chowder. This girl didn't share much at all."

"Where did she work?" Claire asked.

"At a dress shop in Blue Mountain Beach. I can't remember the name of it."

Claire would have to drive down there and ask around in the shops. "Did anyone come here and ask you about her?"

"No, not until today." Irma smiled. "Can I get you another piece of banana bread or more coffee?"

"No, thanks, this has been a wonderful treat." Claire finished the coffee in her cup.

Irma set her own cup down. "Actually, now you mention it, a couple of days after Ruby left a man came here and asked if he could look in her room. He said he and Ruby were friends and she had borrowed a book from him."

"Did you let him look?"

"Yes, I let him in. That day I had my bridge group here. Sarah Jane went upstairs with him while he looked around. I was busy making more tea. Apparently, he never found his book."

Claire thought about this piece of information. She wondered if this man was related to the burglars who had ransacked her house, Abby's house and Hank's boat. What could he, or they, have been looking for? It was a mystery.

"Have you heard from Ruby's parents or friends about her disappearance?"

"What do you mean, disappearance? She just up and left." Aunt Irma eyed Claire suspiciously.

Claire decided to tell her about Lauren Reynolds and Tammy Schulz. "After I heard about those girls going missing, I remembered what you told me about Ruby. It's a similar story."

"Does this have anything to do with Dax's murder? Is that why you're interested?"

Claire blushed. "Well, yes. I think Dax and Samantha Marshall were both working on finding these missing girls."

Aunt Irma reached over and squeezed Claire's hand. Worry clouded her features. "Claire, you need to leave all this to the police. With two murders and three girls missing, we can surmise that there are some evildoers involved in some malevolent wickedness. Leave well enough alone."

Claire smiled uncertainly. "I'm just trying to understand why Dax died." She waited a beat, then said, "Did Ruby have a boyfriend or any girlfriends you got to meet?"

Aunt Irma shook her head. "I never met any of her friends. At first, she spent every evening up in her room. A few weeks before she left, she did have an uptick in her social life. She'd come home from work, change clothes, and then stay out until quite late. I always heard her when she came in. I don't know how she got up in the morning after so little sleep."

"Do you think she was into drugs or heavy drinking?"

"I don't know about that. But what do young people do late at night? From what I read, it usually involves alcohol or drugs these days."

"But she did go to work the next day?"

"Yes, but her schedule was erratic. It changed from week to week."

"Did someone pick her up when she left in the evenings?"

Aunt Irma's forehead furrowed. "Claire, I wish you'd give up this personal investigation. Leave it to the police."

Gently, Claire repeated her question.

Aunt Irma sighed and played with her spoon, turning it over and over. "Yes, someone picked her up."

Claire smiled sheepishly. "Last question. Where did you send Ruby's stuff? You said she told you to get rid of it, but you sent it to her home. Do you have the address?"

Aunt Irma studied the spoon. After a few seconds, she grumbled, "I think it's still here on the fridge." She got up and removed a three-by-five card from under a magnet depicting a colorful parrot. She handed the card to Claire. Claire studied the address written on it: Ruby Branson P. O. Box 1033, DeFuniak Springs, FL 32434. "That's bizarre. DeFuniak isn't that far away. Why wouldn't she just pack up her stuff and drive up there?"

"I don't know, Claire." Irma got up and began to clear the table.

As Claire carried her plate and cup to the sink, she heard Aunt Irma's friend Louise yelling, "Yoo-hoo!" The front door banged shut as Louise came in.

"I better get going," Claire said.

Aunt Irma hugged her before she left. "Claire, please be careful."

"I will. Don't worry. And thanks for the fabulous banana bread."

Chapter 34

Claire spent the morning visiting houses with Bill and Anne Johnson. They were leaving a big house with a sprawling yard in an Omaha suburb. Anne would have liked more of a yard with the houses they visited, but land was too expensive along the Emerald Coast. They looked at a house west of Dune Allen and then as far east as Inlet Beach. Bob especially liked a house in Watersound. Claire suggested a trip out to Bramble Bay in the afternoon and they agreed. Claire dropped them off for lunch in Rosemary Beach at the Wild Olives Wine Bar, where they could sit outside and enjoy the sunny afternoon. They agreed to meet her in an hour at the office.

Claire needed to make some notes about the houses they'd seen that morning. She wanted personal annotations along with the information on the MLS. Little by little she hoped to familiarize herself with properties up and down the coast. Barbara was busy with an elderly couple when she walked in. Consuelo was at her computer and Hal was on the phone. Claire glanced back at Lilly Rose's office. It was empty.

Claire got a bottle of water from the fridge and pulled out a protein bar from her desk drawer. A little while later, when she saw that Barbara had escorted her clients to the door, Claire went over to say hi and ask a question that had popped up when she was reading Samantha's notebook the previous evening.

"Is that all you're having for lunch?" Barbara asked as she eyed the half-eaten protein bar.

Claire laughed. "I had a gigantic piece of wicked chocolate-chip banana bread this morning. It probably provided enough calories for the entire day."

"I've got a salad in the fridge and I've finally got time to eat it." Barbara made her way over to the staff utility room.

Claire followed her. When they were unlikely to be overheard, Claire asked. "Did you talk to Drakos about spotting Dax and Samantha in Watercolor?"

"Yes. I went to the Sheriff's Department and made an official declaration and signed an affidavit." Barbara opened the door to the fridge and pulled out a plastic container and a bottle of Tuscan Italian dressing.

"I wanted to ask you something."

Barbara drizzled some dressing on the salad. Then she looked up at Claire. "What about?"

"Well, do you remember where it was you saw the two of them together? I mean, do you know which house they were coming out of?"

Barbara forked a cherry tomato and studied it pensively. "Yes, I do. It was on Silk Grass Lane. I remember because I was showing a house next door to a couple from Boston and they had their dog in the car, a chocolate lab, and it got out and ran over to your husband. I remember he bent over and patted it and grabbed the leash." She smiled at the memory, then set the tomato down and stuck the dressing bottle back in the fridge.

Claire felt tears in her eyes. Dax had loved dogs and they'd been thinking about getting a puppy. Through Barbara's description, she could see Dax in her mind's eye patting the dog.

Barbara picked up her salad and headed back to her desk. "Could you write down the address for me?" Claire asked.

"Sure, but I don't know what difference it would make now."

Claire shrugged. "You're probably right. But I might drive by there anyway."

The front door opened, and the Johnsons stepped in. They were ready to drive out to Bramble Bay. They decided to take their own car and follow Claire because they were going to a reception at the hospital later.

It was a quick trip out to the development. Claire parked in the same spot as on that eventful afternoon only a few days before. She avoided looking across the street to the place where Samantha's body had been discovered. Ann and Bill Johnson parked next to her and got out. They looked around with pleasure.

"I saw some houses with kids' bikes and a skateboard in the driveway." Anne was beaming. "There are families living here. It feels more like a neighborhood; like what we're used to back home."

"Let's go into the office and I can show you a miniature model of the Bramble Bay development," Claire said.

Inside, Harrison came out of the back office. He looked impeccable today in a yellow dress shirt, striped tie and slacks. He smiled warmly at Claire and she introduced the Johnsons.

"Ava is here today manning the fort," Harrison said. "I could accompany you on the visit, if you would like?"

"That would be nice." He certainly knew more about Bramble Bay than Claire did. The next time she came out here, she would feel more comfortable doing the visit on her own. Today she would listen carefully.

They looked at the miniature layout of the development and Harrison did his spiel. Then they walked through the three larger model homes. Anne Johnson was thrilled. She loved the layout of the Brier Rose. There was a master suite on the first floor with a cozy sitting area. Upstairs were four bedrooms. Anne envisioned the kids being upstairs, and she and Bill could escape to the sitting room when things got too chaotic. "I love my kids, but sometimes it's nice to have some peace and quiet," Anne said.

Bill liked the fact that it would be a short drive to the hospital from the development. He also liked the idea of learning to kayak. Anne felt she would be able to make friends with people who had children. She could do yoga at the recreation center and go for bike rides with the kids. As far as Claire could tell, the Johnsons were sold on Bramble Bay. There would be no going back to the houses they'd seen that morning.

It turned out there were two Brier Rose models nearing completion. The Johnsons agreed to come back the following morning and choose the kitchen cupboards, counter tops and painting scheme, et cetera. "We've got to go," Bill said, with a glance at his phone. "The reception at the hospital is at three-thirty."

After they'd left, Harrison spent time with Claire reviewing the choices of granite and quartz counter tops; Colonial, Shaker or Heritage kitchen cupboards; and many more choices. She felt grateful and found him to be an excellent tutor. Ava was working in another office with a couple who were empty nesters. Claire could hear the rumble of their voices.

"Thanks so much for helping me," Claire said.

They were sitting close together. Harrison looked into her eyes and smiled. "It has been a pleasure. You're obviously quick on the uptake. I think you'll do great tomorrow."

She glowed at the praise. "I do feel more able to complete this transaction now that I have a better feel for Bramble Bay."

Harrison accompanied her to the door and out to her car. "Do you remember the last time you were here, I invited you for dinner. We never had time to finalize the date."

"Yes. That was right before they discovered the body." Claire paled at the thought.

Harrison looked concerned. "Are you all right?"

She forced a smile. "Yes, I'm fine."

"So how about it? Shall we have dinner Saturday night? I'll pick you up and we can drive over to Baytowne Wharf."

"Okay, that would be great."

Once Claire was in the driver's seat, Harrison shut the door. "Take care," he said, and tapped the roof of the car. Claire pulled away, wondering why she'd felt put off by him the last time she was there. He was really such a nice, sincere guy.

Chapter 35

It was still early, so Claire figured she had time to drive up to DeFuniak Springs before her dinner date with Hobbs. She zoomed down 98 and turned north on Highway 331. From there it was a direct shot up to DeFuniak Springs. The traffic was light, and she made good time. She pulled into the parking lot of a Waffle House and typed US Post Office into her phone. It was a quick trip from the Waffle House, and she soon pulled up in front of a nondescript brick building.

At the door, she saw that the Post Office closed at four-thirty. It was four-twenty now. She had ten minutes to find out who owned P. O. Box 1033. She went inside and saw a pretty African American woman behind the service counter. Her long cornrow braids were festooned with multicolored beads. As the woman looked up at Claire, the beads jingled like muted Christmas bells. Her deep brown eyes glowed with life and her eyebrows rose in sharp quotation marks. The name tag on her chest read Dashay Washington.

"We're almost closed. How can I help you?" She gave Claire a quick once-over, probably looking for a package or a letter.

"Hi. I'm here to get some information about a P. O. Box." Claire glanced at the long wall in the back, lined with a series of shiny-doored post boxes from floor to ceiling.

"I'm sorry, I can't give you that information." Dashay had taken on a self-righteous air.

Claire pulled the address card Aunt Irma had given her from her purse. "It's P. O. Box 1033. Can't you tell me who owns it?"

"I can't divulge that information. There are privacy laws." Dashay turned away and busied herself with a stack of packages.

"A few months ago, several boxes arrived for a Ruby Branson. They were sent to P. O. Box 1033. Can you tell me if they were picked up?"

Dashay turned around and eyed Claire curiously. "Do you know Ruby?"

Claire sighed. "Not really. But she kind of disappeared and had a friend of mine send her things to this post box. We're wondering if she picked the stuff up and if she's all right."

Dashay looked up at the wall clock. It was getting close to quitting time. She probably was dying to get out of there and go home. "Listen, those boxes arrived here, but 1033 wasn't her box. She didn't have a post box here, but her granddad does."

Claire's eyes opened wide. "Her grandfather lives here? Did she come back to live with him?"

Dashay looked around as if someone might be listening in. "Well, those boxes arrived here and sat around for a while. Then Mr. Holmes, he's the postmaster, he finally got Mr. Branson to pick up the boxes and take them home."

"Mr. Branson is Ruby's grandfather."

"Right."

Dashay came around from behind the long counter and walked to the door, her beads jingling all the way. She pulled the glass door open. "I've got to close up now. You better leave."

"Can you tell me where Mr. Branson lives? You understand, I just want to find out if Ruby is all right."

Dashay began to laugh, a low rumble. "That girl was always in trouble. I doubt she's back living with her granddad. They never saw eye to eye."

"Please…tell me where he lives."

Dashay looked annoyed. "Over at the Sunrise Trailer Park."

Claire beamed at her. "Thank you so much. I hope I find Ruby." She walked outside; thankful her trip hadn't been entirely useless.

Back in her car, Claire pulled out her phone and googled the Sunrise Trailer Park. It lay on the outskirts of town. Claire followed the instructions on her GPS to the trailer park's entranceway. It looked like a nicely kept camp. She parked in front of a double-wide with a dark green awning. An elderly man sat in a rocking chair beneath the awning, smoking a pipe.

Claire got out and approached him. "Hi, I'm looking for Mr. Branson. Could you tell me where he lives?"

The man leaned toward her. "Grandson, you say?"

Claire figured he must be partially deaf. She raised her voice and enunciated as clearly as she could. "No. Mr. Branson."

"Oh, Branson."

Claire nodded.

The man kept rocking, and gestured with his pipe. "He's down that-a-way. The fifth trailer on the right."

"Thank you." Claire got back in her car and drove down the shady road. She pulled in close to an ancient green sedan and got out of the car, then looked up and down the street. It was quiet in the afternoon heat. The trailer home looked old and tired. She mounted the short metal staircase and knocked on the door. After a minute or so, it opened. A skinny old man with hardly any hair glared at her. "What do you want?"

"Mr. Branson? I'm Claire Simmons. I'm wondering if your granddaughter, Ruby, is home?"

His scowl deepened. "Ruby? Why would she be here? She's long gone."

"She didn't move back here a couple of months ago?"

"No." He began to shut the door.

"Could I come in and talk to you?"

His face darkened. "Why?"

"Ruby's disappeared. We're worried about her."

"Disappeared? That girl disappeared from here, and I said good riddance."

"Could I please come in and talk to you?" Claire said again.

He looked across the way, trying to decide. Claire turned and saw an emaciated woman sitting under a tree, smoking a cigarette. The woman gave a thumbs-up. Ruby's grandmother?

"Well...okay," he said. He stepped back, let go of the doorjamb and made his way into the room, holding on to the edge of a bookshelf and then to the back of an armchair. Claire spied a metal walker in the corner, but apparently the old guy preferred to get around without it.

He fell into a recliner and took several deep breaths. Mr. Branson was definitely not in the best of health. "Sit down and tell me what you want," he barked.

Claire noted that his light-blue short-sleeved shirt appeared to have been washed a million times. His khaki pants were similarly spotless. He was clean-shaven and wore old leather shoes with a high shine. Personal care must be high on his list. She glanced around the living area and the kitchen. The carpet had been vacuumed recently, and the whole place looked neat and clean. Beside the sink was a drying rack with one cup, one plate, and a fork and knife poking out from a plastic container. The solo dishes struck her as poignant and sad. Mr. Branson must live alone.

Claire took the nearest seat, a flowered chintz armchair. Mr. Branson was staring at her. "So, what do you want to know?"

Claire told him about the missing girls but said nothing about Dax or Samantha. She started with Lauren Reynolds and Tammy Schulz, then told him about Aunt Irma and the boxes of Ruby's possessions being sent to the Post Office here in DeFuniak Springs. Mr. Branson listened to all this with a scowl that seemed permanent.

"Ruby seems to have disappeared like the other two girls," Claire said, finishing her story. "The police are looking into it."

"How come they haven't contacted me?"

"I only found out about Ruby's disappearance today. I haven't gone to the police yet. I just drove up here on my own."

He regarded her critically. "Well, young lady, I don't see why this is any of your business."

How to explain her interest in Ruby's vanishing act? "My friend, Aunt Irma—that's who Ruby was living with—has been concerned for her safety for a while. I agreed to come up here and make sure Ruby was all right."

Mr. Branson raised his bushy eyebrows in disbelief. Then he looked down at his gnarled hands, rubbing them together in his lap. "Ruby isn't here. She left this place a year ago and I've never heard from her since." He was staring at the floor. "We never got along. My wife, Ruby's grandmother, always smoothed things over. After my dear wife died, Ruby got into some real trouble. I kicked her out."

He looked up at Claire, his eyes sharp with challenge. "She was just like her mother. Too pretty and too foolish. I said, if you don't want to abide by my rules, then you can leave. So, she did."

"You never heard from her?"

"No, never."

They fell silent. After a moment, Claire said, "What did you think when the boxes arrived with her things?"

"To tell you the truth, I didn't know what to think. Holmes, he's the postmaster, called me and told me they'd been sent to my P.O. box. He said to come on over and pick them up. At first, I thought she was coming on home and had decided to say she was sorry. But then, she never called or..." Claire saw tears in his eyes. He grabbed a Kleenex from the box next to his chair, dabbed his eyes and blew his nose. The scowl came back, as fierce as ever. "So, what more do you want?"

"Could I look in the boxes? Maybe there's a clue to where she's gone."

He shrugged. "Help yourself. They're down the hall in the room on the left. The door is shut. I don't go in there."

Claire got up, went through the kitchen area and down the short hall to what she guessed had been Ruby's bedroom. There wasn't much space to move around. To the right of the door, boxes were stacked along the wall. Under the window, a single bed was covered with a Disney Princess bedspread, and a colorful troupe of stuffed animals were piled high on the pillow. On the opposite wall stood a chest of drawers loaded with mementos: ribbons, a softball, a jar of scrunchies, make-up and a jewelry box. Claire bent to look at a picture of a blond girl being hugged by a smiling older woman, probably Ruby and her grandma. The image evoked love and warmth. She straightened and looked around some more. On the walls were posters of One Direction, Justin Bieber and other teenage heartthrobs. How old was Ruby? The room seemed like it belonged to a pre-teen, Claire thought.

The boxes were well sealed with duct tape. Claire yelled down the hall to Mr. Branson, "I'm going to borrow a knife. These boxes are taped shut."

"Help yourself."

"Do you want to come in here while I look through the boxes?"

"What do you think? They've been here for months and I've never opened a one."

"Okay, just asking."

Back in the bedroom, Claire got to work. The first box was all clothes, carefully folded. She could imagine Irma taking care to fold each tee-shirt just so. Claire put everything back in the box and moved on to the next one. The second box didn't yield anything of great interest, either. Claire felt uncomfortable going through the sad-looking underwear and ragged shorts. Clearly, most of Ruby's clothes came from Walmart or Target.

The third box gave Claire pause. It held a couple of expensive evening dresses: a slinky black number and a royal blue dress with a blue-sequined bodice. Where did Ruby wear these elegant dresses, Claire wondered as she held them up. The last box contained shoes: gym shoes, flip-flops and flats, along with a pair of high-end stiletto heels in a plastic bag. Claire pulled them out and checked out the soles.

Unlike the other shoes, they showed no signs of wear and tear. Where had Ruby worn them?

At the bottom of the box was a dark grey backpack. Claire reached down and pulled it out. It looked like a bag Ruby might have had in high school. There were stickers on the back flap and several miniature plastic animals dangling from the top strap. Claire unzipped one compartment and then another. At the bottom of the side compartment, under a pencil case, was a small book. Claire pulled it out. On the pink plastic cover, My Diary was written in sparkly script.

Normally, Claire wouldn't have dared open something so private, but today she felt compelled to learn anything she could about Ruby. She looked over her shoulder to see if Mr. Branson was watching at the door. The hallway was empty. She unhitched the plastic clasp and opened the journal. On the first page, she read:

To my darling Ruby,
Take time to write down your thoughts and activities. You will be glad to read it later in life. Love, Grandma

Claire read the first couple of entries. The writing was round, with little hearts for dots over the letter "i". Ruby described her thirteenth birthday party, then later she wrote about an argument with her girlfriends and about a cute boy in her math class. Claire leafed through the pages, looking for something more recent. About halfway through, the writing changed. The entry was dated a year ago, when Ruby arrived on the Emerald Coast. Claire smiled as she read it. The girl was still pretty immature.

I found a place in Grayton Beach. There's a bedroom and a sitting room. It's pretty cheap. The old lady who owns the house wants me to call her Aunt Irma. She's nice, but I don't want to spend time with more old people. I mean, I just escaped from Gramps.

Leafing through the pages again, Claire saw that Ruby had written short entries every couple of days. She looked at her watch and was surprised to realize how late it was. She didn't have time to read the whole diary right then. She had to get back to Grayton Beach to meet Hobbs for dinner. What to do? She shoved the diary into her purse, with a horrible guilty feeling. *I'm only borrowing it for the next week or so. I'll mail it back to Mr. Branson as soon as I'm finished with it.*

After packing the boxes back up, Claire shut the door on the sad little room and went out to the living room. Mr. Branson had fallen asleep on his recliner. His mouth was open, and he was snoring loudly. Claire debated about waking him up. He probably napped off and on all day. She noticed a little whiteboard on the wall in the kitchen, with a short shopping list: milk, bread and peanut butter. Claire took the marker that hung next to it by a string and wrote Thank you along with her name and phone number.

Outside, she closed the trailer door quietly. She looked across the street. The skinny lady was still there at the picnic table, smoking. Claire went over and introduced herself. "Hi. Mr. Branson is asleep, and I didn't want to wake him up. Could you tell him he should call me if Ruby comes home? I wrote my number on the whiteboard in his kitchen."

"Are you a friend of Ruby's?" the woman asked in a raspy voice.

"Not really..."

"That girl put her grandfather through hell. He's a nice man, you know. He didn't deserve all that."

What happened, Claire wondered, but didn't have time to ask. "Right...well, I better go."

Chapter 36

As Claire drove back down the highway, she thought about everything she'd learned in the last few days. She needed to sit down and take the time to organize her thoughts about the people she'd met and what they'd told her. It would be a good idea to put it down in writing like Samantha Marshall did.

She was itching to get back to the diary. Maybe Ruby had written something about what she'd been doing before she disappeared. At the least, Claire was hoping for the name of the shop where she'd worked and the names of her friends. Tomorrow, after going back to Bramble Bay to finalize the deal with the Johnsons, she would do more sleuthing. Dax would have been glad she wasn't giving up.

There was no time to go home before meeting Hobbs. She was already late by nearly half an hour. She pulled up in front of the restaurant where they'd arranged to meet and took a minute to comb her hair into a high ponytail and apply fresh lipstick. Over in a corner of the lot, she saw Hobbs's truck. Hopefully he wouldn't be too upset.

A feeling of sadness came over her. The Grayton Seafood Company was one of her favorite restaurants. She and Dax had come here often. She sighed in quiet resignation, got out of the car and walked over to the entrance, and took a deep breath before pulling open the door.

The place was so tiny, she spotted Hobbs right away. He was at a table in the corner nursing a beer. Claire walked quickly over and slipped into a chair "Hi. I'm so sorry to be late. I've got lots to tell you."

Hobbs looked disgruntled—unusual for him, but she could understand. "I had to beg them to seat me without you here. I already ate an appetizer since I was monopolizing a table."

The remnants of a plate of fried calamari and tomato sauce sat in front of him. She and Dax used to share the calamari and the fried green tomatoes. She felt a dark cloud descending over her. Forget the past, she told herself. Here was her friend Hobbs sitting across from her. She had to live in the present.

"I was up in DeFuniak Springs and I let the time get away from me."

He raised his eyebrows. "DeFuniak Springs? Did you go up there with H. R.?"

Claire frowned. "H. R.?" No clue who you're talking about. I drove there by myself."

"Mr. Harrison Reed. I saw he was entertaining you this afternoon."

"Entertaining me? Give me a break. I have clients that are going to buy a house in Bramble Bay, and Harrison helped me close the deal. He was great." She broke off and studied Hobbs, noting the heightened color in his face. Then, slowly, she smiled. "Did you think I ran off with H. R.?" It hit her that Hobbs might just be a little bit jealous, and she laughed.

He looked at her sheepishly. "I just don't like the guy and I don't trust him."

Claire quit laughing, taken aback. "Really? I think he's nice and kind of…" She searched for a word, "…suave…sophisticated."

Hobbs leaned forward. "Don't trust him, Claire. There's something fishy about that guy."

"Fishy?"

The waitress arrived in time to hear the question and smiled at both of them. "Everything here is fishy."

They chuckled politely. Without looking at the menu, Claire ordered a glass of sauvignon blanc and the shrimp and grits. Hobbs got another beer and the fried oysters. When the waitress left, there was a moment of silence. Then Claire said, "Truce?"

"Okay. Truce. Now tell me about your trip to DeFuniak. I've never been there."

Claire needed to share some of what she'd discovered with someone. It would help her to process what she'd learned and maybe get a new angle. She began with her visit to The Emerald Times and then what she'd learned on Hank Robbins' boat. Then she told Hobbs about visiting Abby and the discovery of the red notebook.

He frowned, clearly concerned. "Shouldn't you turn it over to the police?"

"I will, but I wanted to check it out before I gave it to Drakos."

"Where is it now?"

"I put it in the safe."

The server delivered their food and they began to eat.

"You haven't told me why you went up to DeFuniak Springs," Hobbs said.

"Okay, let me backtrack. From Samantha's notebook, I learned she'd been investigating the disappearance of two girls. Someone at work told me they'd seen Samantha and Dax together. Then Drakos told me he thought they'd been working together on the missing girls' disappearance. That's why I went to the newspaper office and to see Hank and Abby."

"Okay, I get that, but why didn't the police know about these girls vanishing?"

"Because somebody cleverly managed to make it look like they had to leave town for a family emergency. So no one raised a red flag for quite a while." Then Claire explained how she had gone to see Mary Sullivan at the Department of Missing Persons, and what she'd learned there.

Hobbs took a sip of beer. "I don't get why Dax, being police chief and all, didn't get the Sheriff's Department investigating these missing girls. Why did he keep it quiet?"

Claire put down her fork and picked up her wine glass. "That's what I've been wondering." She took a sip, gazing thoughtfully across the room.

"Maybe it had to do with people in the Sheriff's Department," Hobbs said.

That thought made Claire shiver. "Which could mean Dax was killed by someone he was working with." But surely not any of the officers she knew. She felt certain none of them were involved in his murder.

"Maybe it was someone in the county council or the Board of Commissioners," Hobbs said. "From what you've told me, Samantha had already caused them a lot of problems."

Claire thought about that. She didn't know much about what went on at the county level. She pushed away her plate, suddenly not hungry. She finished her wine and signaled to the server that she wanted another.

"You still haven't said why you went to DeFuniak."

Claire told him about Ruby Branson's name in Samantha's red notebook, then about her visit to Aunt Irma and finally to Ruby's grandfather in the trailer park. She described the bedroom and the boxes, but she kept the theft of the diary to herself. She really didn't feel good about that.

Hobbs leaned forward. "Claire, you've got to stop your private investigation. Make an appointment with Detective Drakos and tell him everything you've told me. Then leave it to him and his team."

Instead of answering, Claire downed half of her glass of wine and kept her eyes on the golden liquid.

"Claire, these people are dangerous. They've killed two people for sure and maybe three more. I'm worried about your safety."

Claire took another sip of wine.

Chapter 37

Claire couldn't wait to get home and dive into the diary. After locking up and putting on the security system, she went upstairs to the boudoir with the diary in hand. For the next hour she read through the entries, starting with Ruby's arrival on the Emerald Coast. After several interviews, Ruby got lucky and found a job at Coastal Magic, a clothes store that specialized in beachwear, sunhats, funky jewelry and the like. Claire wondered what she got paid there. It couldn't have been much. No wonder she had chosen to live with Aunt Irma. Claire knew Aunt Irma didn't charge much for rooms. Claire's friend Amy had called it a sweet deal.

Ruby was lonely at first, complaining that the other shop girls were mean and stuck-up, and that she wouldn't ever make any friends. Then the other girls invited her out one night. She went with them to bars in Panama City Beach and other places up and down the coast. Claire figured she must have had a fake driver's license, since she couldn't have been more than nineteen. Much of the language she used was immature and childish. She mentioned meeting guys, but no one special.

Claire began to think this diary wouldn't lead anywhere. She pressed on, unwilling to give up just yet. In the next entry, Ruby described going to Hook'd Pier Bar in Panama City Beach with another girl. It was hard to decipher the girl's name...maybe Gretchen, Claire decided.

I was just sitting at the bar minding my own business when this really hot guy started talking to me. I was into him right away. I liked his looks and I could tell he liked me. He bought me a couple of drinks and we talked, I mean, really talked...not like the other skuzzballs I meet. He wanted to know about my family and my friends. I told him everything, about how I only had my grandfather. I told him we'd had a fight and I was on my own now. He said I was brave and "admirable." I gave him my cell number. He texted me when I got home. We're going out tomorrow night. I am so sighked.

156

Claire smiled at the spelling…"sighked" instead of "psyched." She'd found frequent, similar misspellings throughout the diary. She kept reading. From that night on, it seemed Ruby went out with this wonderful man a couple of times a week. His name was James and he was older but still fun. He was good-looking and he told her how special she was, not like the other girls he'd met. It was obvious to Claire that Ruby had fallen head over heels in love.

Then, about two weeks into the relationship, he took her to his house.

James's house is pretty small, not much bigger than Gramps's trailer. There's a living room, a small kitchen and two bedrooms. He uses one bedroom for an office. The living room has cool leather furniture and a really big TV. I can tell he's very neat…just like Gramps. There's a fence and bushes around the house so you can't see the neighbors and they can't see into James's yard.

Tonight, we went over to James's house again. James said he needed to make love to me. That he wanted me so much. That he couldn't wait. No one has ever talked to me like that. I mean, when Eddy and me got in the back of his dad's truck, he just slobbered all over me and yanked off my clothes. I went along because I wanted to do it, but it was nothing like with James. WOW!

James and I don't go to bars or restaurants anymore, just right to his house. It's our special place. We drink wine and he's got some weed, really good stuff. We drink and smoke and then he makes love to me. I mean, it's love, I can tell. He tells me I'm beautiful. I can't wait to see him tomorrow.

James is teaching me how to pleasure him. That's what he calls it, to pleasure him. He says I'm sexier than any girl he's ever met. Sometimes he does stuff to me I don't really like. I need to be more open, he said. Tonight, James gave me a necklace and a matching bracelet. I know he loves me.

Claire looked up from the page, feeling uneasy. She drew a deep breath and made herself read the next entry:

Tonight, James had a couple of lines of coke on the glass table in the living room. He wanted me to snort some before we went to bed. I told him I don't do drugs like that. He got kind of angry, so I said OK. We did have terrific sex after that.

Claire put down the diary, went downstairs and poured herself a glass of ginger ale to settle her suddenly queasy stomach. This James character had been exploiting Ruby. Claire felt like a voyeur, reading these intimate details of Ruby's life. She wanted to scream at Ruby to dump the guy. She paced the great room until she'd calmed down a bit, then went back upstairs and picked up the diary again.

After more entries dealing with kinky sex, Ruby's story took an unexpected turn.

Tonight, James had a surprise for me. On the bed, he'd laid out three fancy dresses. I could never afford dresses like this. One is black. James says you have to have a "little black dress". One is red. It's short and kind of gathered on one side at the waist. It looks beautiful on. The other one is blue with sequins. I look pretty hot in that dress, too. Along with the dresses, there were two pairs of stiletto heels. Shit, I am going to have to learn to walk in those things. James says we're going to parties and I need to look exquisite...he said that...exquisite. To go with the dresses, he bought me sexy underwear. I mean, you can see through them. It's almost like you have nothing on. Tonight, I tried on the underwear and walked around in the stiletto heels. James said I was more beautiful than one of those beauty queens.

Most nights I get dressed in one of the outfits and we drink champagne. James wants me to learn how to walk in the shoes. He complains about how I sit and how I hold the wine glass and how I talk. Tonight, we had a big fight. I said I'd had enough of all the rules, but then he started kissing me and he gave me a pill to calm me down. I'm not sure what it was but I felt like I was floating, and we made terrific love. I love James more than anything.

Claire put the diary down again. What was James up to? Reading all this made her feel dirty. She went into the bathroom and brushed her teeth, then took a shower, as if she could wash away the images of James and his manipulations. Out of the shower, dried off and in her pjs, Claire looked at the time. It was midnight. She should go to sleep, but she needed to finish the diary. Curled up in bed, she continued to read.

Ruby complained some more about her job. Apparently, she arrived late a lot and the boss was giving her a hard time. One day at work, Samantha Marshall came in. She was doing a story about the shop. Claire sat up straight, her eyes racing through the entry.

Samantha was really nice. She asked me a bunch of questions and took pictures of the shop. She's writing an article that will be in the paper. Maybe she'll mention me. Katy says she's an important journalist. She gave me her card so I could contact her if I thought of anything to add.

Claire leaned back against the pillows and closed her eyes. This was a significant piece of information—the first connection between Samantha and one of the missing girls. But Claire couldn't see how this chance meeting could have anything to do with Ruby's disappearance. She went back to reading.

James wasn't always available in the evenings and Ruby wondered if he had another girlfriend. Once she reported that she'd seen a dress in the closet that wasn't hers—a green dress, petite-sized. She accused James of having another girlfriend, but he claimed the green dress was for her; only after it arrived did he realize he'd ordered the wrong size. He told her he would never look at another girl, that he loved only her, that she was special…blah, blah, blah.

For a couple more weeks, Ruby practiced walking in the stilettos. James seemed to gain more control over Ruby, who would do anything he asked like a well-trained puppy. It all made pretty tedious reading. Then an entry caught Claire's attention.

Tonight, James fell asleep after we made love. I was bored, so I got up and went to watch TV. But there was nothing on. I looked at Instagram for a while. James never wants me to go into his office. It's usually locked but I saw the door was a little bit open. I went in and looked around. There wasn't much in his desk drawers. The closet was locked, and the file cabinet was locked, too. I sat down on the desk chair and looked at his iPad. It had a list on it…names, addresses and dates. Halfway down I saw my name with two other names. I scrolled up to the top of the list, but I couldn't figure out what it was about. I pulled out my phone and snapped a picture of each screen, all the names. Then I heard the toilet flush and I slipped out of the office before he came out of the bathroom. He never knew I was in there.

A list. Claire remembered Samantha had written Ruby's name and the words THE LIST in her red notebook. Had Ruby sent the pictures of the iPad list to Samantha? But why would she do that? Because she'd met Samantha once at Coastal Magic? Or had Ruby gotten into trouble and reached out to Samantha? The poor girl was so naïve, but if she realized she was in trouble, maybe Samantha Marshall would have seemed like someone she could trust. And now Samantha was dead, and Dax was dead…and probably Ruby was, too.

There were only two more entries in Ruby's diary. In the last one she announced that the next night, she and James were finally going to a party. She was excited. She would wear the red dress and put her hair up in a chignon like she'd seen on TV. She mentioned that James wanted her to be nice to the other guests at the party. Claire could imagine what that meant.

After that, nothing. Claire checked the date on the final entry. She needed to ask Aunt Irma when Ruby had gone missing. It might have been that very same night.

Before going to bed, Claire put the diary in the safe along with Samantha's notebook. She couldn't be sure the burglars—whoever they were—wouldn't be back to tear apart her house.

Chapter 38

In the morning, Claire stumbled downstairs, blurry-eyed and headachy. She'd barely been able to sleep after reading Ruby's pitiful and unsettling story. She put on a pot of coffee and pulled open the door to the deck. A gentle breeze blew in and she drew the fresh, salty air into her lungs. When the coffee was ready, she poured a mug and went out on the deck.

It was a beautiful morning. The sea oats waved on the dunes. She spotted a reddish egret strutting along the sand and a laughing seagull dive bombing into the water. Dax had been an amateur bird watcher. Sometimes they would sit on the chaise lounge together, wrapped in each other's arms, while Dax pointed out the birds that flew overhead.

Tears filled her eyes. God, she missed Dax. She missed his arms around her. She missed sharing her day with him. She missed his kisses and she missed their lovemaking. She was thirty-two years old and too young to be a widow. But how would she ever find another Dax? She rubbed her eyes with the palms of her hands and stifled a sob. No, she couldn't go down that path, into that big, black cloud of depression threatening to engulf her. Claire picked up her mug with both hands and took a determined sip. She remembered the story Seijun had told her. She had to get rid of the burden that was bringing her down and live in the present.

With a sense of resignation, Claire picked up her phone and scrolled through her email. Most of the messages weren't important, so she deleted them. She noted a voicemail from Drakos and played it. "Mrs. Simmons, Claire, we need to talk. I understand you've been doing a little investigating on your own. This is unwise…even dangerous. Please call me."

He was probably right, but he wasn't getting anywhere, and she had uncovered a lot of information on her own. Why should she stop? Whoever James and his gang were, they knew nothing about what she was up to. She was peripheral to the case. Nonetheless, she realized she should tell Drakos what she'd learned. She returned the call, and Drakos picked right up.

"Hey, Claire. Did you get my message?"

"Yes, that's why I'm calling. I've learned some things I need to share with you."

"Claire, you've got to stop involving yourself in police matters. Let us do the investigating."

"But I found another missing girl you didn't know about. I've got her diary and it's very revealing. It explains how the other two girls might have disappeared. It also points to a connection with Samantha Marshall."

Drakos sighed in frustration. "I would be happy to see what you've got, but then you've got to stop. Please, Claire."

"When could we meet? I'll tell you everything I know." Claire said.

"Not until next week…five days from now at the earliest. I'm going to Orlando for a police convention, leaving today."

"See you in five days, then. I'll bring you what I've got."

"Take care of yourself, Claire. Don't do any more investigating."

Claire pretended she didn't hear him and hung up.

***

Claire dressed for work in a burgundy jumpsuit and sandals. Since she would be driving right through Watercolor on her way to the agency, she decided to check out the house where Barbara had seen Dax and Samantha. It was probably a waste of time, but she'd feel better once she'd eliminated the image in her mind of the two of them together.

The house was ginormous. A horseshoe driveway encircled an impressive fountain of spouting fish, and even from her car, Claire could see the carvings of vines and birds all over the massive oak front door. A three-car garage jutted out along one side of the brick driveway. Claire sat in the car, inspecting the mansion, when a woman came out of the house next door. A small, fluffy white dog with a pink bow around its neck trotted beside her. Short and rotund, the woman wore a pink bathrobe and matching pink mules. Pink was definitely her color. At the bottom of a short flight of steps, she and her matching dog stopped while the little bit of fluff scooched down to do its business. Claire hopped out of the car and walked over.

"Hi," she said, with a friendly smile. "I'm Claire Simmons. Could I ask you a couple of questions?"

"You sure can, honey…but my husband would tell you I don't know much." The woman laughed. "I've got to walk Lilliput up to the corner."

"She's very cute," Claire said as they moved down the sidewalk. "What kind of dog is she?"

"She's a Maltese. She's tiny but I can tell you, she rules the roost."

They stopped walking as Lilliput sniffed a purple pansy.

The woman smiled at Claire, displaying small, even white teeth. Blue eyes sparkled in her round, pink face. "You probably think I'm lazy, but I've been up forever. I just haven't got dressed yet. So, what do you want to ask me about? I'm Dotty Smith, by the way."

"I'm wondering about the house next door. Do you know who lives there?"

Dotty glanced over at the house. "The people who own it are never there. They live in Houston and I understand they have houses all over the world. Their name is Ralston." They stopped walking again so Lilliput could examine a palmetto plant. "I think it's oil money."

Claire tried to think how to ask her next question. "Oh, I thought they were here last March."

"I don't really know, but they do rent the house out for parties. It must be like an Airbnb."

Claire frowned. "What do you mean?"

"Every so often we see lights next door and cars pull up, and they have a little party. But it's all over by the early morning hours."

"Isn't that a disturbance?"

"No, not really. We sleep on the other side of the house, so we don't hear much of anything."

"Who comes to these parties?"

"I don't know. I've never gotten a good look at anybody. That big garage blocks our view of the driveway." Louise giggled. "My husband says it's the Mafia. I have seen big muscle-bound guys walking around sometimes. In the morning, these little cleaning girls in pink dresses arrive, and they go in and clean the place up."

"Little girls in pink dresses?"

"You know, short little Hispanic women."

"A cleaning crew?"

"Right. They spend a couple of hours in there and then off they go. They come in a white van decorated with flowers."

"A white van decorated with flowers," Claire repeated. Why would Lilly Rose, Inc. be cleaning this house after a party? She would have to ask her.

***

That day Claire picked up a new client. The Marianis were an attractive retired couple down from Toronto. They wanted to buy a townhouse, with plans to live in it over the winter months and rent it out during the high season in summer. Like a lot of American and Canadian snowbirds who lived in the frigid north, they wanted to escape the winter cold but enjoy the summer at home. Claire took the Marianis to visit several townhouses up and down 30A. They were particularly taken with two townhomes in Prominence. Over a late lunch of hamburgers at The Hub, they went through the pluses and minuses of the homes they'd visited. By the end of lunch, the Marianis were set on a three-bedroom townhome on Milestone Drive. They went back to the office to draw up the papers, and Claire headed home at five o'clock after a successful day.

As she was pulling into her driveway, the phone rang. It was Morgan. "Claire, guess what. I'm coming to the Emerald Coast for a quick trip to help out with a wedding on Saturday night. I'll be available on Sunday evening to get together. How would that work with you?"

"Wonderful, I can't wait to see you. I'll call Olivia and see if she can join us. It will be like old times. Would you like to spend the night here?" Claire asked.

"I can't. I've got an early morning meeting on Monday and then I fly out. It will just have to be Sunday evening."

"Where do you want to go?"

"How about The Bay? I've got so many happy memories of that place."

Chapter 39

When Claire got home, she changed into shorts and decided to go for a walk up the beach instead of a run. She had lots to mull over and needed some quiet time to think. After locking up, she headed west along the shore. She'd end up passing by Senator Jupiter's castle, but there was no reason to avoid it. As long as she walked below the high-tide mark, his henchmen wouldn't bother her.

As she walked, she went over everything she'd learned from Ruby's diary, from Samantha's notebook, and from her visit that morning with Dotty Smith. What did she know?

She knew that Ruby, along with two other girls, had disappeared. All three were alienated from their families, young and inexperienced, and therefore easy marks. Before disappearing, they'd each started to date a mystery man who gave them gifts. Friends and acquaintances reported that they were into drugs or alcohol. Had James lured all three girls and prepared them for these parties? Whoever he was, he personified evil in Claire's mind. How many other naive girls had fallen into his clutches? Claire shivered, and instinctively turned to look behind her. The beach was empty except for a fisherman way down the coast.

Claire faced forward again and kept walking. She splashed through a little pool. The water was warm from the sun. Her mind went back to her ruminations.

Parties! She'd learned the Ralstons' house in Watercolor was the location of some of these gatherings. Did similar parties take place in other empty homes? Too bad Dotty Smith hadn't been able to tell her who attended the parties. A description might have been useful, even of total strangers.

Then there was the list on James's iPad. Ruby had found her own name on the list, along with other names and addresses. Claire figured Ruby might have found the party list. She wondered who else attended the events. No way to know without a copy of the list...and maybe not even then. Are the names of guests, or of party girls?

The more she thought about it, the more Claire felt certain the list was the key to everything. Dax and Samantha had likely been killed because of the information on it. Undoubtedly, the burglars had been looking for copies of it at her house, at Abby's house and on Hank's boat. Yes, the list seemed to be the key.

Claire's thoughts went around and around. She barely noticed when she reached the stretch of sand adjacent to Juniper's castle. The mansion loomed over the beach like a medieval fort. Why did Juniper build this monstrosity along the beautiful Emerald Coast, a vacation wonderland?

As she approached the building, her eyes traveled up to the slits of windows on the turrets. Claire frowned. She thought she saw a white face staring down at her, but then it disappeared. Was it a trick of the sun's glare, or had she really seen someone—a modern-day Rapunzel, trapped in a tower? As she stared up at the turret, a familiar voice, deep and sonorous, called out to her. "Claire—Claire Simmons." A few seconds later, Senator Juniper stepped into view on the parapet.

Claire waved up to him, though she felt unsettled. Did he spend all his time surveying who walked by his château? "Hello, Senator."

"Come up for a drink," he shouted. "I could use some young and beautiful company."

Claire blushed in spite of herself. She debated whether it was a good idea to take him up on the invitation, but he was a friend of Lilly Rose. She should be polite.

"That would be lovely." She trudged up the sand to the house. A burly guard came down and opened the steel gate that blocked the entrance to the stairs. He nodded at her but didn't crack a smile.

Senator Juniper came to greet her. He wore a bright Hawaiian shirt depicting yellow pineapples and red hibiscus. Pale legs stuck out from green cargo shorts. Claire smiled inwardly. The Senator definitely looked better in long pants. She reached out for a handshake, but Juniper bent over and kissed her cheek. He smelled of some woodsy cologne.

"Let's sit out here. We can view the sunset." He led the way to a grouping of deck furniture in lime green, turquoise and white stripes. "I like this spot in the evenings when I'm down here. I enjoy the quiet after the hustle and bustle of Washington. The rhythm of the waves calms my soul." He gestured for her to sit down.

"I can imagine it's a big change. Life in the capital must be exhausting." Claire sat on a deep, cushioned chair and the Senator sat across from her.

"What would you like to drink? I've got a bartender on location who can make you anything you'd like. Me, I'm going to have a martini. Henry makes the best." As he spoke, a slim Asian girl appeared out of nowhere. She was exquisite, with long, dark hair and delicate features. She wore a long, red silk cheongsam and her feet were bare.

"I'd just like a glass of wine; chardonnay would be fine," Claire said.

"Are you sure? How about a daiquiri or a margarita?"

"Well, okay. I'll have a daiquiri. That sounds festive."

The girl smiled and nodded. Then she disappeared into the house.

Juniper settled back in his chair and smiled at Claire. Again, she thought he would make the perfect President on some TV sitcom. He was a handsome, well cared-for metro male who probably had regular facials and had his hair trimmed and styled daily. His hands were manicured, and his bare feet looked as though he'd probably had a pedicure as well.

"Lilly Rose tells me you're an ace realtor and you're taking over the office." He chuckled at his own joke.

Claire forced a laugh. "Actually, I met my first client here at your cocktail party a few months ago.

"Oh? Who was that?"

"Oscar...Oscar Snell."

"Ah, yes. Oscar. He's a fine individual, a fine American. He's been useful to the country."

Claire wondered what that meant. "He actually knows my father, so he wasn't really a client out of the blue. We had a connection."

"You know, Claire, that's really what success in life is about. It's about connections. We all form webs of friends and acquaintances. It's nearly impossible to make it alone."

Claire considered the statement. "That's true. Oscar sent a friend of his to me. That was my second client."

"You see? That's what I mean. Lilly Rose is excellent at establishing contacts and maintaining relationships."

The Asian girl came back just then with a tray. She handed Claire a daiquiri and a small linen napkin, then served the Senator. Lastly, she placed a plate of mini hors-d'oeuvres on the table between them. There were crab cakes, sushi rolls, spring rolls and mini tacos. Claire thanked the girl as Juniper dismissed her with a flick of his hand.

"Help yourself," he said as he picked up a crab cake. He popped it into his mouth and raised his glass. "Here's to a deepening and meaningful relationship. I like you, Claire. You're a smart girl."

Claire smiled uncomfortably and raised her glass. "Here's to a pleasant evening." The toast sounded lame to her own ears. "Tell me how you got to know Lilly Rose," she continued.

The Senator sat back and smiled. "We've known each other a long time. We both worked as interns in Washington back in the day. It was a twelve or fourteen-hour day; exhausting but incredibly exciting. Once in a while, in the late evenings, we would meet for a drink and compare notes. Lilly Rose worked for Senator Jacobs, a cantankerous old fellow who had a lot of clout. I worked for Senator Massy. He was a wily SOB, wanted to turn Washington upside-down with all the bills he brought to the floor. Our respective bosses couldn't stand each other. But Lilly Rose and I got on fine."

He looked out at the water and laughed softly. "Little did I know I would become a Senator someday. I'd just finished law school and thought I was going on to become a lifetime corporate lawyer, but here I am. Washington gets under your skin with all the power and money." He laughed again and then turned to her, eyebrows raised. "What were you doing before you turned to real estate?"

"Out of college, I had this job and that. Then I started at Safetynaps and became marketing director. My boss wanted me to work 24/7. I finally got fed up and escaped down here to the coast. For a number of years, I sold Brazilian leather bags and purses across northern Florida." Claire sipped her daiquiri. "This is delicious."

Juniper gestured to the canapés. "Help yourself." He devoured a sushi roll and took a sip of his martini.

Claire reached over, picked up a spring roll and dipped it into a little bowl of sauce.

The Senator's face took on an expression of solicitude. "I'm sorry to hear about your husband. I understand he was a damn good sheriff... ran a tight department."

"Thank you," Claire said, her throat suddenly tight. "Yes, he was good at his job."

"What have you heard about the investigation into his death?"

Claire sighed. "They really are getting nowhere. Then this latest murder…Samantha Marshall…"

"The newspaper reporter? Have they figured out who killed her?" Juniper gazed at Claire over the rim of his glass. The look in his eyes was strangely flat.

Claire gripped her glass, uncomfortable again. "I don't know. I was there when they discovered the body. It was a terrific shock."

"It must have been." He finished his martini, and almost instantly the Asian girl appeared with another. "Would you like another daiquiri?" he asked.

"Thanks, no. I'm fine." Claire smiled at the girl.

"It must be difficult to sit on your hands and wait for the police to do something," Juniper said.

Claire nodded. She didn't want to share any information with this man she barely knew. He didn't need to know about the connection between Dax and Samantha or about the missing girls. Bad enough that she'd brought up Samantha's murder right after talking about Dax's. "Yes. I've asked around, questioned friends and acquaintances, but I haven't learned anything."

He popped another crab cake into his mouth. "You're probably better off developing your real estate clientele and leaving the investigation to the police."

Chapter 40

Claire wanted to walk home along the road, but Juniper insisted on having his chauffeur drive her home. As they descended the thickly carpeted stairs from the main floor to the entranceway, Claire was again taken aback by the grandeur of the house. The sweep of the curved stairway and the sparkling crystal chandelier were breathtaking. As they walked across the marble floor to the massive front door, Claire asked, "How often are you down here on the Emerald Coast?"

"Not often enough," the Senator quipped.

"Do you keep a staff on hand while you're gone?"

"Yes, a place like this requires a large staff on-site."

Claire eyed the burly guard standing by the door. "And why do you need these security guards?"

Now, the Senator looked irritated. "I've pushed through a lot of controversial bills. You never know who might go after you."

"I suppose," Claire said.

They stepped outside, and the Senator ushered her into a black SUV. Claire thanked him again for the drink. In spite of Juniper's surface charm and his skill as a host, Claire was relieved to escape the house and his presence. There was something oppressive about the mansion.

The chauffeur knew where she lived and within just a few minutes, she was home. She headed inside and, after locking up, she looked into the fridge. The appetizers at Juniper's castle had been delicious, but she needed something else. In the freezer she found a half-full pint of dulce de leche ice cream. Perfect. Claire got out a spoon and dug in.

She'd just taken her second bite when the doorbell trilled. She couldn't imagine who would stop by at this hour. She pressed the intercom and viewed the camera feed. It was Hobbs.

Claire went downstairs and let him in. "Hi. What are you doing here?"

"I need to talk to you. I was here earlier, but you weren't. I tried your cell phone, but when there was no answer, I got worried." Hobbs looked stressed. He wore jeans, a wrinkled denim shirt and flip-flops. His longish blond hair curled at his neck.

Claire frowned. "What were you worried about? I was down at the castle with royalty...his majesty Senator Juniper, and I forgot my phone at home."

"Can we go upstairs?" Hobbs still looked upset.

"Sure." She turned away, with a nod for him to follow.

In the kitchen, she poured him a glass of pinot noir and decided to have one herself. "I'm just finishing off this ice cream. You want a bite?" She held up the container.

"No, you finish it." No smile. That wasn't like him.

They sat side by side at the island counter. "Tell me why you're in a twit?" Claire said.

Hobbs sipped his wine and then turned to look at her, still visibly disturbed. "I think you're being followed."

"What? What do you mean?"

"Last night, when we left the restaurant, you pulled out before me. I had a text message from a client, and I was about to respond, when I noticed this dark sedan switch on its lights and take off after you. I waited a couple of seconds and then I pulled out after that car. I'm sure he was following you. He continued down the street after you pulled into your driveway. I pulled into the neighbor's drive next door and switched off my headlights. That car turned around and headed back down Lemon Cove Drive. Do you remember noticing any car behind you?"

A dark sedan... "Not last night," Claire said slowly. "But there have been other times recently when I wondered if someone was following me. Like when I went to talk to Samantha's boyfriend on his boat." Claire got up and went over to the sliding glass doors, made sure they were locked, then pulled the curtains. When she sat back down near Hobbs, she asked, "Who would be following me?"

He gave her an exasperated look. "You've been actively investigating your husband's and Samantha Marshall's murders, and the missing girls. My God, yesterday you drove all the way to DeFuniak on a fishing expedition. Claire, whoever these guys are, they don't want you looking around and asking questions. Don't you think that's why your husband was killed?"

Claire ran a hand through her hair and took a long sip of wine. Hobbs was making her nervous. "I haven't told you about having a drink with Senator Juniper. I was walking down the beach after getting home from work, and he spotted me and invited me up..." She proceeded to tell him about her visit, the daquiri on the deck and the attractive Asian girl. He looked irritated, and she could tell he was only half listening.

She continued anyway. "Remember the housewarming at the castle?"

Hobbs crossed his arms over his chest. "Yeah."

"Remember I met Oscar Snell, my dad's friend. Oscar and I talked, while you went on a tour of the place."

"Right."

"How many floors did you visit? Did you go up in those turrets? You know, the two stone towers?"

He was looking more puzzled than annoyed now. "No. We went downstairs and visited the kitchens, which were enormous and had all the latest appliances. Then we went back to the first floor and saw a library filled with books, a big dining room with a table that could sit twenty, and an impressive technology center with computers, speakers and video screens. After that, we visited two floors of guest suites. I think there were, like, five on each floor complete with bedrooms, sitting rooms and luxurious bathrooms. It was out of sight." He shook his head in amazement at the extravagance.

"But you didn't go up in the towers?"

"No. Maybe that's where the servants live."

Claire thought about that. "You're probably right. This afternoon, when I was walking near the castle, I thought I saw a face in one of those narrow windows that encircle the turrets. I felt like the person was looking right at me. Then he—or she—disappeared."

"You probably did see someone. I bet they need an army of servants to keep that place going." Hobbs got up and poured himself more wine. He gestured to Claire. She nodded and he poured an inch into her glass.

"Hobbs."

"Yes."

"There's more that I haven't told you." She looked into his concerned blue eyes. "Yesterday, when I went up to DeFuniak, I found Ruby Branson's diary. She's the girl that lived with my friend Irma for a while and then disappeared."

Hobbs sighed in frustration. "Okay...and..."

Claire took a deep breath. "She was lured into a weird relationship by a sexual predator, some guy named James. I think he was involved with her disappearance." She gave Hobbs a run-down of what she'd learned from the diary. He listened intently, periodically looking into her eyes. The skepticism in his gaze bothered Claire, but she kept on going.

"So, after all this blah blah about how wonderful James was and all about the kinky sex, one night he falls asleep afterward. Ruby goes into his office, which is usually locked, and finds a list of names and addresses open on his iPad. She took shots of the list with her phone."

Hobbs downed the rest of his wine. "Where is all this going, Claire?"

"I think she sent that list to Samantha Marshall. On the final page of Samantha's notebook, she'd printed Ruby's name and the words THE LIST in caps."

"So…?" Hobbs got up and walked around the island to rinse his glass.

"Don't you get it? Samantha and Dax were killed because they had the list and knew whose names were on it. I think some powerful people are involved."

Hobbs looked intrigued now. "And the bad guys have been searching everywhere for the list."

"Yes. They tore my house apart, and Abby's house, and visited Hank's boat."

Hobbs glanced around the room. "Maybe the list is here. We need to figure out where it's hidden."

Chapter 41

Hobbs walked around the great room, peeking behind the sofa cushions and into a decorative blue vase. He picked up a porcelain statue of a flying fish perched on a turquoise wave and looked underneath. "Where would Dax have hidden something? This is a big house, but maybe you remember where he might have put something like that list."

Claire felt a sense of relief. Finally, Hobbs was starting to believe her. Together they would figure out what had happened to Dax and to the missing girls. "I doubt we'll find anything here. The burglars did a pretty good job of taking this room apart. You should have seen the mess. They also emptied the kitchen cupboards."

Hobbs glanced up at the ceiling. "What about upstairs?"

Claire had a thought. "There are a bunch of envelopes in the safe, with our birth certificates, our marriage license, passports. I didn't open them all up when I went through the contents after the robbery."

"Let's go look." Hobbs started across the great room toward the hall.

In the office, Claire removed the painting and keyed in the code to the safe. It clicked open and she drew out the contents. She placed the guns and the ammo on the desk.

Hobbs's eyes widened. "Are those yours, or were they your husband's?"

"They're registered to both of us. I used to be a pretty good shot back in the day. But I haven't been on a range for a long time."

"I'm impressed. I've never shot a gun. They make me nervous." He turned away. "May I look in the file cabinet? Is that invading your privacy?"

"No. There are no big secrets in there. Most of the stuff is from my previous job. I probably should throw it away."

Claire sat at the desk and opened the envelopes one by one. She shook them out and rifled through the papers. No list. She shuffled through the stash of fifty-dollar bills. Nothing there, either.

"Did I tell you what else I found in the safe when I opened it after the burglary?" Claire asked, her voice subdued.

Hobbs was searching through the files. "Uh-uh."

"I found a pair of lacy pink underpants. Not mine."

Hobbs looked up.

"Initially, I thought Dax was having an affair. Later, when I learned about Samantha and the girls, I realized I was wrong. Anyway, I gave them to Detective Drakos. Maybe they were Ruby's, or belonged to one of the other missing girls?"

"Maybe. They can probably do a DNA test and compare it with some of her clothes." Hobbs went back to the file cabinet.

Claire put everything back in the safe and slammed the door shut. Next, she opened the desk drawers and quickly reviewed what was in them. Everything was neat and tidy. She hadn't been using this desk since she'd left Letízia. The two drawers Dax had used contained real estate brochures and listings. She hadn't thought anything about them right after the burglary; she'd stuffed them back in the drawers without a second glance. Now she wondered why Dax had acquired them. He'd never mentioned to her any plan to move. Immediately, she thought of Dax and Samantha coming out of the house in Watercolor. Had they been looking into real estate as part of their investigations?

"Oh my God." Claire jumped up. "Hobbs remember when you asked me about the little x's on my map of the Emerald Coast?"

He was rummaging in the bottom file drawer. "What do you mean?"

"I just found a bunch of real estate brochures describing gorgeous houses."

"So?" He looked up at her, his expression nonplussed.

"I'm wondering if the little x's on the map match real estate listings?"

"Huh. That's worth a closer look." He stood and went over to the wall, grabbed each side of the picture frame, and pushed up to unhook it and lift it down. The heavy frame slid in his hands. He grabbed the left-hand corner before the map fell, and his fingers pushed up the backing. Something small fell out and hit the floor. A USB flash drive.

Hobbs and Claire exchanged a wide-eyed glance. "Bingo," Claire said as she knelt and picked it up.

She stood, went back to the desk and inserted the thumb drive into her Mac. She clicked through the windows that opened up and there it was, a list of names and addresses. Hobbs placed the map next to the laptop. Together, they looked at the screen. The list was organized in four columns: dates, initials and last names of three or four people, three or four female names, and finally an address. Claire ran her finger across the date at the top. "March first." She studied the names. "Hey, look. It says T. Roberts. Could that be the governor, Thomas Roberts?"

Hobbs pointed at an entry farther down. "What about this one. L. Chambers…Larry Chambers. Isn't that the Kansas Senator who was in the news recently?"

"Here's F. Bigelow. I've seen that name before, but I don't know who he is."

"He owns a football team. I think he's a car dealer in L.A.," Hobbs said.

Halfway down the list, Claire spotted the name L. Richardson. Excitement and nerves gave her a queasy feeling. "Oh my gosh, could that be the Vice-President?"

They stared at each other. "If it is…holy shit," Hobbs said.

The third column had three names for March first: Tammy, Beth Anne and Mia. Tammy Schulz was one of the missing girls. Claire didn't recognize the other names. The address was in Rosemary Beach.

They continued to look down the list, exclaiming over the initials and last names. Some individuals appeared two or three times. Some names, they didn't recognize. Others seemed to be well-known movers and shakers on Wall Street, or TV personalities. Several girls' names were repeated often: Tammy, Lauren, Beth Anne, Mai-Li, Ginger, Grace. On the second page, Claire saw Ruby's name for the first time. It was repeated further down the page. The addresses varied, with some repetition, but were located up and down 30A.

Claire read out several addresses, and Hobbs found them on the map. Each time he verified that Dax had put an x on that very address. Finally, Claire stood and ran her hand through her hair. "This is a list of the parties that scumbag, James, was organizing. Ruby was being groomed as a party girl."

Hobbs nodded; his eyes narrowed. "If we're right, and these names are who we think they are, this is a bombshell. These are important men down here, taking part in a sex ring."

"And James is pimping them out. It disgusts me. He lured a young, inexperienced girl into this web of sex and drugs." Claire's next thought sent a chill through her. "Where are these girls now? Are they being held prisoner somewhere? Or are they dead...like Dax and Samantha?"

Chapter 42

Hobbs didn't go home for another hour. They discussed what they'd learned and how they should proceed. They decided that Claire would call the Sheriff's Department in the morning and detail everything to those working on Dax's murder case. This situation with the missing girls and the parties required a full-scale investigation.

Before he left, Hobbs took a picture of each page of the list, as did Claire. Then, they put the flash drive back behind the map and hung the map back on the wall. Before they left the room, Claire looked out the window onto the driveway. Was anyone watching them from across the road? She quickly closed the blinds.

***

The next morning, Claire called and texted Drakos, but received no reply. He must have his phone off, she guessed. At eight AM she called the Sheriff's Department. Officer Nilsson picked up and sounded surprised to hear Claire's voice. After a little chitchat, he sent her to Bob Rogers.

"Bob, I've discovered important information dealing with Dax's death as well as Samantha Marshall's. I know Detective Drakos is in Orlando, but someone needs to act now. Who could I talk to?"

There was silence on the line. Then Rogers said, "Claire, it's been months since those murders. You can rest assured, Detective Drakos is working tirelessly to solve these crimes."

Anger pulsed through Claire's body. "If he's working so tirelessly, why the hell is he off on a vacation?"

"It's not a vacation. It's important training." Bob sounded irritated, unlike his usual calm self. "Why don't you call back next week and talk to him."

Claire saw red. "It's probably a good thing Dax was killed so he can't witness what this lazy-good-for-nothing department has become."

She clicked off and raged around the kitchen island, searching for something to punch. After a few minutes she got hold of herself, took a calming breath, and called back. This time, Nilsson sounded a little wary. Bob must have spread the word that she'd lost her marbles. Claire asked to be put through to Mary in Missing Persons. But Mary was off again, something to do with the twins. When she asked to speak to the new Chief, Nilsson told her Chief Kincaid was in a meeting and couldn't be interrupted. Claire hung up in frustration.

She crossed the room, pulled open the sliding glass door and stomped out on the deck. It was another exquisite day, with brilliant sunshine and a glorious blue sky. The weather seemed to be mocking her. Outside it was bright, light and buoyant. Inside her heart, she felt dark, gloomy and tense. Why did the Sheriff's Department have no sense of urgency? The obvious answer hit her, and she felt the tears coming. Dax had been dead six months and they had yet to find out anything. To them, another couple of days made absolutely no difference.

***

Claire was not herself at work that day. Luckily, no new clients came in. At noon, she went out for lunch on her own. After crossing 30A she walked along South Barrett Square to Main Street and down to the Cowgirl Kitchen. She snagged a table outside and ordered a blackened shrimp quesadilla and Perrier with lemon. The other tables were occupied by families on vacation. Laughter and excited chatter filled the air. Clearly, the tourists were all thrilled to be down at the beach and carefree. Gazing at a giggling ten-year-old girl, Claire felt envious. When would she be free from this darkness that settled over her? She was convinced the answer was to solve Dax's murder and bring the perpetrators to justice. Dax deserved justice. Until then, she would not be able to rest.

While waiting for the food, she opened her phone and went to the photos of the list. Last night, she hadn't zeroed in on the dates. Now, she scrolled down and noted there was a party at the Ralstons' on March 22nd. Thinking back, she realized Dax had been killed the evening of the 24th. The very next day, March 25th, Samantha Marshall had disappeared. Claire figured Dax and Samantha had visited the Ralston home sometime on the 23rd, after the party. That would be when Barbara from the agency had seen them together. That day, they'd probably discovered who organized the parties and provided the call-girls. Dax must have called the perpetrators that afternoon, and within a few hours he was dead.

When her food arrived, Claire took only a few bites. The quesadillas were one of her favorite dishes at the Cowgirl Kitchen, but she'd lost her appetite. When the server reappeared, Claire gestured for the check and a doggy bag for her lunch. Maybe she would eat it later.

As she was walking back to the office, Hobbs called. Claire told him about her frustrating phone calls to the police.

"You've got to understand, the investigation is on the back-burner," Hobbs said. "They probably have lots more pressing cases in the works right now."

"You're right. But we have a lot of new information that should make a difference."

"It sounds like you'll have to wait until Detective Drakos gets back."

"I feel like it's urgent, though. When I read Ruby's diary, she became real to me. Now I'm worried about her. I want to find her and make her safe."

Hobbs sighed. "When Drakos gets back, he'll be able to get things moving. Until then, you stay safe. Keep the security locks on at home."

"No kidding." Then Claire told him about the dates of the Ralston party and Samantha's and Dax's deaths almost immediately afterward. "I wonder what they learned that day, that got them killed?"

"Hopefully, Drakos will find that out. Leave it to him, Claire. Listen, I've got to go. Just wanted to see if you're all right."

"So far. You stay safe, too." They hung up.

***

When Claire got back to the agency, Lilly Rose came out of her office. "Claire, could you please go over to Bramble Bay this afternoon? Ava is alone there. Harrison has been called away."

"Sure, I'll drive over there right now."

"Oh, and Harrison said he'll pick you up at seven tonight. Apparently, you two are going out for dinner."

"Yes, that's right."

Lilly smiled. "I'm sure the two of you will have a great time."

As Claire left the office, she wondered why Harrison Reed had shared their dinner plans with Lilly Rose. She found that bizarre.

Chapter 43

When Claire arrived at Bramble Bay, she briefly looked across at the palm tree and newly planted pansies that covered the spot where Samantha's body had been found. The memory of that day still filled her with angst. The vision of the corpse, dripping water, haunted her dreams. She quickly turned away and walked up the porch stairs and into the agency.

The reception area was empty. Ava must be in her office. Claire took a deep breath and walked back. The last time she'd been at Bramble Bay, Ava had snubbed her, just as she had done when they first met. Today Claire decided to be her most friendly. She reached Ava's office and knocked on the open door.

"Hi, Ava. I'm here to cover for Harrison. Lilly Rose said he'd been called away."

Ava kept studying her computer screen. "You don't need to be here. Things have been slow today. I can handle it."

Claire smiled. "I'm sure you can. But Lilly Rose told me to come over, so here I am."

Ava still didn't deign to look at her.

"I'll just go hang out in Harrison's office," Claire said.

That got Ava's attention. She glanced up, her sharp gaze seeming to evaluate Claire. "I don't think you can get in there. He always locks up when he's not here."

Claire smiled uncertainly. "I'll just sit out in the reception area, then, in case someone walks in. I've got my laptop."

"Okay, Miss Sunshine, you just do that."

To hell with acting friendly. "You are being incredibly rude," Claire snapped. "I don't know what you've got against me. Ever since the first day I walked into the office, you've had it in for me. Why?"

Ava stood up. She wore ropes of beads over a dark mauve flowing dress, and the beads jingled as she leaned over her desk. "Because you've become Lilly Rose's little protégée. I've been working my butt off but now you've managed to get these prime deals."

"I didn't get anything through Lilly Rose."

"What about the first deal…Lilly Rose sent that guy to you."

"No, she didn't. Oscar Snell knew my dad. I ran into him by accident."

Ava snickered. "You thought that was an accident? I saw Snell in Lilly's office. She shut the curtains so they could have a little chat. Two days later, he walks in as your client."

Claire was taken aback. "Really?"

"Yes, really. God knows why, but Lilly Rose is putting you on the fast track to success."

"But…I bumped into him at this party at Senator Juniper's house. I wasn't even going to go; I changed my mind at the last minute. Oscar said he was planning on contacting me because of my dad…"

Ava rolled her eyes. "That must be a story they dreamed up."

"Who's they?"

"The powers that be…Lilly Rose, Harrison, maybe even Consuelo."

Claire sank into the seat across from Ava's desk. "I don't know what to say." She rubbed her forehead. "Why would Lilly Rose do that? What am I to her? It makes no sense."

Ava was looking a little less hostile now. "I don't know, but they definitely set up that sale. And that Snell guy was in on it."

Feeling dizzy, Claire closed her eyes. It made no sense. She couldn't imagine why Lilly Rose wanted to help her out. Didn't Oscar want to buy that house? Why would he lie to her?

"Are you all right?" Ava asked.

"I'm probably hungry. I didn't eat much lunch, and all this is freaking me out."

Ava got up and came around from behind her desk. Claire heard her booties click down the hallway. Moments later, she was back. "Here, drink this. It'll give you instant energy."

Claire opened her eyes and saw Ava was holding a can out to her. "What is it?"

"A protein energy drink. You'll feel better."

"Can I be sure you're not trying to poison me?" Claire asked.

Ava's mouth twitched. "I don't poison. I go straight for the jugular."

Claire smiled uncertainly, popped open the top and sipped. The energy drink was a berry-flavored liquid that tasted a little like a milkshake. She drank down half the can. The cold liquid tasted good. She looked at the nutrition label. The drink had all sorts of vitamins and twenty percent of one's daily protein requirements. "Thank you, it's delicious, Claire said.

Ava sat back down behind her desk. She rested her elbows on the smooth surface and tented her fingers. "I'm sorry for being such a bitch. I realize it was uncalled for."

"Apology accepted. But right now, I'm worried that I've been manipulated. I probably should confront Lilly Rose."

"Why? It kick-started your career in real estate. Since then, you've made several sales on your own, right?"

"At this point, I don't know. Maybe they set me up with the Morehouses and the Johnsons, too." She gulped down the rest of the drink and got up to throw the can away. "I'll talk to Harrison tonight. Maybe he can clarify what happened."

Ava sat up straight and raised a brow. "Why are you seeing him tonight?"

"We've got a dinner date."

Ava shook her head. "Be careful of Harrison. I wouldn't trust him."

***

Claire and Ava talked for the rest of the afternoon. Only one couple came in, and Claire took them through the models, but it was obvious they had no plans to buy a house at Bramble Bay. On the way home, she spotted a text from Hobbs inviting her for dinner. After she'd pulled into her driveway, she texted him that she was busy. Some other time?

Inside and upstairs, Claire got ready for her date. She chose a jade-green wrap-dress, gold jewelry and black sandals. Harrison arrived right on time. Claire hurried downstairs to greet him. She'd decided not to invite him in. After all, they barely knew each other.

Harrison looked relaxed and handsome in a blue Vineyard Vines polo shirt and white shorts. "You look ravishing. That dress is perfect with your green eyes," he said.

Claire blushed. "You look pretty good yourself."

Harrison drove a black Mercedes. He came around to the passenger door and held it open for her. Then he handed her the seatbelt buckle. Once she was settled, he closed the door quietly. He was really quite the gentleman.

After seating himself, he turned to her and touched her forearm. She felt a shiver go down her spine. Was she attracted to Harrison, or did he turn her off? She certainly had reacted to his touch, but she didn't feel entirely at ease with him.

He seemed oblivious to it. "I thought we'd go to Baytowne Wharf. We could walk around. Get a drink at the Daiquiri Bar. Have dinner at the Marlin Grill. What do you think?"

Claire's first thought was she'd had her quota of daiquiris for the week, but she said, "That sounds great."

Harrison started the engine and backed out. The sound of classical music filled the car. "Are you familiar with Baytowne?" he asked.

"Yes, I had a couple of clients there. I used to go fairly regularly. The village has a nice vibe."

He looked at her and smiled. "Clients?"

"Yes. I represented a Brazilian company that made purses and bags. I dealt with a couple of gift shops in the village."

The drive to Baytowne went by quickly. Harrison had little stories, all of them entertaining, about various agents who worked for Lilly Rose. One day Consuelo let herself into a house that was supposed to be empty. She and her client walked into a bedroom and found a naked man taking a nap. They had to scurry out. Then there was the time Hal got bitten on the rump by a dog that was supposed to be locked up. Once, Barbara had showed a house where the utilities were turned off, and the client's little boy had used a non-working toilet. The mother was so embarrassed that she'd fled the scene.

They laughed over that.

"So, in other words, anything can happen in this profession," Claire said.

"That's for sure." Harrison turned to smile at her again. He had a really nice smile.

When they got to the village, they parked and walked to the Daiquiri Bar. There was a line to get in, so they decided to go directly to the Marlin Grill. Since it was a perfect night, they sat outside. The air was warm and soft with just a little breeze. Harrison ordered a bottle of Mayo Zinfandel and toasted their newfound friendship. They split an order of duck spring rolls. For an entrée, Claire had a filet mignon with bleu cheese and Harrison got a strip steak. The entire meal was delicious, and Claire felt happy and satiated.

During dinner, Harrison asked questions about Claire's family and her life before moving down to the Emerald Coast. He showed a sincere interest in her life and her interests, which she found refreshing. When she asked him about his background, he told her he was part of a big, boisterous family and his parents were still alive and well, living in Arizona. "I don't like the desert, but they can't stand the humidity in Florida," Harrison said.

"I know what you mean. There are pro-Florida people, pro-Arizona people and pro-California people."

Harrison chuckled. "Anyway, we usually get together for the holidays. It can get pretty rowdy when my brothers and I are hanging out."

Claire liked that. Dax had had a large, close-knit family, and she felt that his solid background had added to his stability as an adult. She smiled at Harrison. Why had Ava warned her against him? Ava must be jealous of his success in the real estate market, like she'd been jealous of Claire. Reluctant to spoil the mood, Claire decided not to bring up the Morehouses or the Johnsons. Even if Lilly Rose had pointed Oscar Snell Claire's way, they were probably legit. She'd been silly to think otherwise.

On the way back to Lemon Cove, Harrison mentioned Dax and asked her how she was doing.

"Highs and lows," she murmured.

"Are they close to catching the killers?" His voice was warm and sincere.

"No. It's very frustrating. I need to talk to the head detective, but he went out of town. I'll have to wait until next week."

"You should leave it to the police."

"Everyone tells me that, but I feel like I won't have closure until someone is in jail. I've learned some things recently that should move the investigation along. I uncovered a key piece of information that could help them nail Dax's killer and maybe Samantha Marshall's. There are also some missing girls." Claire was dying to confide everything in Harrison, but something held her back.

Harrison didn't respond. He was concentrating on passing a truck that was going at a snail's pace in the left-hand lane.

Back in Lemon Cove, Harrison accompanied her to the door. He bent down and kissed her. It was a perfect kiss, softly demanding. At first, she gave in, then gently, she pushed him away. She wasn't ready for that.

"Thanks for a great time," she said and turned to open her door.

"I enjoyed your company. Let's get together again soon. Maybe you could come over to my house and I could cook you dinner."

"Sounds fun. We'll talk soon."

Claire waved as he drove away.

Chapter 44

In bed that night, Claire thought about Harrison. He was a first-class act, a true gentleman and intelligent as well. During dinner they'd discussed books and he knew all about the latest bestsellers. He'd recommended several novels Claire might like. Since Dax's death, she hadn't been able to lose herself in a book. On Monday, she promised herself, she'd stop by the Hidden Lantern or Sundog Books and buy one of Harrison's suggestions.

***

Claire spent the next day at Bramble Bay. Several interested couples came through, and the hours flew by. She didn't have time to talk to Ava. They were both too busy. At six o'clock she was ready to head home. As she was getting into her car, Hobbs pulled up beside her. Still in a hard-hat, he looked hot and dusty.

"Looks like you were busy today. I saw all the cars," he said.

"Yes, non-stop clients and they seem to be serious customers. Several are coming back tomorrow."

He grinned. "Great, you must have the touch."

Claire laughed. "I've got my spiel down pat now. I feel comfortable showing these houses."

Hobbs lowered his voice. "Anything new in terms of the investigation?"

"No. I guess I'll have to wait until Drakos gets back."

"Good, leave it all to him." He took off his hat and wiped his forehead with the back of his arm. "Are you busy again tonight?"

"Yes, my friend Morgan is here from California. We're having a girls' night out."

"Have fun!" He started his engine and drove away.

***

At home, Claire showered and changed into a blue-and-white striped top and white jeans. Within a half hour she was on her way to The Bay. When she arrived, she found Olivia and Morgan already installed at a table. A retro band was playing and there was a party atmosphere. After hugs and exclamations, they sat down and ordered a bottle of wine and appetizers: Point Washington spring rolls, Thai shrimp lettuce wraps and spicy sweet Brussels sprouts.

Morgan pulled out her phone and they oohed and aahd at the latest pictures of Harper. She was really a cute baby and, according to Morgan, exceptional in every way.

After the appetizers arrived, Morgan told them about the gigantic wedding she had helped organize. "It was pretty over-the-top."

"Like Victoria Palmer's wedding?" Claire asked. They all remembered when the famous media star had staged her wedding at the Magnolia. Victoria had been beautiful but an egomaniac. She'd been killed during the wedding reception, a tragedy that turned the whole event into even more of a crazy media extravaganza.

"Not as outrageous as that." Morgan forced a smile. "I'd rather not remember that one. Let's talk about something else."

Olivia told them she was dating a new guy who worked at McDonald's corporate offices in Chicago. "He gets down here every couple of weeks and I go up there when I can. It's hard being so far apart."

"Could you change regions and work in the Chicago area?" Morgan asked.

"Right now, I can't. Corporate wants me down here. It's an impossible situation." Olivia turned to Claire. "Tell us what's new with you?"

"Yes, how are you doing?" Morgan asked.

Unexpectedly, Claire's eyes filled with tears. "I'm doing better." She laughed. "I don't know why I've got tears in my eyes. I guess it's because I'm happy to be with you guys, my dear friends…" She smiled at Olivia and Morgan.

"What about the job?" Morgan asked.

"I'm actually enjoying real estate. I enjoy meeting new people and helping them find the perfect home."

Olivia looked at her over the rim of her glass. "What about a social life?"

"I've got a man friend."

"Ah-ha," Olivia said, raising her eyebrows.

"No, really, he's just a friend. We have an arrangement. Sometimes we have dinner together, but you know, nothing fancy. And I went out last night with a business associate. Nothing meaningful." She poked at the sauce on her plate. She felt ambivalent about Harrison.

"Good." Morgan laid her hand on Claire's arm and looked into her eyes. Morgan's were full of compassion. "What's the latest with the investigation into Dax's death?"

Claire wanted to tell them everything; about Samantha Marshall, about Ruby Branson, about the list with its famous names, but she didn't think it was a good idea. They would tell her to leave it to the police, just like everyone else. No one understood her need to personally bring the killer to justice.

"The detective continues to follow leads," she said instead. "So far, they don't have any answers."

"Just be patient. They'll find the guy and lock him up," Morgan said, with fire in her eyes.

Claire drove home later, feeling on top of the world. It had been great seeing her two best friends. She sang along with the radio as she headed down Lemon Cove Drive. She stopped at the mailbox and pulled out several advertising brochures, a couple of bills, and a letter from her mother, who still communicated via snail mail.

She continued up the driveway and parked under the house. As she turned off the engine, a sense of something not quite right made her uneasy. What was different? Looking up, she realized the light over the front door had burned out. Relief, and mild annoyance, replaced her brief anxiety. She would have to climb up there tomorrow and put in a new bulb.

She got out of the car, slammed the door shut and locked it. At the entryway to the house, she punched in the code. As she reached for the doorknob, strong arms came around her and someone pressed a cloth to her face. She smelled something slightly sweet, and then everything went black.

Part III

Chapter 45

Ajax Drakos sat at a table with three guys. The hotel bar was crammed with detectives sharing war stories, and he often felt he learned more during these impromptu discussions than in the workshops. Other detectives freely shared their successes in the field, and often Ajax learned a new strategy or two.

The conference had dealt with the latest technologies in law-enforcement, including state-of-the-art police wearables. Hands-free smart watches were giving first responders access to real-time information. He'd also gone to a workshop about drones that were revolutionizing many aspects of police work, and to a presentation on how to turn your in-car video system into a license plate reader. As representative from the Sheriff's Department, Drakos was taxed with the job of bringing back the latest technology to Walton County. The question was whether or not the department had the funds to purchase the latest software or equipment he'd learned about.

The other detectives at his table were discussing Jeffrey Epstein's suicide in prison. The entire country had followed the coverage of the Epstein scandal. Allegedly, the man had sex for years with underage girls and provided them to his important friends. It was said Epstein frequently invited royalty and wealthy individuals to his private retreat in the Virgin Islands, as well as to his Zorro Ranch in New Mexico. He was eventually imprisoned and hung himself one night when his guards were busy shopping online.

"I don't think it was suicide," a big guy with red hair said, his voice loud and aggressive as he hunched over a glass of Scotch in both massive hands. "A lot of people wanted to see that guy dead."

"Right, Epstein was going to sing like a canary. All sorts of powerful men were worried he would reveal their names." This from a thin, dark-haired detective with a marked scar down one side of his face. Drakos knew the guy had made quite a name for himself in Dade County.

The redhead gulped Scotch. "So, somebody got to him in jail. The suicide is still being questioned by one of the forensic pathologists."

"Yeah, but then someone buried the investigation," the third detective said. Drakos didn't know much about this guy. He was younger than the rest of them, probably in his early thirties, with sharp eyes and a cocky air.

"I'm telling you he was going to sing like a canary," the scar-faced man repeated.

Suddenly tired of the conversation, Drakos stood and threw some money on the table. He needed to get to bed. There was one more presentation in the morning and then he would start home. He planned on spending tomorrow evening with his sister in Tallahassee and the next day he would be back on the Emerald Coast.

"Calling it a night, Drakos?"

He nodded. "Time to get my ZZZs. I'll see you guys in the AM."

***

Olivia tried again. Still no luck. She'd called Claire several times, but the phone had only rung once and then gone directly to voicemail. Claire hadn't answered her texts, either. They had planned to have breakfast in the morning. When Olivia looked at her calendar later, she realized that she wouldn't be able to get together after all.

Claire should be home by now. Why didn't she pick up?

***

Hobbs felt a certain amount of guilt. He didn't want Claire to think he was stalking her, but he needed to check that she was safe. What he'd learned the day before, seeing that USB drive and the list of names on it, made him very nervous. Some really bad people had killed Dax and Samantha because of that list. He was sure of it. If they thought Claire knew about the list, knew anyone on it, they wouldn't hesitate to eliminate her as well.

He'd worked late in the trailer that served as a makeshift office at Bramble Bay. Then he'd picked up some barbecue and gone home. After a long shower, he'd had dinner and then sat down at his drawing board to work on a hotel landscape design. He'd managed to lose himself in his drawing, and it was already eleven when he next looked at the clock. He knew Claire had gone out with her girlfriends, but she might be home by now. Without thinking, he grabbed his keys and took off.

In Lemon Cove, Hobbs drove slowly down the street and past Claire's house. Her car was in the driveway and everything was dark.

Good. Claire was safe at home. He turned around and headed home to bed.

Chapter 46

Drakos decided to skip the morning session and take off early. He wanted to get back to the Emerald Coast, the sooner the better, though he couldn't have said why. He'd called his sister and they had agreed to meet for lunch. She was disappointed that he wasn't going to stay in Tallahassee longer, but he felt a certain urgency to get home and back to work. As he drove, he called in for updates from the department. He talked briefly to Chief Kincaid, then he was passed to Bob Rogers.

"Hey, Drakos. How did it go?"

"I learned new technology, new apps, the latest equipment. Now all we need is a big donation of a couple of million dollars to upgrade the department. Anyway, I'm on my way home, should be in to work bright and early tomorrow morning."

"Good thing, too. You need to talk to Claire Simmons. She's losing it," Bob said. "Yesterday she called and wanted to talk to someone about Dax's murder. She claims she has new information. I told her you'd get in touch. But man, she was nuts, called back in maybe two minutes and wanted to talk to the Chief."

"She just needs someone to listen to her. Then she'll calm down." Drakos ran his hand through his hair. He felt sorry for Claire, but he knew she could be a pain in the ass.

"Right. I'll see you tomorrow." Bob hung up.

***

Olivia tried to call Claire again, but to no avail. Well, at some point Claire would look at her phone. If she arrived at Another Broken Egg Café and Olivia didn't show, she could just enjoy breakfast on her own.

***

In the Uber on her way to the airport, Morgan tried texting and then calling Claire, but there was no answer. She left a message: "Hey, Claire. I'm on the way to the airport. Just wanted to say goodbye. I hope you're planning on coming out and visiting us soon. I know your godchild would love to see you and so would her mom. By the way, I was happy to see you've started a new life for yourself...the job sounds great and I'm glad you've got a man friend. Bye-bye. Take care. Love you."

***

Ava Hines felt frazzled. Where was Claire? As usual, she'd opened at ten. Claire should have been there. As soon as Ava'd turned the lights on, two couples came in simultaneously. Ava began with the Bramble Bay miniature model, keeping an ear out for Claire to show up. Then, just as she was about to take everyone through the model homes, a family with two rambunctious kids arrived. She'd sent them over to look at the pool and the Club House, where the kids could climb around on the playground equipment. While the two couples without kids inspected the family room of the first model, Ava texted Claire. No reply. While they went upstairs to check out the bedrooms, Ava called Claire. No answer.

As they exited the second model, Ava saw another car drive up. Not Claire's car…more clients. Damn, where oh where was Claire this morning? As soon as she could manage it, Ava called the Lilly Rose Agency. Consuelo answered.

"Hey, it's Ava. I'm over my head here at Bramble Bay. Claire is supposed to be here, but she hasn't shown up. I need help."

"Okay, cariño. I'm not busy. I'll be there as soon as I can. Don't you fret."

"Is Harrison there?"

"No, neither is Lilly Rose. I'll see you soon."

"Okay, thanks."

Fifteen minutes later, Consuelo showed up. Ava could have hugged her. Another couple had just shown up.

As Consuelo accompanied the new customers back to the office, Hobbs drove by. He waved Ava over. "I just noticed; Claire's car isn't here. I thought she was working at Bramble Bay all week."

Ava nodded. "She's supposed to be here, but I can't get her on the phone, and she doesn't answer my texts. Thank God Consuelo's filling in." But Ava had barely finished her last sentence before Hobbs gunned his engine and took off down Bramble Bay Boulevard toward the highway.

***

Hobbs raced down Highway 98 towards 283. He tried calling Claire several times as he drove. There was no answer. A feeling of dread grew in the pit of his stomach. When he got stuck behind a slow-moving truck, he passed it on the shoulder. In Lemon Cove, he gunned the engine and took the curve along the beach at a breakneck speed, his heart beating frantically.

The house looked quiet. Claire's car was still in the carport under the house. He pulled in behind the vehicle and got out. As he strode up to the entrance, he noticed all the mail scattered by the entryway door. He walked up to the door and realized it was partially open.

He barged in and raced up the stairs. "Claire, hello Claire. It's Hobbs. Are you here?"

He went through the entire house, calling her name. The house was empty, silent.

He took out his phone and called 9-1-1.

***

Claire opened her eyes. She didn't recognize the room. She closed her eyes again and turned over on her side. The movement made her feel woozy. Had she had too much to drink last night with the girls? She couldn't remember. She blinked and opened her eyes again. She was lying in a queen-sized bed, under a white comforter. Across from the bed were an armchair and footstool. Recessed lighting from overhead illuminated the space.

This had to be a nightmare. Claire closed her eyes and rubbed her face. Was she awake or dreaming?

She opened her eyes again and forced herself to sit up. The change of position made her dizzy, and she closed her eyes to let the feeling pass. When she felt better, she opened her eyes and looked around. The room was triangular, with the bed on one long wall, the armchair and foot stool opposite. To her left was a curved wall of stone, with a narrow vertical window in the middle. Claire felt a frisson of fear. That single narrow window made her think of the white face she'd seen during her walk on the beach, the evening she'd had a drink with Senator Juniper. She got quickly to her feet. A wave of nausea gripped her, but she fought it down and made her way to the window. She stretched up on her tiptoes and looked out. All she could see were the tops of trees. What had happened? How had she gotten here? Was she in Juniper's castle? Why?

Claire turned back around, holding the wall as another wave of nausea rolled over her. Beside the armchair was a white table with a straight-backed wooden chair pushed under it. On the floor was a grey carpet. Opposite the curved stone wall was a heavy wooden door with a small window in it. Two white-painted doors flanked the wooden door. Claire walked unsteadily towards it. She grasped the handle and pulled. The door didn't budge. She tried to push it open, to no avail. She was locked in.

Panic swept through her. She banged on the door, yelling, "Help! Somebody! Help me!"

Chapter 47

Drakos turned off Highway 10 and found his way to the Panera where he was supposed to meet his sister. He was fifteen years younger than Helen, and they'd never been close, but he'd done his best to stay in touch since she was the only family he had. They'd grown up in North Dakota where their parents ran a family-style restaurant. Both of them had spent every minute out of school and during summer vacations in that restaurant, working side by side with their parents.

It had been a hard life. His father had died of a heart attack at fifty-five, his mother of cancer five years later. Neither had been especially loving, probably because they were too busy and too tired. There had never been vacations or even days off. In the small town where they lived, the restaurant was open every day except Christmas. On Thanksgiving, they served dinner to half the town.

Helen had done well in school and had become an English teacher. She'd moved down to the Florida Panhandle and found the job in Tallahassee where she'd taught for thirty-five years. Now she was retired and spent her money on two trips a year, traveling with fellow retirees. Helen had never married, and he hadn't either. Why was that, he wondered. Had their parents' dispassionate marriage put them both off the idea?

He'd fallen for a girl when he was twenty, but she'd dumped him and married his best friend. He'd dated now and then in the years since, but he'd never felt a desire to push it further than a couple of dates.

Years ago, he had followed Helen down to Florida. He'd gone to the Police Academy in Niceville and taken a job in Walton County. Through the years, he and his sister had only seen each other on the occasional holiday. He had a feeling Helen didn't approve of his profession and looked down on him intellectually.

Helen was seated in a booth, a bowl of soup in front of her. Helen had soup for lunch every day. That was why she'd chosen Panera...for the soup.

Drakos bent over to give her a kiss on the cheek, but she brushed him away. "I didn't know if you'd show. I waited fifteen minutes and then I got my soup." Helen's back was rod straight, her brown eyes sharp and her hair a metallic grey cap. As usual, she was wearing a pressed long-sleeved blouse. Her glasses hung by a cord around her neck. The archetypal English teacher, Drakos thought.

"Sorry. Construction on ten. I couldn't get here any faster." Whenever they were together, he converted to his role as irresponsible little brother.

She gave him a faint smile. "Go get something to eat. I've got a meeting at the library in a half hour. We'll have to make this fast."

He went over to the counter and put in an order for a ham and Swiss on multigrain with chips and a Dr. Pepper. He got his drink and while he waited for his sandwich, his phone rang. He stepped back into a corner and answered the call. It was Officer Nilsson.

"Hey Detective, sorry to bother you, but I thought you would want to call this guy."

"What guy?"

"His name is Scranton. Hobbs Scranton. He called 9-1-1 because he thinks something's happened to Mrs. Simmons. He sounds pretty frantic. We've got a patrol car going over to her house. He says he absolutely needs to talk to you."

Drakos felt his gut twist. He'd dreaded something like this. He knew Claire wouldn't let it go. "What's his number? I'll call him."

Nilsson gave him the number.

The girl at the counter called out, "Ajax, order for Ajax."

He went over and got his sandwich, took it to the booth and sat down. Helen was cutting her apple in neat slices.

"Just a minute, Helen. I've got to call this guy," he said.

Helen rolled her eyes and shook her head. He knew what she was thinking: Her little brother couldn't spare five minutes to talk to his sister.

He smiled apologetically at her, his ear to the phone. "Hello, this is Detective Drakos."

***

After Hobbs called 9-1-1, he went into Claire's office and quickly verified that the flash drive was still there behind the map. No one had touched it. He palmed it, planning to lock it up in the glove box of his car. Then he went back outside to wait for the police. Sirens wailed in the distance. He looked down at the mail strewn on the cement driveway. Claire must have dropped it when someone surprised her. He walked over and looked in her car. Her phone lay on the passenger seat. He tried opening the door, but it was locked. He went back to the house and looked around the entryway. After a moment, he saw the thin strap of her purse. It had fallen behind the planter he had given her. More proof Claire had been violently abducted.

Hobbs's phone rang. He answered it.

"This is Detective Drakos," said the voice on the other end. "What's going on?"

"Detective, Claire…Claire Simmons has disappeared. I'm at her house. Her car is here, but she isn't."

"Could she be out walking on the beach?"

"No, she's been taken. I'm sure of it. There's some information…a list…we thought, Claire and me, that her husband and that reporter, Samantha Marshall, were killed for this list. There's mail strewn on the ground outside her front door, and her purse—"

Drakos stopped him in mid-sentence. "Mr. Scranton, you're not making any sense."

"Sorry. I'm frazzled." Perspiration dripped down Hobbs's face. He wiped his forehead with the back of his arm.

"Listen, I'm in a restaurant," Drakos said. "I'll be on the road in twenty minutes. I'll call you back, and you can explain clearly what you know. Meanwhile, talk to the officers when they get there."

Hobbs nodded.

"Scranton, did you hear me?"

"Yes, sir. Okay." As he hung up, two patrol cars swung into the driveway. Right then and there, Hobbs decided he wouldn't talk to these guys about the list. That information was dangerous. But Drakos needed to know.

***

Claire's knuckles were bleeding. Her throat was raw from screaming. No one was coming. Through the little window in the door she could only see muted light. She started to sob. As tears streamed down her face, she turned around and leaned against the door. What had happened? How had she gotten here? She remembered dinner with the girls, the drive home and then nothing.

She pushed away from the door and tried opening the smaller white door to her left. Inside was a closet with shelves, drawers and a wooden pole with hangers. No clothes were on the hangers, there was nothing in the drawers.

Then she looked down at herself, smoothing her hand over her stomach. She was wearing white silk pajamas with light blue piping along the edges. The top had long sleeves and there was a small breast pocket decorated with the same blue piping. Underneath the pajamas, she was naked. She gave a screech of horror. Someone had undressed her while she was out of it and taken her clothes away.

Shaking, she turned to the white door on the right. Beyond it was a small bathroom with a narrow shower stall, a sink and a toilet. There were towels and a series of toiletries in bottles attached to the wall. A blue plastic cup was placed on a shelf. Claire filled the cup with water and gulped it down, filled it up again and drank some more. Then she used the facilities.

Back in the main room, Claire threw herself onto the bed. She felt empty and headachy. She closed her eyes and tried to think. Clearly, she'd been kidnapped and drugged. It probably had to do with the list. Here she was in Juniper's castle, unless she'd been transported to a castle in Liechtenstein. Not bloody likely.

A gentle knock came at the door, followed by the click of a lock being turned. Claire sat up and looked towards the door. It opened slowly. On the threshold was the Asian girl, the one she'd seen the night she had drinks with Senator Juniper. The girl wore a purple cheongsam and was carrying a tray. Behind her was one of Juniper's burly bodyguards. The girl scurried in and placed the tray on the white wooden table, avoiding Claire's eyes. Then she turned and darted out of the room.

Claire rose from the bed and rushed toward the door. "Can I get out of here? Please can you help me?" But someone—the girl, the bodyguard—pulled the door shut, and Claire heard the click of the bolt.

She walked over to the table. On the tray were shrimp and grits, a green salad and a dish of cut-up fruit. It all looked delicious and smelled even better. Claire didn't know how long it had been since she'd eaten, but the fact that she was being held prisoner won out over her hunger pangs. She picked up the plate of shrimp and grits and threw it across the room. The plate smashed against the door and the food fell on the floor in globs. Next, she threw the salad and the fruit. They broke into a hundred pieces, strewing lettuce and pineapple across the room. Finally, she threw the glass of ice water at the door. It made a satisfactory crash. Then she stood with her arms at her sides, her hands in fists, and screamed. Sobs wracked her body. She fell into the armchair and curled up into a ball.

As she huddled there, she heard a voice...distorted, but somehow familiar. Who was it? The mocking tone sent chills down her spine. "Claire, you shouldn't have done that. You were very foolish."

Claire looked up at the door. Her gaze circled the room and then moved to the ceiling, where she noticed a camera in one corner. Good God, they'd been watching her.

"That's right. You see the camera. Someone will be watching you at all times. We can hear your screams, too." There was a chuckle. "But we can turn down the volume."

Anger made her sit up straight. "Why am I here? What did I do? I want to go home."

"You wouldn't give up, Claire. Everyone told you to leave it alone, but you just wouldn't. We're deciding now whether you should live or die. For now, we're tired of your antics. You'll be put back to sleep."

"Who are you? What are you talking about? I don't know anything," Claire pleaded.

"We think you do."

"Can I talk to Senator Juniper? I know I'm in his mansion."

But the voice had gone silent. Minutes later the door opened. Two bodyguards and a muscular woman in white carrying a hypodermic came in. They crunched across the floor littered with food and broken dishes. Claire screamed as the men held her down. The woman jabbed the needle into her arm, and she lost consciousness.

Chapter 48

Drakos spent the allotted twenty minutes listening to his sister's complaints about the mismanagement of the library board, followed by a tirade concerning bad grammar and misspellings in the local paper. As he listened, he wondered if she was ever really happy. That made him think of himself. Had he ever really been happy? Had their childhoods turned them into lonely nitpickers? Goodness knows he was a stickler for facts.

He ate his sandwich quickly and crunched on his chips as Helen went from one topic to the next. He found it difficult to concentrate on her diatribe. His mind kept returning to Claire Simmons. He needed to get through this lunch and get on the road. Claire could be in real danger.

When Helen stood to leave, they shared a brief hug. Then they went their separate ways. As soon as he was on the road, he pulled out his phone and called Hobbs Scranton. "Drakos here. What do you have to tell me?"

"I don't know where to start. Claire learned a lot about those missing girls recently, the ones her husband was looking into. And she was being followed. I'm sure of it."

"Start from the beginning. Why were you at her house this morning?"

"I actually went by her house last night. Her car was there, and I thought she was all right."

Drakos's hackles went up. "Why did you go there last night? Have you been stalking her?"

"No, no. That's not it." The guy sounded aggrieved. "After I saw this car following her the other night, I got worried and decided to go and check on her."

"So why did you go back today?"

"This morning I drove by the realtor's office in Bramble Bay and her car wasn't there. I talked to Ava Hines, who works there too. She was upset because Claire hadn't shown up and they had a lot of business. I got a bad feeling and decided to drive over to Claire's place."

That made sense, though Drakos didn't like where this was going. "Why do you think she's been kidnapped?"

"When I got there, the door was partially open, there was mail strewn on the ground, and her purse had fallen behind the planter. Somebody must've grabbed her and she dropped everything. I went inside the house, I kept calling her name, but she wasn't there. So I called 9-1-1."

Scranton sounded frantic, probably with good reason. In spite of frequent advice to leave matters to the police, Claire Simmons had continued with her own private investigation. Damn! Drakos banged the steering wheel with his palm. He should've taken the time to listen to her when she'd called him before he left for Orlando. If he'd heard her out, maybe she would be safe at home now. He banged the steering wheel again, then reined in his frustration. "How much do you know about what Claire learned, Mr. Scranton?"

"Pretty much all of it."

"Okay, fill me in."

Drakos leaned back and listened while Scranton told him about another girl's disappearance—a girl named Ruby Branson, who'd been living with a friend of Claire's. "And this Aunt Irma never reported Miss Branson as missing?"

"No. The girl texted her, said she was going to Texas and to dispose of her belongings. But Irma had an address for the girl's grandfather in DeFuniak Springs, so she sent Ruby's stuff up there.

The story felt all too familiar. Drakos realized it was pretty much what had happened with the other missing girls.

"So Claire drove up to DeFuniak and went to see Ruby's grandfather," Scranton continued. "She went through Ruby's stuff and found her diary. From what she read in it, she thought Ruby got lured into a weird relationship with a sexual predator—some guy named James. If she's right, this guy's involved somehow with Ruby's vanishing act.

"But here's the most important thing. Ruby discovered a list on James's computer that contained dates, addresses and names of important men. She took a picture of the list with her phone. Later, we think she sent it to Samantha Marshall at The Emerald Times."

Drakos frowned. "What important men?"

"Politicians, rich guys in Silicon Valley and Wall Street…movers and shakers. Then there were the names of girls and addresses off of 30A."

Drakos tried to wrap his head around all this information. "Who were the girls?"

"We recognized two of them, Tammy and Lauren, as the ones that disappeared last spring. Tammy Schulz and Lauren Reynolds. Plus Ruby, and some other names."

"You sound like you've seen this list."

"I have. It's on a USB flash drive. I've got it locked in my glove box. I also took a picture of the list with my phone." Scranton took a breath. "Claire got hold of Samantha Marshall's notes, too. She found Ruby's name and 'the list' printed in capital letters."

"Samantha's notes?"

"Her notebook, that she used for her stories. Samantha'd made notes on Lauren Reynolds' and Tammy Schulz's disappearances, too. A couple of days ago, Claire went to the Missing Persons office to learn about those missing girls."

"Yeah, I heard that. Listen, I'll be back on the Emerald Coast in a couple of hours. Why don't you meet me at five-thirty in my office? We'll sit down and get all this on paper."

"Five-thirty? Sure, I'll be there. I want to help. I really care about Claire."

Drakos could hear the desperation in his voice.

***

Claire felt as though she was drowning. She kept trying to swim up for air. She could see the light above her, filtering down through the water. Could she swim up and burst into the light? But something kept pulling her down. She felt panicky and tried to kick off her assailant. She kept kicking, trying to get free.

Her eyes shot open. Where was she? It took her a few moments to recognize her prison cell. No light came through the narrow window. The overhead lights had been dimmed and she could just make out the furniture in the room. It must be nighttime. Her legs were tangled in the bed sheets. She reached down and pushed the sheets aside, then slowly sat up. Like before, she felt dizzy and queasy.

"Hello, Claire," a voice said. The same voice as earlier? "You've been a bad girl."

Fear clutched at her heart. Who was watching her? The voice was muffled but had a cadence she thought she recognized. If only she could place it...

"I'm sorry I made that mess, but I want out of here. Why are you keeping me locked up?" Claire whimpered.

"I told you, Claire. You wouldn't stop your little investigation. We had to remove you."

The best strategy was to act dumb. "What do you mean?" Claire said, as innocently as she could.

"You went to The Emerald Times, then you talked to Hank Robbins, that small-time fisherman. And that pitiful retard, Abby, who's one fry short of a Happy Meal. Then you started investigating the missing girls. We know you went to the police station and then all the way up to DeFuniak. It had to stop."

Claire didn't know how to deny these accusations. Hobbs had been right. They—whoever they were—had been following her for some time. "So what if I did all that? I don't know who you are, and I never learned why Dax died."

"Oh, I think you did. You found the list, didn't you? Ruby sent it to Samantha Marshall. She told us she did. We didn't need to twist her arm. She'll do anything to gain our approval."

"List? What list?" Claire twisted a corner of the bed sheet in her hand.

"The list of parties and attendees. Come on, don't bullshit me, Claire."

"I don't know what you're talking about. Please, can't you let me go? I'll stop asking questions and talking to people. I promise."

There was no response.

"Hello? Are you there?"

No response.

Claire lay back down and closed her eyes. She needed to play along with these people. If she agreed to do whatever they wanted, maybe they would let her go. Then she could figure out how to escape them for good. She clutched at the comforter as tears trickled down her cheeks.

Chapter 49

Drakos stopped at Amavida for a large cup of black coffee. He needed the high-octane stuff this morning. On his way out, he picked up a copy of The Emerald Times. There was a picture of Claire Simmons front and center.

The headline proclaimed, Police Suspect Foul Play. The article began: Claire Simmons, wife of Chief Deputy Sheriff Daxton Simmons, who was murdered last spring, has been abducted. She disappeared yesterday in the early morning hours...

The piece went on to describe how Dax's body had been found on the beach. The article ended with a plea: If you see this woman, please contact the Sheriff's Department.

Ajax knew they'd be getting hundreds of bogus calls. Checking them all out would take over-the-top manpower, but it had to be done. Yesterday afternoon, they'd canvassed Claire's neighborhood, but no one had seen or heard anything. The lots were large, and the houses were far apart. They figured Claire had been abducted late at night, so most of her neighbors were sleeping.

Yesterday evening, Nilsson went to The Bay and interviewed the waitress who had served Claire and also contacted her friends. The waitress remembered what they ordered and the nice tip, but she didn't remember Claire Simmons. According to the friends, they'd left the restaurant at ten forty-five. Claire had been fine and full of conversation that evening. Neither Miss Barnes nor Mrs. Perry had any idea who could have kidnapped her.

Last night, Drakos had worked with Hobbs Scranton until the early morning hours. Scranton had repeated what he'd learned from Claire, while Drakos took copious notes. Together they'd written out a timeline and organized the information Scranton provided. After the landscaper handed over the flash drive containing the list, Drakos had sent it to the lab for fingerprints. He wanted to verify that Chief Simmons and Samantha Marshall had handled it and were thus aware of the parties.

On the list, he found the address he'd gotten from Barbara Larson at the Lilly Rose Hamlin real estate agency. It was the house where she claimed to have spotted Dax and Samantha. Hobbs Scranton said Claire had checked the dates of that party and had verified that Dax and Samantha were killed shortly after that visit.

He stared at the list. "Three names on here are girls who disappeared or were abducted. But they were scheduled for parties well after their disappearance. So they were still alive. Right?" He looked at Scranton across the desk.

"Right," the young man said. He looked like he was imagining Claire might be among them now.

"What I'm wondering is, where are they keeping them? They have to be available to attend these parties, so they must be lodged somewhere nearby."

Scranton shrugged, without much energy. "Maybe in another vacant house."

Drakos continued to study the list. "And who rents these houses?"

"I've googled a couple of them. They're not on Airbnb or on local rental sites." Scranton ran his fingers through his hair in frustration.

"But they're rentals, right?"

"They must be if these parties can take place while the owners are away. Someone is handling them."

"So whoever's handling the rentals is in cahoots with the organizers of the parties. They know when someone is away, and they invite all these bigwigs for a cozy get-together."

"Right."

"Who could I question about this without raising suspicions?"

A thoughtful look crossed Scranton's face. "I'm wondering if you could show the addresses to Ava Hines, over at Bramble Bay. She'd know enough to be useful. She's a loner, doesn't hang out with the other realtors in the area. She told me once that she didn't trust anybody at the Lilly Rose agency and preferred working alone."

"I don't want to raise any red flags. We have to be very careful."

Scranton looked down at his hands, clenched in tight fists in his lap. "If they figure out what Claire knows, they could kill her just like they killed Dax and Samantha. They'll do anything to keep this secret."

Drakos leaned back in his chair, crossing his arms over his chest. "I don't think you should be involved with this. I'll take it from here. These miscreants might have seen you with Claire. Maybe they'll be coming after you."

"I can't just sit by and do nothing. Let me talk to Ava. I can ask her unofficially if she's familiar with these properties and it won't raise her suspicions. I'll say I'm looking into designing gardens in the area."

Drakos sighed and put his hands on the table. "Okay, go ahead and talk to her. Obviously, only show her a couple of addresses, minus the names."

"Right, I'll do that." Scranton stood, running a hand through his blond hair again. "We've got to find her."

Drakos looked down at his computer screen. He didn't want to see the anguish in Scranton's eyes.

***

"Good morning, Isabella."

Claire's eyes flew open. She was lying spread-eagled on her back.

"Good morning, Isabella," the Voice repeated. That was how she'd come to think of whoever this was…the Voice, with a capital V.

"I'm not Isabella." She rubbed her eyes.

"You are now. Introduce yourself as Isabella."

"Why?"

"Don't ask questions. Do as you are told."

Claire turned on to her side. She felt a wave of nausea.

"We've decided to give you a chance, if you agree to work with us."

"What does that mean?"

"You're attractive. You've got a good body. You could be an asset for us and join our stable of fillies. Anyway, recently we lost an uncooperative party girl."

Claire rubbed her eyes again. She felt a stab of fear. Who was she replacing? "I don't understand."

"You will attend our parties and provide entertainment for our guests."

Claire sat up. Dizziness rocked her, and she waited for it to pass. Sunlight was pouring through the narrow window, and she could see a thin slice of blue sky. Remembering what she'd decided last night, she made an effort to sound compliant. "I'll do whatever you say. I want to live. I'll be good."

"Remember, we will be watching you at all times. Do not question the other girls. They all know it is forbidden to talk about their previous lives."

"I'll do whatever you say. Thank you." She looked up at the camera and felt tears wet her cheeks.

"Take a shower now, Claire, and change your pajamas."

Claire got out of bed and went into the bathroom alcove. She showered and brushed her teeth. Then she changed into another pair of silk pajamas, with pink piping, that she found in the closet along with a matching silk bathrobe. As she was combing out her hair, the door opened. The Asian girl stood there, gesturing for her to come out of the room.

Claire exited her prison cell and found herself in a sort of rotunda. Ten doors around it opened on to the central area. On one side, a dining table was set for ten. On the other side of the round room were several white sofas and matching armchairs. There was a large TV screen and a stack of magazines on a glass table. Claire looked up and saw skylights that illuminated the room with natural light. She also noted several cameras focused on different areas of the room. Someone was always watching.

As Claire moved further into the round room, the other doors opened. Girls stepped out of them and walked toward the dining table. They smiled at Claire but showed no surprise or other real emotion. Like her, they all wore white silk pajamas with blue or pink piping. Claire figured none of them could be more than twenty years old. She was definitely a senior citizen here.

The Asian girl gestured to Claire to join the rest at the table. When they were all seated, a white-uniformed woman arrived with a trolley and dishes covered with silver domes. The woman put the dishes on the table and uncovered them. Along with scrambled eggs, there was a dish of fruit and whole wheat toast. The Asian girl poured them each a glass of orange juice. She stepped back, as the other woman did. The girls began to eat. There was little conversation except to ask someone to pass the eggs or the toast.

Claire looked nervously around the table. "Hello, my name is Isabella. I'm new."

The girls nodded and smiled at her. She looked across the table at one of them, maybe Lauren Reynolds. "What's your name?"

The girl looked at her uneasily and then glanced around the table, as though uncertain how to respond. Finally, she said, "I'm Lauren."

"Hi, Lauren. What about the rest of you?" Claire looked around the table. Shyly, they told her their names. Tammy was there, with her curly dark hair and petite body. As with Lauren, Claire recognized her from the photo at the Missing Persons department. Next to her was Ruby. Her voice held no inflection when she said her name. Claire wanted to go over and give her a hug, but didn't dare with the cameras active. The lively young woman who had become so real to Claire in her diary had turned into an anesthetized robot.

"Are we not supposed to talk?" Claire asked.

The girls looked at each other and then up at the cameras, their expressions like guilty schoolchildren. Claire's spirits sank. She had her answer.

At the end of the meal, the white-uniformed woman handed each of the girls a pink pill. The other girls swallowed it with a sip of water. Claire did likewise. She didn't want to take it, but she felt it was important to show she was falling in line.

Then they all stood and headed to their rooms. Claire got up and followed suit. When she entered her cell, the Voice came over the speaker. "Today, you will participate in yoga and aerobic exercise. Your workout clothes have been placed on your bed."

Claire saw that the bed had been made and a set of black yoga pants and a black tank top were laid out. She went into the bathroom to change. If she stood behind the partition close to the wall and in front of the toilet, she figured she wasn't in the camera's arc. Not that she knew what good that did her—yet—but it was something.

Back out in the rotunda, the other girls were standing in line, all dressed in black workout clothes. Two well-muscled, white-clad women were there, one in front and one in back of the line. They led the girls out through a metal door and along the parapet between the two towers. It was nice to be out in the sunshine, however briefly. Claire glanced towards the crenellated wall to her right. It reached her shoulders. Unless they walked right near the outer wall, they would not be visible from below. But the girls followed their leader, close to the inner wall.

They went through another metal door into the second tower and were ushered into an exercise room. Yoga mats were laid out on the floor. The Asian girl stood in the front of the room, dressed in a similar black yoga outfit. Each prisoner went to her assigned mat.

Claire walked over to the Asian girl. "I'm Claire—no, Isabella. What's your name?"

The girl gave her an empty gaze. Ruby piped up, "Her name is Mai Ling. She's deaf and dumb. You can't talk to her."

Claire smiled at Mai Ling. She needed to make friends with everyone. They all could be useful at some point. Mai Ling gestured to a mat, and Claire walked over and sat down. She looked around the space, feeling mellow and happy…yes, happy, in spite of the fact that she was a prisoner in some weird jail.

The yoga workout was vigorous. Claire noticed the other girls moved smoothly and with strength. They all had great bodies and worked hard. After they'd toweled down, they went into an adjacent alcove that was outfitted with five bikes and five treadmills. One of their white-clad guards put on a timer. Claire was ushered to a bike with four other girls and told to ride. The rest of the girls jogged on the treadmill. Then they switched. As she rode and jogged, Claire observed the other girls. They rode or ran like automatons, in complete silence. Their ponytails swung back and forth. Watching them, Claire thought they were exactly like a stable of thoroughbreds, as the Voice had said.

At one point, Claire tried to initiate a conversation with one of their female guards. "Hi, have you worked here long?"

"That is of no interest to you," the woman barked.

Both of their jailers wore white short-sleeved shirts and white pants. They were heavyset and muscular. Claire imagined they could wrestle her to the ground if she got out of line. Mai Ling was beautiful, with a kind expression, but the two guards in white had cold, hard features. They probably despised their attractive prisoners. Privately, Claire thought of them as twin Brunhildas. This made her giggle.

As she rode on the bike again, a warm glow of pleasure flowed over her. Being here wasn't so bad. She would be in shape and have no worries. She didn't know what else they would do that day but she didn't care. Looking up, she could see the bright blue sky. Looking forward through the narrow window, she could see a bit of the beach and the water. She smiled and turned to Ruby, who was riding at a terrific speed.

"This is fun." Then she started to laugh, for no reason at all.

Chapter 50

In the late afternoon after dismissing his work crew, Hobbs pulled into a parking spot in front of the Bramble Bay rental office. He was in luck; only Ava's Jeep was parked in front. He got out of his truck and clumped up the stairs and across the porch. He took off his muddy boots and left them by the door. Inside, he took off his hard hat. The front reception room was empty. He continued down the hall past the closed door to Harrison J. Reed's office and down to Ava's open door.

When he walked in, she was standing by the window, the phone to her ear. She gestured for him to sit down and continued her conversation. Hobbs sat and studied her. Today, Ava was dressed in Indian regalia. She wore a brown top with beadwork and fringe around the bottom. Her skirt was long, with more fringe. Around her neck was a turquoise beaded necklace. All she needed was a headband with a feather to join the tribe, he thought.

Once Ava was off the phone, she turned to Hobbs, her eyes glazed with concern. "God, what a tragedy. I'm so sorry about Claire. Tell me what you found when you went over there." She sat down behind her desk.

He told her about the scattered mail, the open door and the dropped purse. "It was obvious to me she'd been surprised and abducted. I called 9-1-1."

"What's the latest? Have you heard anything?"

"Not really. I think they've got the entire Sheriff's Department out on a hunt to find her, though."

Ava shook her head. "What could be going on? I mean, her husband was murdered and now they've gone after her. It's got to be drugs...maybe a bust that went wrong."

Hobbs shook his head. "I can't see Claire involved in that. It wouldn't make sense."

They were quiet for a minute. Then Hobbs pulled out a short list of addresses. He'd ascertained that most of the parties took place in ten homes. He had copied down just three addresses on a piece of paper, not wanting to arouse Ava's curiosity.

"Hey, I've got three houses that seem to be rentals, but I haven't been able to figure out who handles the properties. Somebody asked me about them...would you mind taking a look?" He felt himself blush. He wasn't adept at lying.

"Sure, no problem."

He pushed the paper across the desk to Ava. She frowned, then turned to her laptop and started typing. "One of these I know is Lilly Rose's. She's got some special clients...close friends." She scrolled down. "M-m-m, all three are her special accounts. They're only visible on the Lilly Rose Agency's internal site."

"What do you mean, they're her special accounts? What's the deal?"

"She handles those rentals exclusively. I guess the owners don't want just anyone in their houses. They probably have lots of valuables...something like that."

This information caused a silent explosion in his head. Lilly Rose Hamlin must be involved with the parties. Hobbs rubbed his chin, hoping his face wasn't giving him away.

Ava looked over at him, her grey eyes locked on his. "What is this really about?"

He shrugged. "I'm interested in their landscaping...might make a pitch to the owners."

Ava frowned, unconvinced.

***

After their workouts, the girls were weighed. Then they were led back to the other tower. Claire was told to go into her room and shower. A clean pair of white silk pajamas lay on her bed. She put them on, and then the door opened and she was ushered out to the dining area for a kale salad with grilled shrimp. It was delicious.

After lunch, Claire was told to return to her room. She lounged in a chair and picked up one of the novels laid out on the table. It was a title she'd heard about recently. She read avidly for an hour or two until the Voice came over the speaker.

"Hello, Claire. It was reported to me that you performed well this morning. We are proud of you. If you keep doing as you are told, your future looks bright."

Claire giggled. "Thank you, I feel great." She giggled again.

"Mai Ling will be taking you for a massage and a hair appointment. Enjoy your afternoon."

A minute or so later, Mai Ling opened the door and beckoned her forward. Claire followed the Asian girl out through the metal door and back to the tower where they'd done yoga. Besides the workout room, there were several cubicles. Claire was ushered into a small room with a massage bed in the middle. One of the Brunhildas stood beside the bed.

"Take off your clothes," the woman commanded.

Happily, Claire disrobed and lay down on the massage table. For the next half hour, she was pounded, pummeled and kneaded like a loaf of bread. After she put her pajamas back on, Mai Ling returned, and she was taken to another cubicle set up like a beauty salon with a black swivel chair. Mai Ling produced several bottles of shampoo and a color agent. Claire watched her, but the truth was she didn't really care what Mai Ling did. She closed her eyes and let her thoughts wander. Time flew by. When Mai Ling had finished blow-drying her hair, Claire opened her eyes and looked in amazement at the brunette in the mirror. Her hair was a rich dark brown with red highlights. Her eyebrows had become black swallowtails. It made her giggle again. Everything made her giggle.

While she was sitting there, one of the Brunhildas came in with a small box. She told Claire to lean back in the salon chair and open her eyes wide. The woman washed her hands and then she held Claire's left eye wide-open with two fingers and placed a contact lens in it. She did the same with Claire's right eye. When Claire next looked into the mirror, her eyes were dark brown. This sent her into gales of laughter. She looked like one of Lucca's Brazilian cousins. What a hoot.

Back in her cell, she spent several minutes admiring her new self in the bathroom mirror. Now she could be a spy, and no one would recognize her. She looked this way and that, viewing herself from every angle. Then she started to laugh.

Dinner was salmon and vegetables and a small dish of vanilla ice cream. The girls seemed to think this was a special treat.

"The food here is very healthy," Claire said.

"Yes, they want us to stay in shape and not get sick." Tammy slowly licked her spoon.

"Do you go outside sometimes?" Claire asked.

"For parties," another girl said. She glanced up at a camera and blushed.

Claire was lazily curious. "Tell me about the parties."

"We get dressed up," Lauren said.

Another girl added, "We take special pills and there's champagne at the party."

"What happens at the parties?" Claire asked.

A voice came from the speaker. "Girls, please get up now and go into the living room."

They did as ordered, Claire included. They watched Dirty Dancing on Netflix. Everyone was immersed in the movie, and no one talked much. After the movie, a Brunhilda appeared with pills for everyone, along with small glasses of a purple smoothie. Claire obediently swallowed her pill and drank the sweet drink.

Back in her room, she heard the turn of the lock. In the bathroom, she removed the contact lenses and put them in the little container they'd given her. Then she brushed her teeth and fell into bed. She yawned and felt a wave of fatigue pour over her. Those evening pills must be a potent sedative, she thought as she drifted into a deep sleep.

***

Hobbs sat in Drakos's office, waiting for the detective to return. He'd been doing a lot of thinking. Since he'd learned that Lilly Rose was involved in the management of the party houses, he felt pretty sure she must be involved in the actual sex parties as well. This led him to think about Senator Juniper. Claire had said Lilly Rose and Juniper had some special relationship that went back years. Apparently, they'd been in Washington together right out of college. He remembered when he and Claire had attended the house-warming party at Juniper's mansion; how amazed they'd been at all the famous people there. Juniper was well-connected. In his position as Senator, he used people and they used him. What had Claire said? It was a case of you rub my back, I'll rub yours.

So, what could he surmise? Lilly Rose and Juniper had to be at the center of the sex party organization. Juniper had the power and the connections. Lilly Rose must provide the locale and the girls. But where were the girls?

He got up and paced the room. He knew he was on to something.

Chapter 51

The following days were so similar, they blurred in Claire's mind: breakfast, yoga, bike and run, lunch, read, pedicure, manicure, a facial or massage or more exercise, dinner, video, sleep. Claire floated through the days feeling fuzzily happy. The only thing she missed was her phone and her computer.

On the second night, three girls were being readied for a party. That afternoon they had their hair done and got fresh manicures. At nine o'clock when Claire and the other seven girls were finishing the video, the three party girls exited their rooms. They looked fantastic: beautiful dresses, perfect make-up, full glossy hair, and they smelled divine. They made Claire think of Chinese courtesans. Everyone applauded as they left through the metal door. In the morning, they didn't appear for breakfast.

The girls were fed pills in the morning and at night. Claire drifted through the days without worries or concerns. One night, she dreamed that Dax had appeared and joined her in bed. His love-making had been different, he'd stroked her and quickly brought her to climax. In the morning, she wasn't sure if it had been a dream or real. She was sore and found her pajama bottoms on the floor. Had someone been in her room? Had she been raped? But in her drugged state, she didn't much care.

Every couple of days, some of the girls left for a party. They were dressed and primped before leaving. They all seemed excited and ready for the night.

On the morning of the sixth day, Claire slept late. When she awoke, she felt somewhat normal, although groggy. Knowing they could be watching her, she remained motionless, her face turned away from the camera, her eyes closed. Her heart began to race, and a sense of panic overcame her. Every day she was being drugged into a robotic state. The last five days, she had been happy but oblivious to what was going on around her. If she were ever to escape, she needed to refuse the pills, but she knew that if she did, they might kill her. Her survival depended on following the rules.

How could she avoid the pills when the Brunhildas, Mai Ling and the cameras were watching constantly? She wracked her brain. Memories of her father filled her mind…all the magic tricks he used to do, to entertain her and her friends when she was a kid. He had taught her some of the simpler sleight-of-hand tricks. She had gotten pretty good at making a coin disappear. Could she make those pills disappear? It was all about fooling the eye of the observer. She needed to practice, but she knew if she took her allotment of pills that morning, she would be too insanely happy to manage it.

She would have to make it happen without practice. As she opened her eyes, she heard the Voice.

"Good morning, Isabella. We are pleased with you. In a few days, you will attend a party. You will need to be on your best behavior."

"I will do whatever you want." Claire stretched and forced a happy smile.

The Voice chuckled. "Good girl."

She had a feeling she was being ridiculed. Someone was glad to have a docile, obedient Claire.

There was no time to practice her magic trick, but that morning she would try to make the pill disappear. If they caught her, she could just say she'd dropped it. During the breakfast of yogurt, berries and granola, she rehearsed in her mind the actions she would take. Her hand was shaking as she brought a spoonful of yogurt to her mouth, dreading the moment Brunhilda would hand her the pill.

When the moment came, she took the pill in her right hand. As she raised the glass of juice in her left hand to her mouth, she let the pill drop into the long sleeve of her pajamas. She swallowed the juice and let her right arm drop to her lap, where the pill rolled into her palm. She patted her mouth with a napkin and let the pill fall into the breast pocket of her pajama top. She looked up, sweat running down between her breasts. Without the happy pill, she needed to put on the best show of her life.

Claire went to her room to get ready for yoga, smiling all the way. In her room with the door closed, she went behind the bathroom partition and sat on the toilet seat. What should she do with this pill? She could flush it down the toilet, but maybe a stash of pills would come in handy in the future? But where could she hide them? Looking around the little bathroom, her eyes fell on the toilet paper dispenser.

Three rolls were threaded on a metal stick. She removed the top two rolls, took the pill from her pocket and pushed it between the cardboard roll and the white paper. Then she dropped the paper roll back to the bottom of the container and placed the other two rolls on top.

Still sweating profusely, she wiped her face and neck with a towel. Then she flushed the toilet and ran water in the sink. Back in the room, she walked lazily over to the bed where the yoga clothes were spread out, all the while aware that someone might be watching her every move.

***

Ajax Drakos hadn't wanted to listen to Hobbs Scranton when he brought up his theory: that Senator Juniper and Lilly Rose Hamlin were the masterminds behind the sex parties and maybe the murders of Chief Simmons and Samantha Marshall. But as he went over the details Scranton had enumerated, it began to seem plausible. The problem was, they had no real evidence and they both agreed that approaching Lilly Rose directly could backfire. She'd likely close down the organization, and they would be no closer to bringing her and Juniper to justice or finding Claire.

What Drakos wanted was to arrest Juniper and Lilly Rose and send them to jail.

Now here was Scranton, facing him across the desk, with a crazy idea…a crazy idea that might just work. He'd have to run it by Chief Kincaid, make sure they had back-up and coordination.

"We need to infiltrate the organization. We need someone to attend a party and bring us proof that Juniper and Lilly Rose are running a prostitution ring."

Drakos smiled wryly at the term "we." Apparently, Scranton had decided he was part of the police force. "What's your plan?"

"I've got a friend in Washington. He's a congressman. He's been there for a couple of years."

Drakos straightened a paper clip. "So?"

"His name is Clifford Huntington. We've known each other forever. He's a real straight arrow. We went through scouting together. I dropped out but he went on to become an Eagle Scout. He attended Yale and became a lawyer before he ended up in Washington."

Drakos concentrated on the paperclip. He began to fashion a pinwheel with the thin metal. "So…" he said.

"So I think we should get Cliff to attend party."

Chapter 52

After avoiding the pills, Claire's morning became a series of mine fields. It was essential that she appear drugged up and docile. She mimicked the facial expressions of the other girls as they went through their paces, doing her best to look like a happy-go-lucky robot. As the morning wore on, she became increasingly more alive. The drugs she'd taken before today were wearing off. She drank lots of water with the hope that she could flush the poison out of her system...poison that had so completely changed her personality. She was becoming increasingly angry at Mai Ling, the Brunhildas and whoever was the mystery voice...and Senator Juniper, who had to be in the mix.

Claire felt on edge much of the day. Playing a role for hours and never letting down her guard worked on her nerves and left her exhausted. At lunch she tried to keep her head down and her eyes on the food. She worried that her guardians would spot a change in her. During the free time after lunch, she kept her nose in a book.

Several more days went by. Each morning and evening, she palmed her pills. Time crawled at a snail's pace. Coping with this place had been easier when she was drugged up. One afternoon, after her massage, Mai Ling came into her room carrying a strapless, short red dress. Red was a color Claire wouldn't normally wear as a dishwater blond, but as a brunette with big dark eyes, it looked spectacular. Claire put the dress on and inspected herself in the closet mirror. She knew she'd lost weight, and her body was in great shape with the forced exercise routine. Mai Ling had also brought diamond-encrusted stilettos and diamond earrings. She smiled at Claire and gave her a thumbs-up.

Then the Voice came over the speaker. "You look sensational, Isabella. I think you will become a favorite of our clientele. Walk around for me, so I can see how you manage in high heels. Some of the girls have problems."

Claire walked slowly around the room, swaying her hips gently.

The Voice whistled. "Very nice. Very nice, indeed."

It hit her then and she almost tripped, catching herself before she fell. This experience made her think of Ruby and James, from Ruby's diary. Was James the voice over the speaker? It had to be. He had lured all those girls here and imprisoned them. Anger bubbled up. No, she couldn't show emotion. She clenched her hands in tight fists.

"Are you all right?" the Voice snapped.

"Yes, I'm fine." She looked up at the camera and willed a slow, sensuous smile. "I love the dress."

"Good, it looks fabulous. Maybe you better practice walking in those shoes."

"When will I go to a party like the other girls?"

"Soon. Very soon."

Mai Ling helped her undress and took the clothes out of the room.

***

After the meeting with Detective Drakos, Hobbs lost no time in calling a familiar D.C. number. Three rings, and then Cliff Huntington's voice came over the line. "Hey, Hobbs, how are you, man?"

"Me? I'm fine, never better. How's Washington?"

Cliff sighed. "Frustrating. I ran for office because I truly thought I could change things in the Capitol. But it's incredibly difficult to get anything done. My fellow congressmen are more concerned about getting reelected than doing the right thing."

"I hear you, man. From the news, it sounds like there's a stalemate in Congress. How are Louise and the kids?"

"I miss them. Louise thought she should keep the home fires burning instead of relocating with me, but I'm lonely. I've got this studio apartment here in Washington, but I don't even want to go home at night."

"Maybe you need to rethink the course your life is taking."

"Yeah, maybe. Sorry, you got me at a low point. I am grateful to have been elected. But why are you calling? I'm sure it wasn't to hear me bitching."

Hobbs tensed up. "Have you heard about any parties lately?"

"Parties…as in political parties?"

"No." He breathed deep and took the plunge. "Parties in Florida. With call girls."

Cliff started laughing. "Are you thinking an orgy will solve my problems?"

"Not quite…"

Cliff chuckled for a moment longer, then broke off. "As a matter of fact, now I think about it, last week I was at a fundraiser for the President and I happened to walk by Senator Juniper. He was having a conversation with Willard Barnes, the senior Senator from Montana. They were talking about a party."

Hobbs's heart beat faster. This was incredible luck. "What did they say, exactly?"

"I didn't really listen. I was just passing by. It sounded like some in-joke, Hobbs. I don't really know either of those Senators well."

"But you remember their exchange. Why do you think that is?"

"Hmmm." Cliff paused, as if evaluating his reaction. "I guess it was their behavior. Looking left and right as they talked, like my kids being naughty and hoping they won't get caught. I don't know. That sounds over-dramatic."

"I'm going to tell you a story." Hobbs explained to Cliff what had occurred on the Emerald Coast; the murders of Chief Simmons and Samantha Marshall, the parties, the list with its well-known names on the USB drive, and finally about Claire's abduction and Juniper's possible involvement. When he'd finished, there was silence on the other end.

"Cliff, are you there?"

"Yes, I am. This is a lot to get my head around."

"We need your help. That's why I called. We need someone to attend a party so we can nail those responsible. You'd be perfect."

Cliff went silent again. Hobbs could imagine him thinking, chewing on his bottom lip like he had when they were kids.

"So, you want me to get invited to one of these parties?"

"Yes. The detective working the case went to the new sheriff, Chief Kincaid. The department's brought in the FBI. If you agree, they'll get in touch with you."

"Will it be dangerous?"

"They don't think so. You'll just be the decoy to get inside the house where the party is. Then they'll move in."

More silence. Cliff was still thinking it through. Then, slowly, he said, "Okay, I'll do it. But I don't want to get caught with some hooker. What if my constituents got wind of it?"

Relief made Hobbs feel weak in the knees. "It won't get to that. Thanks, Cliff."

Chapter 53

Claire was beginning to give up hope. Every day felt incredibly long. She had to be hyper-vigilant to maintain her cover. Each morning, when she slipped the pill down her sleeve, she lived in mortal fear of discovery. One false move and they would be on to her.

One day, a tall redhead named Cleo freaked out after a party night. Without any warning, she got up from the breakfast table, kicked back her chair and began to scream. She ran for the elevator door and pounded on it. "I want out. Let me out."

Within minutes, both Brunhildas were on her. They grabbed her and threw her to the floor. Claire heard a crack as Cleo's head hit the ground. She was still screaming as they dragged her to her cell and locked her in. They left the rotunda, and came back minutes later with Mai Ling, who carried a hypodermic. Cleo didn't appear again for a couple of days. When she finally showed up again at breakfast, she looked like a zombie. She'd lost weight and her hair hung lank around her pale face. Claire reached out under the dining table and squeezed Cleo's hand, but the girl was unresponsive.

Claire never saw the Voice, but she felt the weight of his presence. Or was it several people that were watching her? The thought of some unknown number of scummy goons staring at her on a monitor made her stomach turn. She and the other girls were like lab rats. Every day, they came out of their cages and had to run on a treadmill or ride the bikes, just like hamsters running nowhere on a wheel.

Lying in bed each night, she went through the events of the day, trying to imagine how she could escape. Each time she came to the same dispiriting conclusion. Only a party would provide the opportunity to get away.

***

Hobbs was getting out of his truck at the gas station when his phone rang. It was Cliff.

"It's tomorrow night. I'm going to a party," Cliff said.

"How did it go down?"

"I talked to a guy who's pals with Barnes. Barnes's secretary called me and said a woman would be getting in touch. A few minutes later, some woman with a Southern accent called. She told me there'd been a cancellation and there was a vacancy for a party tomorrow night. She asked if I could come down to Florida for a fabulous evening. I said yes. She asked me how I'd heard about these private events. I kept it vague, told her, 'Just around the Senate floor.' Then I said my wife was back home and I needed company."

"She believed you?"

"Yes, but here's the kicker. It costs three thousand dollars for this evening of fun."

Hobbs's eyes widened. "Wow."

"She wanted the money transfer immediately. My contact from the FBI made the funds available to me."

"Do you think they did a background check to see if you were on the up and up?"

"Probably. I don't know. It seemed like fast approval."

"Did she say where this party would take place?"

"No. They're going to pick me up at the hotel and take me to some house. It's all very hush hush."

"What about the FBI? What have they told you?"

"I'll have a wire, and agents will be following me at all times. Once I'm in place, they'll close in."

***

That morning, Claire woke up to the Voice. "Good morning, Isabella. Tonight, you will attend a party."

She knew she had to put on the best act of her life. The party offered her a chance to escape. But she had no idea where she would be going, who would be there and what would happen. She was pretty sure there'd be several important, rich men, and her job would be to entertain them and probably go to bed with them. Could she just blurt out that she was a prisoner? Would somebody be watching her all the time? She shivered. Probably.

The morning crept by even more slowly than usual. When she went into her room after yoga, she turned on the shower. While the water ran, she sat on the toilet seat and removed the roll of toilet paper that contained the pills she'd been hoarding…the morning happy pills and the nighttime sleeping pills. She shook the sleeping pills into her hand and then rolled them in a piece of toilet paper. That night when she left for the party, she would tuck them in the bodice of her dress or in her shoe. Maybe she could pop them into someone's drink.

Sitting there with the twist of paper in her hand, she admitted the truth to herself. James and Juniper were running a high-end prostitution ring. Deep down, Claire feared she'd be raped by one of tonight's party guests. She hadn't really acknowledged it until now, but her captors were her pimps, grooming her as a drugged-up call girl. She buried her head in her hands and soundlessly let the tears flow. Getting through this day and night would be difficult. She had to escape.

In the late afternoon, Claire was taken to the massage room. They shaved her legs, plucked her eyebrows and waxed other parts of her body, then rubbed her all over with a lavender body lotion. Now that she was alert and aware, having Brunhilda's strong hands caressing her was an embarrassment. After the cream was rinsed off, her skin felt smoother and softer than it ever had.

Mai Ling washed and conditioned her hair, and styled it into smooth waves around her face. Next came her make-up, expertly applied.

Finally, the beauty ordeal ended. Mai Ling led Claire into the hall, where they met Ruby and Lauren. Both girls looked exquisite; they must have gotten the same treatment. Brunhilda gave them all a glass of purple smoothie and a new pill, a different color from the usual ones. When Brunhilda turned to pour more smoothie for Ruby, Claire managed to slip the pill into her pocket. She wondered if it was a form of ecstasy. After their snack, they were led back across the parapet to the tower where their bedrooms were. It was already getting dark.

Back in her room, Claire found the strapless red dress on a hanger with the stiletto heels placed underneath. On her bed, someone had laid out black lacy underwear and a small box. Claire smiled at it all and forced a giggle. In the bathroom, she slipped out of her pajamas and put on the underwear and the dress. Padding in bare feet, she went back into the bedroom and opened the box. It contained the diamond earrings she'd seen before and a thin diamond tennis bracelet. She wondered if these were real. As she put on the earrings, the Voice came over the speaker.

"Good evening, Isabella. Tonight, you will be entertaining some guests."

Claire glanced up at the camera, trying to look dull-minded and happy. "That'll be fun." She giggled.

"You are to do whatever our guests desire. Whatever they want. Do you get that?"

Claire nodded as she fiddled with the clasp on the bracelet.

"We will be with you at all times. Your dress has a tiny microphone chip sewn in it, so we will hear every word you say. You'll never be alone."

Claire frowned as though this was too much to understand. Internally, she felt a pang of terror. How would she escape, if they were listening to her and following her every move? Oh God, she pleaded, please help me.

"Do you understand, Isabella? We will be with you. You will not talk about where you live. You will not use your real name. You will make our guests happy."

She smiled up at the camera. "Yes, I'll make the guests happy. I will be good."

"If you don't do as you're told, you will be punished. Do you understand?"

Color drained from Claire's face. "Please, no, I'll be good."

"Good girl, Isabella."

When the Voice fell silent, she put on her shoes and walked into the bathroom. How much could they hear with this microphone in her dress? She turned on the water, sat on the toilet, retrieved the sleeping pills and slipped them into her bra. Then she flushed the toilet and turned off the water.

A minute later, Mai Ling knocked on the door. She gestured for Claire to follow her. As Claire exited the room, the seven girls staying behind applauded.

"Have fun!" they shouted.

Trembling slightly, Claire smiled and waved her hand. She, Ruby and Lauren started for the elevator.

Chapter 54

Ajax Drakos sat in a van with four FBI agents. All five men wore riot gear and silently watched a couple of video screens. One showed the gate across the private road into Senator Juniper's estate. A car was hidden in the driveway down the street from the mansion, as well as a nondescript vehicle waiting on 30A. They would take turns following any car that exited the place. Juniper was the key to the lucrative sex parties, along with Lilly Rose Hamlin. Drakos felt sure of it. A car was hidden down the road from her driveway as well. There were too many signs that led to both of them.

The third screen showed the entrance to the Watercolor Inn, where Cliff Huntington was staying. He'd arrived earlier in the day and an agent had met with him, posing as a room-service waiter in case Cliff was being watched. The agent had gone through the protocol and procedures devised for the operation and had outfitted him with a wire. The agents in the van would be able to follow Cliff wherever he went and listen to his conversations. He'd been shown pictures of Claire, Tammy Schulz, Lauren Reynolds and Ruby Branson, in case any of them were attending this party. At the moment, it sounded like he was pacing his hotel room.

Things were moving fast. Drakos felt adrenaline pumping through his veins. Soon, he hoped, this nightmare would be over. In the last few days, he had learned from the lab techs that the DNA on the lacy pink underpants from Dax Simmons's wall safe matched the DNA of a girl from Missouri who had gone missing. He wondered if her body was buried somewhere in Bramble Bay. In addition, he'd learned the thumb drive had Samantha Marshall's and Dax's prints on it, meaning they'd seen the list and had known all about the parties.

He glanced around, working out a crick in his neck. His gaze fell briefly on Hobbs Scranton. The landscaper had wanted to be in on the sting tonight. Tarantino, the chief FBI official, was glad enough to get his information and cooperation, but said he didn't have the clearance to participate in the operation. After a lot of back and forth with Drakos and Chief Kincaid, Tarantino reluctantly agreed that Scranton could sit in the van, but he was forbidden to leave it. Drakos knew his chief interest was Claire. They were both hoping against hope to find her safe and unharmed.

It was nearly ten o'clock, the time when Cliff was supposed to be picked up. As they watched, a black SUV pulled up to the entrance of the Watercolor Inn. Minutes later, they heard a buzz and then Cliff's voice. "I'll be right down."

Drakos looked at the other guys. "Here we go."

Just then, the gate across the private road rolled open. A black stretch limousine pulled out and started down Lemon Cove Drive. Drakos looked over at Tarantino who gave him a thumbs up. They'd been right. Juniper must be attending the party as well.

Now they could see Cliff entering the SUV. His voice sounded inside the surveillance van: "Hi, thanks for picking me up." No one in the SUV answered him. "Is the party nearby?" No response. Apparently, the driver wasn't going to be dragged into a conversation.

On the monitor, Drakos saw both vehicles were heading down 30A. They weren't far from each other. They went through Seaside and on towards Seagrove.

Tarantino nodded toward the agent in the driver's seat. "Follow them."

***

Claire, Ruby and Lauren stood silently in the elevator as it descended several floors. A Brunhilda accompanied them. When the doors opened, they exited the elevator and walked down a short hall. Their heels clicked on the cement floor. Brunhilda pulled open a door at the end of the hallway and they entered a garage. A stretch limousine awaited them. Claire recognized two of Juniper's bodyguards standing by the car. The men stared at the girls as if they were pieces of meat.

"Get in," one guy said. He held open a rear door. Ruby and Lauren slid into the back seat. The guard took Claire around to the other side of the car. He patted her backside and she wanted to turn around and slap him, but she giggled instead. She had to play her part.

One guard sat across from them in the back of the car. Claire could see the bulge of a gun under his light jacket. The other guard sat next to the driver in front. The garage door opened, and the car pulled out onto Lemon Cove Drive. Claire couldn't see anything, because the windows were opaque. The guy in front pulled open the divider between the front seats and the back. "You got the address?" he asked the driver.

"Yeah, I put it in the GPS. But we've been there before."

"What's the plan, Mack?" the bodyguard in back asked, in a distinct Southern drawl.

"I'm going inside," Mack said. "Lou here will stick to the front of the house near the car. You'll cover the back."

"Hope they've got some nice deck chairs."

"Don't lie down. You can't fall asleep. You never know if the place is being watched."

Mack closed the divider. Claire felt the car turn onto 30A and head east. Where were they going? A wave of panic rolled over her. She had to gain control. She squeezed her hands tightly together.

The bodyguard reached over and slid his hand up Claire's thigh. "Man, I'd like to get a piece of this ass."

Claire pushed his hand away. Then she giggled, the same chirpy giggle she'd been faking for days.

Mack turned in his seat and pushed the divider back again. "Hands off the merchandise, Clive. H. J. is probably listening. You know the girls are wired."

Clive pulled his hand away. "I'm horny just sitting back here with the three of them."

Lauren and Ruby started laughing. Ruby reached out and touched Clive's crotch. Clive groaned.

"Cut it out, girls," Mack said. "Save it for the party." He slammed the divider shut.

Ruby lifted her hand and licked her lips. Then she giggled.

They drove for ten or fifteen minutes, then turned off 30A towards the Gulf. The car stopped, and Lou rolled down the window and spoke to someone. They'd come to a gated community, Claire guessed.

Moments later, they pulled up in front of a house. Mack and Lou got out of the car and came around to open the doors. Claire could see lights blazing in the entryway to the house. As she got out of the car, a black SUV pulled up.

***

Cliff couldn't get much conversation out of his driver. After fifteen minutes, they turned off 30A and drove up to an open gate. A car in front of them went through, and Cliff's driver pulled up to the gate house. He gave an address Cliff couldn't catch. They were waved through and went down a winding road, then turned off down a narrow lane. At the end was a huge house all lit up.

Some joint, Cliff thought. He wondered who lived in the house, and did they know about these parties? Maybe they got a cut of the three thousand dollars. Back in his hotel room, he'd thought about the money. Who would pay that much for a roll in the hay? Were these girls specially trained to provide kinky sex? It all seemed ridiculous to him. But maybe if you had big bucks, three thousand dollars seemed worth it.

As they pulled up to the house, he noticed a limousine stopped near the front door. A couple of big linebackers got out of the car, followed by three girls. Cliff swallowed hard. He had to put on a good show until the FBI agents broke up the party. He wasn't shy and knew how to carry himself in new situations, but what he was about to do this evening rattled him.

Cliff opened the door before the chauffeur came around. As he stepped out of the car, he found himself standing behind a dark-haired woman in a red mini-dress. It wasn't something Louise would ever wear. This girl had long legs and a slim build. They walked together towards the short flight of stone steps that led up to the entranceway. He felt tongue-tied. His usual gift of repartee had escaped him.

The girl turned to look at him. She had big brown eyes and thick wavy hair. She looked as uncertain of herself as he felt. He thought he glimpsed a flash of fear in her eyes. This wasn't the hardcore hooker he'd imagined. He held out his hand.

"Hello, I'm Cliff." He'd been told not to mention his last name.
"Isabella." Her hand felt cold and sweaty.
"Lovely night."
"Yes," she said softly. She smiled at him. She looked vaguely familiar. Had he met this girl somewhere before?

A bodyguard herded them into the foyer and shut the door behind them. Cliff looked around. They stood in a high-ceilinged room with a coral-colored marble floor. Massive potted palms stood in the corners. A porcelain life-sized tiger sat under one leafy plant, a lion under another. A curved, white-carpeted staircase led up to the floor above. There were doors off to the right and straight ahead, but the rooms beyond were in darkness. To the left, Cliff saw a spectacular living room. The strains of a smooth love song flowed out from it. What was that song, he wondered?

A pretty Asian girl appeared in the living-room doorway and gestured for them to enter. He noticed Isabella seemed to hesitate at the threshold. The decor in the room was eclectic, but it all hung together. Over the mantelpiece was a huge picture of water and flowers. Groupings of sofas and armchairs, white with accents in orange and yellow, dotted the space. A man was seated on one sofa already, and a blond girl hurried over to him. Another guy stood by the fireplace, his hands behind his back. Cliff felt sure he'd seen this man before, maybe on the cover of Fortune magazine. Another girl headed toward Fireplace Man. Cliff couldn't be sure, but he thought he recognized the girls from the pictures the FBI agent had shown him. Maybe Ruby Branson and one of the other ones?

He glanced over at Isabella. It looked like they would be an item tonight. She hovered at the threshold of the living room, seemingly reluctant to go any further.

What was he supposed to do next?

***

Claire looked around the room. A spectacular Monet hung over the fireplace. It must be worth a fortune. Already, Lauren and Ruby had found companions. Claire did a double take when she looked across the room. Lauren was cuddled up on the sofa with Oscar Snell…Oscar, her dad's friend. The thought that he participated in this kind of thing disgusted her. He looked up and right at her but didn't recognize her. Of course, he didn't. She'd become a brunette. He pulled Lauren closer and she nuzzled his neck. They kissed, and Claire heard Lauren's high-pitched giggle. She felt herself blush.

The guy she came in with seemed nice enough, but he might have a dark side when it came to sex. Sudden angst flowed over her. It was hard to breathe. She needed air.

"Are you all right?" Cliff asked.

They can hear every word I say. "I…I…I just feel a little faint."

"Come sit down over here." He led her to an armchair. "Do you want some water?"

Claire thought about the Voice. It would not approve if she fainted. She forced a laugh and tried to sound vivacious. "No water. How about a glass of champagne?"

"Are you sure? You look a little pale."

"Nothing like champagne to make things right," she chirped.

After Cliff left, Claire glanced around the room. Along with the drinks cart, there was a table laden with plates of hors-d'oeuvres. Claire could see oysters, caviar and what looked like a platter of carpaccio di manzo.

She snuck a glance at the other two couples. Oscar's hands were moving over Lauren's body as they snuggled together on a sofa. Across from them, Ruby was sitting close to the other man, gazing up at him adoringly. He had his hand on her thigh. In his other hand was a martini. He was a big guy who radiated arrogance that matched his expensive clothes and Gucci loafers. His watch sparkled with diamonds. Where had she seen this guy before? It hit her a second later. The guy was Cyrus Baker, Consuelo's husband. She remembered Cyrus ogling her at Juniper's housewarming party and shivered with disgust.

Mai Ling brought Oscar a glass of Scotch and took away an empty tumbler. Oscar put the drink to Lauren's lips, and she took a long sip. Oscar licked her lips and she giggled. Claire closed her eyes, not wanting to watch any more. Oscar was an intelligent man with a wife, children and grandchildren. What did he see in this drugged-up girl who seemed to have nothing between her ears?

She opened her eyes and looked away from Oscar and Lauren. Cyrus and Ruby were snorting a line of coke. Claire turned away from them too and took several deep breaths. How would she get through this evening and how would she escape?

Cliff returned with two flutes of champagne. He sat in the armchair next to her. So far, he didn't expect her to sit on his lap. He handed her a glass. She took a sip. "Thanks, I just love champagne."

Silence fell. What were they supposed to talk about? She couldn't reveal anything about herself and he probably didn't want to tell her much about himself.

"Where do you come from?" Claire asked. She took a longer sip of champagne. She felt like downing the entire glass and getting more, anything to deaden her fears. But she needed to remain alert if she was going to escape this madness.

"Washington area. How about you?"

"Minneapolis." Why had she said that? She'd never been there.

"Nice city, but cold."

"Right."

Silence. Claire felt someone's gaze on her. She turned to look across the room. Cyrus was giving her the once-over. She turned back to Cliff. "What music do you like to listen to?" she blurted out.

"I'm pretty much an '80s guy. The Police, Guns N' Roses…"

That was music from before her time, but she recognized the artists. "Like 'Every Breath You Take'. I like that song." What were they going to talk about now?

A strong hand grabbed her arm. Shocked, Claire looked up. Cyrus Baker stood there, staring down at her. She could smell the alcohol on his breath.

"You don't mind, right?" he said to Cliff. "I want her now. You can have her later." He pulled Claire to her feet and held her arm tight. "Let's go upstairs. I want to rip that little red dress right off of you."

Chapter 55

The FBI van turned off 30A and headed toward the site where the party was taking place. Three other units had gone through the guard house already. The FBI had posted an agent in the guard house to control comings and goings. Another agent was stationed down the street from the party house. A third FBI vehicle was parked on the next street over, so they could come in from the back.

Cliff's voice came over the speaker. He was talking to a woman. When she answered him— "What music do you like to listen to?"— Hobbs Scranton looked at Drakos, eyes wide. "That's her. That's Claire. I recognize her voice. She's alive."

Drakos nodded. "Let's hope. We can't be sure."

The glimmer of relief left Hobbs's face. "They're using her to make money. She's one of their call girls. We've got to get her out of there. Someone should go in there now." He stood up in the narrow space between the seats.

"Sit down," Tarantino barked.

Reluctantly, Hobbs sat back down. He gripped his knees, leaning forward, his body tense. "What are we waiting for?"

"We've got to be sure everyone's arrived for the party before we move in."

Drakos thought they were in luck. If Claire was paired off with Cliff, she would be safe. Only, why didn't Cliff recognize her? They'd shown him plenty of pictures of her as well as the other three missing girls. Maybe Hobbs was wrong. Maybe the woman wasn't Claire.

Another voice sounded...a man's voice, muffled. "I want to rip that little red dress right off of you."

Hobbs looked at Drakos. "That's not Cliff. Who is that? What's happening?"

The van drove through the gate. As the agent posted in the guard house waved them on, the driver said to Tarantino, "Sir, another car just pulled up in front of the house. A woman is getting out. She's heading for the front door."

***

Cyrus was big and strong. He started up the stairs to the bedrooms, pulling Claire along behind him. Mai Ling scurried in front of them. She pointed to an open door. Cyrus shoved Claire inside, then followed her and slammed the door behind him.

She barely had time to register a few details—bed, sitting area, drinks table—before Cyrus grabbed her arms. "Man, you are hot. Just what the doctor ordered." He pulled her into an embrace, tight against his body. His mouth was on hers and his tongue slid between her teeth. He tasted of gin. With one hand, he reached down and yanked up the hem of her dress. His hand moved up her leg. When she felt him reach her panties, she managed to push him away.

"Hey, let me have a moment to freshen up." She managed a giggle. "Can you wait that long?" She knew the microphone in her skimpy dress must be picking up everything they said and did. Maybe there was a camera in this room, too. She looked up and scanned the ceiling. It could be anywhere.

"I can't wait too long. Ya'll hurry up." He smiled down at her, his breath boozy and his eyes unfocused.

Claire looked around the room. It was a large space, decorated in deep shades of burgundy and grey. On the far side, French doors led out to a balcony. The bed was king-sized, the sitting area off to one side. The drinks table held bottles of alcohol, more champagne, and snacks. "Why don't you get a drink while I'm gone?" She forced herself to reach up and kiss Cyrus on the cheek. He grabbed her bottom and pulled her back into a boozy embrace. Again, she pushed him away.

The bathroom was off to the right. Claire went to it and closed herself inside, locked the door, and leaned against it, taking deep breaths. The bathroom held an enormous tub, a marble and glass shower stall, gold fixtures, and thick towels. On the back of the door hung two silk bathrobes with blue piping. They made her think of the pajamas back at her prison cell. Anger flooded through her. This was her chance. She had to escape.

Thinking fast, she went over to the sink and turned on the water. Next, she removed her heels, unzipped her dress and took it off. She folded the dress and stuffed it under the sink. So much for the microphone. She put on one of the silk robes.

Across the room, above the tub, was an oval-shaped window. Claire climbed on the edge of the tub and looked down. Below, she could see a deck and a swimming pool. The window was decorative and couldn't be opened. Could she break it and jump? She had no way of knowing the depth of the pool. She'd probably kill herself.

She climbed back down, trying to calm her racing nerves and think. Maybe she'd have to have sex with this guy, but if she could put some of her hoarded sleeping pills in his drink, he would be out, and then she could escape. She removed the small packet from her bra and placed it on the counter, unwrapped the pills, picked up one of her stiletto heels, and started grinding one pill into powder.

A heavy knock came at the door. "Hurry up in there. Get the fuck out here."

"Just a minute," she yelled back.

She ground up four more pills, then wiped the powder into the square of toilet paper, twisted it closed and placed it in the pocket of the robe. Then she turned off the running water. Taking a deep breath, she opened the door.

Cyrus was standing by the open French doors, buck naked, with a drink in his hand. He looked over at her.

"You're different than the other girls," he said, frowning. "Get your cute little ass over here."

Claire walked slowly over to him and gave her practiced giggle. "Of course, I'm different. I'm special."

He put his drink down and reached out, grabbing her into another bear hug and sloppy kiss. She could feel his body heat and his erection through the thin material of the robe. He pulled her towards the bed. Then he fell backwards onto the mattress and she fell on top of him.

Just as he reached down to pull off her panties, they heard banging, yelling and screaming.

"Waz' that?" Cyrus said. Momentarily, he stopped his assault.

Claire heard heavy footsteps and pounding on the door. She pulled herself away just as the door flew open and a big man in riot gear stomped into the room.

***

The FBI van's high beams lit up the driveway. Two agents jumped out of the back and quickly seized the security guard standing by a limousine. Other agents stormed the house, charging up the front steps and bursting into the mansion. Drakos crossed the bricked driveway behind them. He could see lights flashing from the back of the house and heard shouts. As he approached the open front door, he turned on the top step and saw Hobbs following in his wake.

"You better get back in the van. You know what Tarantino said."

Hobbs shook his head. "What if they arrest her or shoot her? I want to be there."

"Hobbs, this is an order. Get back in the van."

"No. I'm going in."

His tone said he wouldn't be deterred. Drakos shrugged. It wasn't his call. Hobbs would have to deal with Tarantino.

Together, they entered the front hall. It was enormous, with jungle plants, tropical trees and life-like porcelain animals. Two officers were pounding up an elegant, curved staircase. Another pair of FBI agents had taken down a well-muscled security guard and slapped him in handcuffs. Tarantino stood on the threshold of the living room, as if momentarily taken aback by the scene. A blond girl wearing only lacy black underwear and high heels was dancing to "Blurred Lines" by Thicke, which blared from some speakers, her body swaying, her arms over her head. Across from her, Cliff jiggled to the beat. On the other side of the room another scantily glad girl sat on the lap of a chubby bald guy. She seemed to be feeding him sushi rolls as his hands caressed her body.

Suddenly the music stopped. The dancing girl looked over at them and froze. Cliff turned, a look of relief on his face. The chubby guy's mouth was open like a monstrous baby bird. The other girl turned to look as well, her mouth forming an O. To Drakos they created a bizarre tableau.

Tarantino barked, "Okay, all of you, get dressed and get out your identification."

From an alcove, a woman in a low-cut green dress strode into the living room. A beautiful Asian girl followed a few steps behind her. "What are you doing? This is a private party. I would ask that you leave immediately."

Drakos recognized Lilly Rose Hamlin. He'd never met her, but he'd seen her picture plenty. Apparently, Tarantino had too. The FBI man stepped toward her. "Ms. Lilly Rose Hamlin you are arrested for..."

Lilly Rose backed away, screaming obscenities. Tarantino and another agent, handcuffs at the ready, closed in. When Tarantino grabbed Lilly Rose's arm, she fought his grip and tried to bite the agent who was struggling to lock the cuffs around her wrists. Drakos tensed, ready to join the fray, but the losing battle was over in seconds. When they finally led her out the front door to the waiting squad car, she screamed, "If you're arresting me, you better arrest Juniper. He and Harrison Reed better not get away."

As several more officers dealt with the girls in the living room, Drakos headed toward the staircase. On the landing above, a dark-haired girl in a short, white silk robe stared down at them. She was accompanied by an agent in riot gear. Tears streamed down her face as she descended the stairs. In a trembling voice, she said, "Hobbs, you found me. Thank God."

Hobbs stared up at her. A frown furrowed his brow. Then his eyes lit up in recognition and he took the stairs two at a time.

Chapter 56

One week after the raid, Claire and Hobbs sat at the kitchen island with glasses of wine, talking while they waited for Detective Drakos to arrive. The detective had interviewed Claire several times after the arrests. Tonight, he was coming over to talk about Dax and Samantha.

Claire fidgeted with the hem of the loose white sweater she wore over black tights. Her hair, still dark brown from the dye job before the party, was pulled back from her pale face, and dark circles ringed her eyes.

"Harrison James Reed," Claire murmured, gazing at her wine glass. "I should have figured out Harrison was the infamous 'James' Ruby wrote about. The night we went out for dinner, he was so smooth. I should have recognized his slimy persona." She looked up at Hobbs, pain reflected in her eyes. "I even thought I was attracted to him."

Hobbs reached over and held her hand. "Don't do this to yourself. That guy was a master con man."

Claire nodded and squeezed his fingers. "Anyway, Drakos told me that after they arrested Lilly Rose, the FBI raided the castle that same night. The Brunhildas and the security guards were arrested, and they rescued the other girls."

"Do you know what happened to the other girls?"

"I understand they've been placed in a drug rehab program. They were all pretty screwed up."

"What about Juniper and Harrison? How did they catch them?"

"Senator Juniper was arrested by FBI agents in his Washington townhouse. Apparently, Lilly Rose fingered him as an accomplice in the prostitution ring."

"Right, I was there. She was crazy mad, yelling like a banshee. She wanted to make sure Juniper and Harrison didn't get off."

Despite the grim topic of conversation, the image of a crazy mad Lilly Rose made Claire laugh. Lilly Rose Hamlin had always been so controlled, the perfect lady. Claire caught Hobbs's eye and they both cracked up. It relieved some of the tension.

When they'd calmed down, Hobbs asked, "And Harrison?"

Claire wiped her eyes with a tissue. "They arrested him at the Panama City Beach airport. He was headed for the Grand Cayman Islands."

Hobbs considered this. "I bet they stashed all their money there."

Claire nodded. "Juniper and Lilly Rose had been in cahoots since their days as interns in Washington. Back then, they provided drugs to congressmen, senators and their staffers. Later, when Lilly Rose settled on the Emerald Coast, she invited the Senator down. They continued a quiet drug business along 30A, but Lilly Rose wanted to branch out. She dreamed up the idea of running an ultra-exclusive brothel. The Senator would supply the johns and she would supply the girls. Initially, they hired local prostitutes, but the girls weren't trained and didn't provide the 'luxurious experience' Lilly Rose desired."

Claire got up and began to pace. "Not long afterward, Harrison Reed joined the real estate team, and one thing led to another. At first, he and Lilly Rose were lovers, then Lilly Rose brought him into their little business. It was his idea to coach an elite troop of beautiful girls in the sexual arts."

Clearly sensing her distress, Hobbs said, "You don't have to tell me anymore."

"No, I want to tell you everything." She continued to pace. "Initially, the call girls were kept in an old house in Panama City, but Lilly Rose worried about raids, and the milieu wasn't elegant and excusive enough. So they moved the girls into the towers of Juniper's castle, even before construction was complete."

Claire took a breath. More quietly, she said, "Harrison lured young girls without close family ties. They fell in love with him. He provided them with drugs and turned them into sex slaves. Once they were hooked, they were imprisoned in the castle." She stopped and looked into Hobbs's eyes. The sympathy she saw there gave her strength to continue. She tore her gaze away and went back to pacing.

"With a growing real estate business, Lilly Rose decided to take advantage of the high-end rentals she handled exclusively for a select group of owners. She knew when the houses were vacant and had the keys. Her maid service set the houses up for the parties and cleaned up when the party was over. All of those women were Latinas and undocumented, and Lilly Rose threatened deportation if they didn't keep quiet about their work for her."

"What a monster," Hobbs said.

Claire shivered and wrapped her arms around her chest. "It was one of those women who cleaned the crime scene in the house in Watercolor and found the bloody underpants...the ones I ran across later, in the office safe. She took a chance and sent the panties to Samantha Marshall, in an envelope with the address of the house and the word PARTY. About the same time, Ruby sent the list of parties to Samantha that she'd photographed off James's iPad. Samantha contacted Dax, and together they visited the Watercolor party house."

Her agitation was giving her the shakes, and she stopped talking. Hobbs got up, came over and wrapped his arms around her.

***

Drakos arrived right on time and Hobbs went down to let him in. After the customary greetings, they sat down; Claire and Hobbs on the sofa and Drakos across from them in an armchair.

Notebook in hand, Drakos began. "Through the interrogations of Lilly Rose Hamlin, Senator Lucius Juniper and Harrison James Reed, we've learned what happened to Dax and Samantha. Are you ready to hear it?"

Claire nodded and swallowed. Hobbs took her hand, but she pulled it away.

Drakos cleared his throat and consulted his notebook, "On March 22nd, Chief Simmons called Lilly Rose and asked to talk to her about the rental of certain properties she managed. She acted surprised and claimed ignorance. At that point, the Chief didn't know of Lilly Rose's direct involvement with the prostitution ring. But when he inquired about several addresses where parties were scheduled, she realized he must have seen a list somewhere. She said she could meet him the following afternoon, but suggested he come to her house rather than the real estate office since they would be discussing sensitive information. That evening, Lilly Rose called Senator Juniper and Harrison Reed. They had a powwow at Juniper's castle."

Drakos tapped his notebook with his pen. "Let me open a parenthesis here. It wasn't just the castle that had cameras. Many of the bedrooms and formal rooms in the party houses had them, too. Juniper used video footage from those cameras to extort information, get votes, and prod the powerful, the rich and the famous to do his bidding."

Hobbs leaned forward. "So, Juniper curried favor by providing illicit sex with beautiful, trained girls. He extorted favors from his clientele, and he made a shitload of money. What a sleazebag."

Drakos nodded. "Juniper pulled strings and got ahold of Dax's cell phone records, and they learned he'd been communicating with Samantha Marshall. They were worried about her; she had a reputation for going after stories like a dog with a bone. They were sure she was the one who got Dax involved. Plus, she'd written inflammatory articles about some of Juniper's cronies. He had it in for her."

"So they decided to get rid of her," Claire said softly.

"Yes. They also figured out how Samantha learned about the list of parties and attendees. When Ruby Branson first took up with Harrison Reed—James—she mentioned meeting Samantha and being interviewed at the store where Ruby worked. He could tell Samantha had greatly impressed her. That evening, Reed pressured Ruby, and she told him she'd taken pictures of the list on his iPad and sent them to Samantha."

Claire nodded. "I read about that in her diary." She shivered, imagining what Harrison might have done to Ruby to get her to talk.

Drakos continued. "All three of them didn't want to lose the revenue stream the parties produced. With two or three parties a week, they were pulling in thousands of dollars. If they didn't shut down Dax and Samantha, they would lose all the money and end up going to jail for kidnapping and running a sex trafficking scheme, not to mention extortion." Drakos looked up, his face grey and aged. "Just like that, they decided to kill them both."

Claire reached out to Hobbs. He wrapped his arms around her. She sobbed quietly and he patted her back. When she calmed down, she pulled away and got up, went into the kitchen and grabbed some paper towels. She blew her nose and wiped her eyes, then came back into the great room and sat back down in an armchair. "So, what actually happened? I want to hear all of it."

Drakos took a deep breath. "The next afternoon, March 23rd, Lilly Rose offered Dax a glass of drugged-up sweet tea. Once he grew drowsy, Mathilde Dubonnet administered the shot of pentobarbital."

Claire felt sick but remained stoic. Drakos, on the other hand, looked like he badly wanted to get this over with. "They stripped him and put on those orange swimming trunks you spotted, Claire. At first, they stashed him in the back of his car. Later that night, they transported him up past Seaside in a Lilly Rose van. With one of Juniper's men keeping watch, two of them took Dax down to the water and dumped him in. They wanted to make it look like he'd drowned."

Claire's knuckles went white as she squeezed her hands together.

Drakos glanced down at his notes. "Lilly Rose lives right on 30A, east of Seaside, and has a three-car garage. They parked Dax's car in a stall, covered with a tarp, for several months. Eventually, they got a truck and drove the car down to Fort Walton Beach. It was Louis Dubonnet's fingerprint we found on the inside of the trunk. We learned much of this story from him. He and his sister were both working for Juniper when they went off the radar. Juniper had a hold on them, and they remained his loyal foot soldiers."

Claire huddled in the armchair, curled up tight. "What about Samantha?"

"The Dubonnets picked her up the next evening when she left Hank's boat. It wasn't until the following night that anyone noticed she was missing. And no one reported it until a day after that. At that time, no one made the connection with Dax."

"So...what happened?"

Drakos looked from Hobbs to Claire and then sighed. "Harrison Reed orchestrated the whole thing. At first, they tortured her, trying to get her to tell them about the list. But apparently, she wouldn't say if there were copies at her house or your house. Eventually, Reed grew so enraged, he strangled her."

Claire blanched.

"The spot where they buried her out at Bramble Bay had been recently excavated, so the earth was loose. The Dubonnets and another one of Juniper's goons had no trouble digging a hole and putting her in. No one ever would have found her if it wasn't for that water leak."

Claire looked at Hobbs. She knew he was remembering the same thing she was—Samantha's body, dripping water and sand, hanging from the bucket of the excavator.

They all stayed silent for a moment. Then Claire said, "What about Mai Ling? I've thought of her often. Where is she now?"

Unexpectedly, Drakos relaxed a bit. "Mai Ling was basically an indentured servant in Juniper's household. She was brought over from China, thinking she was going to work in the medical field. Juniper locked her up. She's not deaf and dumb, either. She's actually pretty smart because she went into her deaf mode when she saw what was in store for her. She's been invaluable in providing evidence on life in the castle. People talked in front of her and she was able to glean useful information." His face turned grim again. "Mai Ling said one of the girls was murdered, and she thinks the victim was buried behind the house. Currently, the FBI is digging in the woods behind the mansion."

Epilogue

Claire and Hobbs invited everyone they knew to a New Year's Day brunch at Claire's house. Ruby came with her grandfather. Claire noticed how attentive Ruby was to his needs. His face was all smiles when she brought him a plate of pulled pork and potato salad. Later, Claire saw Ruby and Poppy talking. It sounded as though the two of them were discussing sharing an apartment.

Alexia and Drakos had hit it off and were huddled together over a platter of spanakopita Alexia had brought. Maybe they were comparing their Greek roots. Mary Sullivan from Missing Persons was there too, with her husband and twins. The babies looked just like their mother with adorable ginger curls and bright blue eyes.

Of course, Ava and Barbara were there. In the past few months, they had joined forces with Claire to form a new real estate company: The Emerald Dream Realty Group. They were in the process of acquiring the Lilly Rose Agency offices. Several former Lilly Rose realtors were pleased to join their firm. Consuelo Baker had disappeared after her husband was arrested. Someone said they'd seen her in Miami, but these days Claire hardly spared her a thought.

Aunt Irma and her friend Françoise were there, along with Celestina. Françoise and Celestina were well-known artists in the Emerald Coast community. Claire had befriended them several years earlier. They were seated around the dining table with Seijun and Claire's friend Olivia, discussing the 30A Songwriters Festival, which was coming up in January.

Hank Robbins and Detective Bob Rogers were at the other end of the dining table, arguing about fishing techniques. At one point, Bob waved his arms and nearly knocked Hank's beer bottle to the floor. They both cracked up.

Claire sat at the kitchen island counter with a glass of wine. Hobbs came over and sat down beside her. "Everyone seems to be having a great time," he said.

Claire smiled. "You were right. This was a super idea. I'm glad we got everyone together. We need to heal and to move on. What better way than to celebrate the New Year."

***

After everyone left, Hobbs stuck around to help Claire clean up. He took out the garbage and Claire put the last few glasses into the dishwasher. When the kitchen was back to normal, they went out on the deck to watch the sunset. They sat on the top step of the stairs leading down to the beach.

Claire turned to Hobbs. "Thanks so much for helping today. I couldn't have done it without you."

"You're very welcome." He smiled at her, his blue eyes crinkling at the corners.

They fell silent and stayed that way while the sun sank lower on the horizon and made the sky a festival of pinks and oranges.

Hobbs took Claire's hand. "You know how I feel, right? I want to be there for you…always."

Claire nodded.

"You know I love you and I always will," he said.

"Yes." Claire squeezed his hand.

"I fell in love with you that first day when I came up to the house with the beach ball. I was right down there." He nodded towards the high-tide mark.

Claire laughed quietly and squeezed his hand again. "I know how you feel. You've showed me in a hundred different ways these last months."

Hobbs drew in a breath. "I want to marry you, when you're ready."

Claire turned and looked into his eyes." I like you, Hobbs. I…I might even love you." She paused long enough to lean over and kiss his cheek. "But Dax hasn't even been gone a year. I'm still grieving, and I don't want to go into something on the rebound. I'm not whole yet."

"I understand, but I'll be here. I'll always be here."

Acknowledgements:

Thank you, Diane Piron-Gelman, *éditeur extraordinaire*.

Thank you, Meg Dolan, *artiste fantastique*.

A big thanks to Jan Matson who graciously shared her original painting *Girlfriends*.

Thank you, Honin, my Zen Buddhist friend, for sharing the story of the two monks.

Thank you, Linda Miller, Randy Rintala and Oliver Robbins who shared information, stories and opinions, about the real estate market on Highway 30A. I apologize for any inaccuracies in my portrayal of the profession.

Most of the restaurants and shops exist along 30A and Highway 98. However, Lemon Cove, The Magnolia Spa and Resort and Beach Mania are figments of my imagination.

Made in the USA
Columbia, SC
24 September 2023